Memoirs From Limbo

Jason Nadle

Old Cart Books

Copyright © 2026 Jason Nadle All rights reserved.

The story, all names, characters, and incidents portrayed in this production are fictitious. No identification with actual persons (living or deceased), places, buildings, and products is intended or should be inferred.

No part of this publication may be reproduced, distributed, or transmitted in any form or by any means, including photocopying, recording, or other electronic or mechanical methods, without the prior written permission of the publisher, except as permitted by U.S. copyright law.

All references to trademarks are under fair use and are not intended to endorse or demean them in any way.

All references to Alice in Wonderland are from Lewis Carrols work under public domain.

ISBN eBook: 979-8-9940855-1-6

ISBN Paperback: 979-8-9940855-0-9

ISBN Hardback: 979-8-9940855-2-3

Cover design by: Inspired: Veteran Made

Library of Congress Control Number: TBD

Printed in the United States of America

For those heroes and warriors who have fought and are still fighting their war.

I hope you find peace.

To all my helpers.

Most of all, to my wife, for her invaluable support with this crazy adventure.

Contents

Prologue	1
Ch. 1 A New Mission	9
Ch. 2 The White Rabbit	30
Ch. 3 Drink Me	39
Ch. 4 Eat me	64
Ch. 5 The Spade Gardner	72
Ch. 6 Cheshire	111
Ch. 7 Alice	165
Ch. 8 Jabberwocky	209
Ch. 9 The Griffon	221
Ch. 10 Red Queen	251
Epilogue	303
Afterword	310
Also by	311

Prologue

Tech Specs

[This is a text based transmission. Often used via text messages or emails.]

<"This is an audio based transmission, typically over radio.">

~This is private communication via other means.~

FEBRUARY 12TH, 2021

The walls were...Peeling? Almost like a time lapse of decades going by in seconds! The paint just peeled and fell away from the wall, sometimes it looked like it was eaten by mildew, but it all was just...dying...I looked around for a way out but there was nothing, just these peeling walls! I need a way out, I need to RUN! There! A weakness in the wall!

I leapt forward at the gap, I could see through the disintegrating dry wall and dove through the studs as a nearly silent cackle began to come from...Everywhere?! I get it, I got the flag on the wall, but I'm not ACTUALLY mad!

Keep moving, don't stop! The corridor flew past as I ran, the continuing disintegration of this house that I don't recognize. Find an escape, find a weapon!

Down a hallway, another dead end. These walls were almost gone, but beyond that was only blackness. It seemed like an abyss of nothingness, and I couldn't make out anything past these dying walls.

"HEY!" A female voice, loud and distant. I turned and saw her, she yelled again. "HEY YOU!" She was very hard to see, just floating in the blackness. More of a ghost than anything else. She had flaming red hair and a rifle, at least I think she did.

I tried to yell for help, but the words died in my throat.

"WAKE UP!" She barked again. Wake up?

BEEP BEEP BEEP

My alarm.

I sat bolt upright, panting. I was back in my room, in bed. I looked around wildly and wiped the sweat from my brow. I stare at the flag on the wall, with the big face of the Cheshire Cat and those words about being mad. Holy shit, what a dream...Maybe I am a bit more crazy than I thought.

SEPTEMBER 17TH, 2021

It was just another day. During lunch break, I went to the BX on base to see what was available, because it changed SO often. But something was off today...While I read the Subway menu over, the colors shifted. Or... Drained maybe? Everything around me was eerily black and white...I looked down at my hands, and they were fine but...What was happening?

I looked around the sitting area...Was I having a stroke or something? Everyone was frozen in time, everyone colorless. The TVs looked like paintings, frozen on their typical Fox News broadcast. An unsettling silence weighed on everything. I felt cold, everything was stiff, like I was trying to walk through Jello.

Wait...Was that a whisper?

"Who's there?" I croak out.

What's happening?!

The shrill siren of tinnitus crept up and broke into a crescendo. Then, it vanished...Color snapped back, the TVs started playing and people resumed walking as if nothing happened.

"You okay, Mas'Sergeant?" I looked at the old man behind me in line for a moment.

"Yeah...Tinnitus is kicking my ass." Truth be told, I couldn't tell for sure. What happened was most certainly not ringing in my ears, this was something much different. I wasn't crazy, and I didn't need to alarm the retirees.

"Welcome to the club." The old man grinned and slapped me on the shoulder. As I came around to my senses I saw his hat, retired army.

"They never warn you about that, do they?"

The old man smiled again. "Try doing artillery for a few years." He grunted.

JULY 1ST, 2022

Oh no...It's happening again! I just sat down in my truck, the shrill whine crept in, and color started to drain again. This can't be right...

The car passing by stopped immediately as if the world pressed pause. Everything was colorless again, it drained into the ether. I gripped the steering wheel tightly, what in the hell was happening?? And why could I move, why did I still have color to my skin??

"Hello again..." It was that whisper from before. Barely audible, but I could hear it this time. I froze, I'm not even sure I'm still breathing. It was...wrong. Inhuman. Yet inviting.

"Oh, don't be shy..." It whispered again. The hair on my neck stood up. Footsteps, off to the left. Moving fast. What do I do? Pretend to be frozen like everyone else? Hide? I scanned quickly and decided to duck my head below the dash, trying to hide silently.

"I'm sure we will meet again..." The voice continued. I couldn't locate the source, it felt like it was in my own ears.

"Shit, it's gone!" Male voice this time, clear and correct. Guess that means I'm not the only one who sees this...whatever is happening.

"What do you mean, 'gone'?" Another male voice, different but still correct.

"Did I stutter?!" First male again, kind of sounds like an angsty youngster.

"Jesus, Ulid, you can be a real shit some days. Come on, let's do a sweep."

"Okay, dad." Second male again, voice thick with teenage sass.

The tinnitus sound was coming back again as the footsteps grew closer. They had to be nearly in front of the truck as the shriek hit a crescendo and the color snapped back into place. I took a chance, picked up my head, and everything was back to normal. But...No sign of the two males... They had also vanished.

I got out of my truck, looking around in front of the hood and down the lanes. No foot traffic. Just that one car and the usual sounds of a parking lot.

Safe to say I was starting to get a little worried.

JANUARY 9TH, 2023

Here we go again. I hadn't even opened my eyes and I could tell, the oppressive silence had already set in. I looked at my clock, 0320 in the morning. How many of these events have I slept through?

I got out of the bed and grabbed the pistol out of my bedside stand. It was a direct copy of my service pistol, an M9. As I scanned, my eyes fell on my sheets...They stood frozen in the air where I last touched them. As if their existence simply paused as soon as I broke contact with them.

"That's new..." I murmured under my breath. Through the silence I could just make out something, some noise coming from outside.

"Good morning..." It was that damned voice again. That wrong voice. I turned my head to locate, this time I was sure it was in my head. It didn't change directions as I scanned. I clicked off the safety. I moved quietly to the front door, peering out the window next to it to locate the initial sounds I heard. "Coffee...?" the voice continued. I felt best to ignore it. Something was wrong about it...

"This way!" It was faint and muffled, but it was a female voice. Oddly familiar this time.

"Don't ignore me, Jake..." That voice cooed again.

"Then show yourself." I spoke softly into the void of the colorless room, as a trio of people appeared on the road outside. They still had their color, and it was most certainly a strangely uniformed combat team. There was a woman with them this time, and somehow, she felt familiar...

"But I'm already here, Jake..."

"I'm afraid I have to disagree." I growled as the trio stopped, one of them was holding some kind of device and looked in the vague direction of my house. It was at this point the laundry room door opened. I had previously identified it as the most center, defensible and hidden room in the house. But this time, it was purely dark. I couldn't see anything in that doorway.

"I'm right here...Come...Don't let your coffee get cold..."

Coffee sure sounds good right now. Wait...I looked around the room again. I don't remember leaving the front door!

But a nice cup of coffee...

STOP IT! I gripped my pistol tighter and backed out to the front door. I had no idea what forces were at play, but humans sounded like a safer bet than a dark door frame.

"Stop playing Jake, your coffee is almost cold..."

"No..." I tried to yell, but it only came out as a soft whisper.

"Jake...." It really was a sweet voice. She sounds nice. "How about some breakfast too? What would you like?"

This isn't right...I need to listen to myself. Go outside!

...

I can't reach the door.

"Oh, it's cold outside, you'll catch a chill, my dear..."

The door swung open on its own, and I turned to look but it felt like my entire body was rebelling, not wanting me to even move. A red headed woman breached, followed by two men, one young and one older. He may have been roughly my age.

"Forsyth, that door!" The woman spoke with authority as the older man bolted around me, producing some kind of device from a pouch on his chest rig. The younger male did a sweep of the room with his rifle as the woman approached me.

"It'll be okay." She seemed to move with an air of elegance, and the familiarity struck me again as she laid a hand softly on my shoulder. Her hair was unquestionably red, and I felt a very old memory being pinged. The room was filled with a slamming door followed by a suppressed, small detonation. "You'll be okay, this is just a bad dream, alright?" She smiled at me. Why do I know her? More importantly, why do I think she's on my side? That I can trust her?

There was a scream that followed the detonation and her words, and it seemed to reverberate in my skull, it felt like the bone would crack but I could move freely again. I dropped to a knee, my free hand on my head. "What the fuck is going on?"

"Some kind of siren, Ms. Steel. Cleared, ready for RTB." The older male returned to my line of sight.

"Siren?" I looked at him. "Who are you people??"

Ms. Steel lowered herself to my level, bending at the knees. "Friends." She spoke smoothly. "All you need to do now is go back to sleep and everything will be okay."

I looked at her, hard. I nodded softly, my head still pounding but it was fading.

"Have a good evening, sir." Forsyth spoke to me, opening the door. "You're safe now." The youngster ducked out of the door, followed by the woman and Forsyth himself, closing the door behind him.

"Think he will remember this?" Sounded like Forsyth as they walked off.

"They never do. This one was close to getting snagged." Ms. Steel. I couldn't tell the tone.

"Damn sirens. Sneaky bastards." Maybe the youngster, but they had made it out of earshot now.

By far the weirdest, most real feeling dream ever. I sat on the couch, no way I could fall asleep again. About that time, the shrill sound of tinnitus came back around, and the color exploded once more around me. "Well, Ms. Steel." I looked at the window. "You were wrong."

Ch. 1 A New Mission

AUGUST 1ST, 2023

Freedom. The golden handshake. Becoming a real boy. Many different names and terms but it all came down to one thing.

Retirement.

And not the usual old gray hair type either. I sat on my porch, watching the sun begin to sink behind the mountains, beer in one hand and my phone sitting on my thigh. I was sitting on my porch, relaxing in the rocker I bought a while back at Cracker Barrel. Yeah, cliche. It was still a nice chair. This place had become my saving grace, a little work here and there to fix it up and make it nicer. It was nestled in the mountains of North Carolina, off a long road that only attached about ten total houses to civilization. Not a place folks just randomly found themselves in. This ain't real yet. This retirement. This...Old bastard shit. Don't think it will be real for a bit...I've already come to grips that my body and I aren't on the same page anymore. It's almost like jumping out of helicopters in full tactical kit is bad for the knees and back...Who would have thought! Yeah, I am fully aware that it's not the only thing that has my body letting me down. But that's not important.

    I sigh heavily. I got a good deal from Uncle Sam, but this was way before I planned and now...Not sure what I am going to do. 12 years, 5 months of service.

> *Greetings, reader. You have arrived at the present day for this memoir. This is most certainly a story driven forward by Mr. Sixx, and I shall not interfere with his memories. However, Mr. Sixx has a tendency to omit certain things that the normal reader may need to understand, or perhaps he is unable or unwilling to make certain observations. This is my dutiful role. I shall explain things that are important to the story, so you can fully enjoy his...idiosyncrasies. I am simply the narrator. Subtitles, if you will. This way, you can enjoy his...particular style...unabridged. I apologize in advance.*

> *Uncle Sam is the US Government. Mr. Sixx served as an Air Force pararescueman for 12 years, 5 months before being medically retired early due to an autoimmune problem that required an injection once a week. Today is the first day of his newly obtained civilian life.*

    Well...It's been a good ride. Maybe I'll start another project car. Always wanted an old GSX, those are pretty slick.

My ears picked up the crunch of gravel and the hum of an engine off in the distance. I closed my eyes, listening. It's approaching, but not an engine I recognized. Sure sounded expensive too. Wonder if one of the neighbors got a new toy?

I opened my eyes again, taking a sip of my beer as the vehicle peeks around the curve. It was a black sedan, looking like an MKZ from a distance. Oh no, was I gonna be one of those old hillbillies counting cars on the side of the road?! Shit. Alright time to do...something. I stood up, maybe I'll change the truck's oil, although it's a bit early for that kind of maintenance. Think I did it last month.

My plans became a little more unsure when the sedan started slowing down, as if it was about to stop, and then turned down my driveway. It wasn't turning around either, that was the distinct sound of it being put in park. Today just got a little more interesting.

I leaned against the railing of the porch, picking out two separate bodies through the windshield as they stepped out of the car. My eyes narrow as I see the driver. It was her, Ms. Steel. I would recognize that hair anywhere. She was dressed smartly, in a very nice blazer with a medium length skirt. She commanded an air about her, one that she knew what was going on and how to turn the tides in her favor. My eyes immediately darted around the area, checking that there was still color to the trees, which they did. Glad she was real.

"You lost, miss?" I called out, kindly but firmly to make sure she knew I was there. The passenger got out too, a small framed younger woman. Blonde hair, evidence of some kind of color highlights, looked like she was in college and dressed to match. T shirt, jean skirt to her calf, with a few strange necklaces. She was nervous, twitchy. Why?

"If you happen to be Mr. Sixx, I am not lost." She spoke with the same smooth, elegant voice as before.

"Well, you found me. But you have me at a disadvantage, miss...?" I know enough that she saved me once before. But I wasn't going to reveal anything more than I needed to, not with so many questions circling around her and those...experiences...

"I hear you're a free agent, and I just so happen to have a job opening. My name is Sarah Steel." She approached calmly towards the porch, I still hadn't moved from my leaning rest, beer resting on the railing in front of me.

"You private contractors don't waste any time, do you? I haven't even gotten my retirement certificate yet." My eyes fell on the young woman, who seemed to have been distracted by a nearby tree. Judging by the look in her eye, it wasn't so simple though.

"You would be partially right. While we do take defense contracts, we have an additional mission as well. One I suspect you would be interested in."

I sigh. "With all due respect, ma'am, I served honorably and I don't intend to change that now." My tone certainly changed, I didn't like the insinuations. Heard about these groups with 'extracurricular' activities.

"Nor do I ask you to do so. We deal with unconventional and non-traditional threats. In short, we provide a service that no one knows they need."   I stared at her for a moment, before looking at the younger woman who had finally become interested in the conversation. I caught a tablet in her hand.

"This isn't wonderland, ma'am. Not sure why you speak in riddles." I stood up from the railing, taking a drink.

Ms. Steel looks at the younger woman and nods. The young lady opens a tablet and taps a few buttons before turning it around. "Does any of this seem familiar?" She pressed play, and it was a video that looked a lot like the room with peeling paint. It was hard to forget a dream like that.

"Looks like a timelapse of an old building in Chernobyl." I looked at her. "Miss...?"

"Oh, sorry, I'm Fae Rosewill. Would this video look familiar to you? Perhaps in a dream?" She was still jumpy, her small voice betraying a forced confidence.

"Should it?" I was firmly in uncharted water here. Without speaking, Fae turned the tablet around, tapped a few more things and presented it to me to take. It was a medical chart.

My chart.

This one had more on it.

It had stuff about my head, unexplained marks on my brain. Indeterminable if they were even a problem or not. Another...something on my right arm and spine. I didn't see half of this myself, and it's my own medical record. But I recognized those signatures. Everything looked correct and legal. Was it being kept from me? I flicked to the next page, it was a Steel Roses document. Most of it is standard legal crap, some medical jargon, but it listed me as...'Limbo Sensitive likely'. The hell does that even mean? The mission report from the team that came and stopped that Siren was even attached. While still looking at the tablet I turned and walked inside the house, leaving the door wide open.

"Where'd you get this?" I asked directly.

Mr. Sixx had a tendency of doing away with certain niceties most people expect such as 'Please, come in.'

Ms. Steel didn't wait, and followed me through the door, Rosewill paused before following cautiously. I called it a cabin, but it was a rustic aesthetic small house with a large attached garage. It resembled a cabin inside and out, and when everyone stepped in, they were greeted with a pleasant living room that flowed into a dining room on one side, and a kitchen attached to that. Wood walls, and comfortable, albeit slightly worn, furniture. Most of the lighting was a tasteful old school with exposed bulbs. It was the place of a man seeking a quieter, old school life. "We have our ways. I believe you may have had some experiences in your past that were unexplainable, and you may or may not remember them."

I stopped, setting the tablet on the table. It was enough for four, but it was pretty clear the table was only used for one and storage. Half of it was covered in old mail, magazines, and gun cleaning equipment. "That's not disconcerting at all." I looked between them both. "I think I need something harder. Ladies?" I grabbed a bottle of rum off the counter. "If you're old enough, Ms. Rosewill."

"I am, thank you. And yes please." She smiled.

"Whiskey, neat." Ms. Steel spoke, her tone betraying she was very much accustomed to this sort of thing.

I paused. "I'm not as cultured as you, ma'am."

She made no expression, but I could hear the tone of amusement. "Simply whiskey in a glass." I nod, grabbing the second bottle out of a cupboard. I definitely made mine a little stronger than normal as I slid their glasses to them on the table and sat down.

"Limbo. What is it?" I threw the opening salvo into the air.

"A mystery." Ms. Steel pulled a chair and sat down with her drink.

"Thought we were past the riddles?"

"Unfortunately, that one is. We call it Limbo because it seems to be the limbo between reality and somewhere else. No one can explain the how or the why." She had no deceit in her eyes or words. She was either very good or very honest, and my gut was thinking the latter.

"We can't even say with certainty when it'll happen." Ms. Rosewill spoke up, I wasn't sure if this was just her bread and butter or the alcohol loosened her up. If so, that was quick. "Some, like myself, can sense its arrival. So..." she takes another sip of her drink, and stares at the table while she speaks. "They vary. Sometimes they last for hours, sometimes seconds. We call the short ones blips, I only get about a five minute warning with those, but the substantial ones I can feel up to 2 weeks in advance."

"Which is why we always have a team on standby." Ms. Steel took back the conversation.

"I assume there are more things such as that siren a ways back, then?"

Ms. Steel nods. "That and much worse. Honestly, Sirens aren't that bad."

I took another drink, a bit longer this time, before setting my glass down. I leaned back in my chair and absently spun the glass on the spot.

"So, you want another shooter for the roster to keep these...things at bay. Do conventional arms even work? If I hit one with a 9 mil or a .308, would it even matter?"

"Oftentimes conventional arms do some damage, depending on what it is. Generally, if you can see through it, bullets and blades won't do much. The rest will feel it."

I felt my eyebrow raise. "See through...?"

"Yes Mr. Sixx. Shadows, shades...think ghosts."

"Who ya gonna call..." I mutter under my breath.

"The Steel Roses are real, I assure you." Ms. Steel smirked. I glanced at her, still processing everything. The situation weighed in the air as if lined by lead. "In an effort of clarity, we have a very big challenge with recruiting. If one does not experience Limbo, they have a tendency to assume we are…well…Insane."

"We're all mad here." I said shortly, finding it convenient Ms. Steel was sitting between me and my flag that said the same thing, with a great big Cheshire Cat smile made out of the words. My eyes widened suddenly. "So, you have absolute green horns on your roster, don't you?"

Ms. Steel made a face that betrayed the truth before she could speak. "Unfortunately, yes. It has been quite a difficult obstacle." This made me lean back in my chair, locking eyes on her.

"Let me guess, again." I picked up my drink. "You're looking for a shooter, team lead and/or instructor." My tone was definitely dripping with an air of frustration. "Need I remind you, I'm retired."

"I cannot refute any of that." Her turn to lean forward. "Is that truly how you wish it to be though?"

I glared at her, letting the words hang. "Retired. Means no longer effective. This Limbo shit break your vocab?" I had begun subconsciously turning my glass on the table again, it spinning smoothly with a little bit of condensation on the glass.

"I don't recall saying that." She was definitely good.

"Uncle Sam did."

"I am not he."

I paused again, eyes falling to my glass. She was quite good at her job, and I was vividly reminded of SERE.

> *SERE would be Survival, Evasion, Resistance, and Escape. A difficult training program designed to teach Air Force warriors how to do the aforementioned and come home safely, and with honor.*

"I made my peace of a quiet life, ma'am. I've done my duty." Hollow words. My voice reflected it. Ms. Steel knew it, and she just waited, whereas Ms. Rosewill kept looking between the two of us, sipping her drink.

I sighed, my tone an air of defeat. "Benefits? Insurance? Time off?" How could I possibly pass up an opportunity to save the world? I mean, it would likely be dealing with young punks basically trying to get themselves killed in combat. I cannot fathom sending this girl into the fire as she is, she would get ripped apart. Who else was just as innocent? Unskilled? I could feel that old familiar nagging in the back of my head saying that if I don't do it, it won't get done. I also knew that's exactly what she wanted.

"I'm sure we can make you quite comfortable on top of your retirement pay, Mr. Sixx. We can discuss that at the office, should you choose to come by." She immediately gave a tone of victory as she spoke, and my stubborn ass was immediately annoyed by it. "You'll find we don't have the strict requirements of military life, and time off is often mission dependent. However, we rotate four small teams, and only two are active at any one time." I nodded, taking another drink. "I would like you to take over team 2. Bill Forsyth, and Joey Ulid. You probably don't remember them, but they were the ones that rescued you from the Siren."

My eyes flicked to her. "What's it mean if I remember that?" They both paused, Ms. Rosewill's eyes went wide.

"That...would be abnormal. Perhaps you have been experiencing Limbo more often than we thought."

Ms. Rosewill leaned forward, her drink nearly empty, eyes wide with excitement. "What does that mean? Is he something new?" She stared at me as if I would change in front of her eyes.

"Started experiencing oddities about two years ago." I paused. Wondering how much I should reveal.

"Any specifics?" Ms. Rosewill pressed for more.

"That siren." I pointed at the tablet, referring to the mission I recall. "Plagued me the whole time. Saw Forsyth...twice. Saw you twice too."

"That's even more abnormal." Ms. Steel leaned back in her chair, a thoughtful expression on her face. "I'm not aware of anyone that has tangible memories when under Limbo corruption."

"Can you sense it?" Ms. Rosewill asked directly, once more.

"Not really? Maybe? I'm just the FNG, I don't have answers."

FNG stood for Fing New Guy. A...kind term for the new person in the unit.

"Yes, of course. Much will come in time with training." Ms. Steel responded, looking pensive.

"I guess it's too much to hope to avoid suffering through another inprocessing week." I shrugged. "Guess some things never change, eh?"

"Suppose you may be right, Mr. Sixx. Would that mean you'll accept our offer?" Ms. Steel tilts her head, a curious expression seeping through her elegant mask. Ms. Rosewill hid nothing, her curiosity and concern mixed loudly. I smirked, probably looking a lot like the Cheshire cat himself.

"You already have the answer, ma'am. Don't need me to say it."

While she didn't smile, or grin, there was a look of cunning victory in her eye as she stood up. "I shall expect your arrival tomorrow morning." As if on a cue she was partially expecting but not quite ready for, Ms. Rosewill pulled a card out of her pocket and slid it across the table. "0800. You need not call me ma'am, either. We aren't quite that formal."

"I'll be there, ma'am." Spotting a wonderful place to be a stubborn pain, I couldn't let that go. She would forever be 'ma'am'. My way of fighting back against her tone of victory. She picked up immediately with a flash of a raised eyebrow but said nothing.

"Address is on the card, tomorrow will be largely admin work so no specific gear or clothes required." Ms. Rosewill was oblivious to the battle of will and wits that had begun.

"Understood, too easy." It was clear Ms. Rosewill didn't understand my phrase, but Ms. Steel didn't wait for her to ask.

"Until tomorrow, Mr. Sixx. I look forward to the future." She paused. "I suspect we can both stand to learn from each other." We all stood up and made for the door.

"'Til Tomorrow, Ladies."

AUGUST 2ND, 2023

The next day was starkly familiar. Inprocessing, paperwork, training videos, all the standard fare of a new assignment. It wasn't the same, but it was close enough. Intel on Limbo was a little sparse, but I suspected that it was due to its unknown nature. Everything on the public facing side was essentially a Private Defense Contractor, which is the fancy term for hired gun or mercenaries. That training and paperwork circled around certifications, licenses, how to engage safely and the like. In between the training and paperwork, I met other members of the group in passing.

Bill Forsyth, plucked out of the North Carolina Highway Patrol. He had been around forever and was extremely knowledgeable at fighting these entities. He didn't say a whole lot, and I certainly got the 'lone wolf' mentality off of him. He had reluctantly been leading Team 2 for about a year now, which essentially meant coordination and paperwork to him.

Joey Ulid, a hot shot loose cannon if I ever saw one. He was the youngest person on the roster and had begun fighting at the age of 16 and still wasn't even legally an adult. He had some early successes that I suspect were largely thanks to Forsyth, and those went to his head. Another member of Team 2.

Fae Rosewill, the same lady as before. I found out she had actually been going to college when she was recruited and is still taking part time courses. Forgot to ask her major…Oops. She had a head for admin work, and I found out she was the best at detecting when Limbo was about to hit.

Going through the building revealed quite a solid operation. Fae had turned me loose with the rest of the team for a bit to give me a tour.

"This is our room over here. Each team has their own off this hall, door at the end is a supply room. Actual supplies like staples and shit, not the fun stuff!" Joey took me to a dead end hall, two doors each side and one at the end. Each had a giant number plastered on the door. The familiarity kept creeping up, echoes of my past. I followed him into our room, Forsyth was over by the coffee machine, he nodded as I walked in. The room was fairly sparse, just your basic furniture and tiny kitchenette not unlike an office breakroom. It lacked character, that's for sure. Ulid plopped into a chair along the wall as I took stock of the area. "We aren't in here much. Either out kicking ass or in the ready room. This is a good nap area though!"

"I can kind of tell. I'm used to rooms like these being covered in heritage."

"Heritage?"

"Yeah, like…Souvenirs. Art work. Plaques and awards."

"Sounds lame." Ulid was already taking out his phone as he spoke, clearly done with the conversation.

"Coffees ready." Forsyth said shortly. "Your uniforms should be delivered here by the end of the week, boss."

"Thanks." I nodded to him and proceeded to make a cup of coffee myself. Forsyth disappeared as I did so, and Ulid was absorbed by his phone. Odd group…"Hey Ulid, what kinda training schedule are we looking at?"

He snorted. "Fuck that." I didn't like that answer, but it's too soon to cause trouble yet.

"We'll see about that." I said simply.

"Yeah, we will."

Clearly, he had a very different plan for the future…Not wanting to throw my freshly made coffee at him, I decided to continue the tour on my own. I left the room, turning down the hall. I still haven't seen this ready room, and there should be an armory and some kind of command post. I found the armory quickly as it was very close to the team area. Door to the side appeared to be a ready room which made sense. I entered the armory through the rather heavy door, pushing past the hand painted sign "Clean your shit, or I'll clean your guts - L". Typical armorer. No sooner than I opened the door, I was greeted with a loud, female bark.

"What?!"

There was a small entry area, a table against the wall and a wall of bars blocking access to all the good stuff. Behind the bars was a very pissed off woman with a latitude of piercings and tattoos and shocking yellow? Green? Lime hair maybe? I wondered if it was powered by a battery.

"Newbie." Her mood turned a little kinder, but she was still pissy. Guess that battery was stored somewhere uncomfortable.

"Jake. Presume you're the magic maker?"

"Gotta be, you jackasses bring me garbage and I make them run. Call me your friendly neighborhood witch." She grumbled.

"I take care of my toys."

"That's what they all say and yet here I am!" She brandished a screwdriver menacingly.

"I get the feeling we are going to be best friends soon." I couldn't hide my smirk, but I could dodge the screwdriver that left her hand, pinged loudly off a bar, and clattered to the floor.

"A smart ass to boot?" She shook her head, turning back to the project she was working on. Her tone was almost disappointed. "I really wish Sarah would hire competent people."

I quietly collected the screwdriver and placed it on the counter, akin to a peace offering. She didn't react, but I saw her eyes flick to the screwdriver.

Her tone dropped again, reluctant but still willing to talk. "We can offer you a plain M4 and some mags with a basic chest rig. Pistols, swords, bows are on your own dime." She pointed to a closet with her elbow. "Arrows are in there. Ordnance on the back wall." She glared at me. "I don't like giving out the ordnance 'toys'." I do believe she was mocking my earlier choice of words… "I can clean and fix whatever you bring me. Backlog ain't short. Everyone gets comms, one scanner per team and I only issue those on the way out. They are worth more than you are."

"Understood, ma'am."

"Lena. Call me ma'am again, I won't miss with the next tool."

"Understood, Lena."

"Fuck outta here. I have too many 'toys' to fix."

I nod and depart, not wanting to press my luck. As the door shut, I spoke to myself. "That went well."

"You survived meeting Lena?" Fae's soft voice nearly caught me off guard.

"She's a sweetheart, what do you mean?" Fae's eyes went wide with confusion and maybe a little bit of fear. "She threw a screwdriver at me." I admitted, Fae smiled at that.

"She's scary." She shakes her head as if purging an unpleasant thought. "Anyway, I brought you an ID card and some paperwork so you can come and go as you please. Have you settled in okay?"

"Thank you, and well enough. Certainly different, but as to be expected." I shrugged. Fae looks at me a little confused, and I shake my head dismissing my comment. Not sure how to explain it anyway.

"Okay then. The only thing left is uniforms on our side, which should be Friday. Gear and equipment you can hash out with Lena…" She flicked a glance at the door and I could tell she was glad she stayed away from the armory. "Perhaps tomorrow…" Faes' expression was hard to read, but I'd call it fear mixed with reverence. I smiled reassuringly.

"I can handle it. I have some stuff of my own anyway. Anything else for today?"

"Nope. You're all set. Team 2 is off duty in about 30 minutes and..." She looks at her notes. "Off for two days."

"Excellent. Thanks."

I spent the last few minutes roaming the halls. I located a nice training area with gym equipment on one side, mats on the floor, and various equipment lining the other walls. It actually looked pretty good. There were two doors clearly marked up as locker rooms on the far side from the entrance too. Retreating to the halls again, I confirmed my suspicion on the ready room, which was essentially some benches and tables with a heavy looking slide open door into the armory. Just the basics to load everything up. Next stop was the medical room. I looked at the closed door and decided I had no interest in going back in one of those any time soon. As I note the time, we were officially off duty.

"Yeah, I can make this work." I mutter to myself.

AUGUST 8TH, 2023

I had just shut my eyes in the break room when the room erupted in red lights and a siren. Instinctively, I was up on my feet, pistol drawn and in front of me by the time my brain processed where I was. I'm in Team 2 break room. Forsyth started chuckling in the corner.

"Breathe, boss." He quickly recovered from his chuckling, but the smirk remained.

"What's going on?"

He had nonchalantly moved to the door. "Limbo. Joey should meet us at command."

Heart rate dropping back down a little, I followed him out the door as I reholstered my pistol. We walked in silence, the alarm's volume dropping considerably after the first few minutes.

"Nervous?" He asked offhand.

"Should I be?" I shot him a side eye glance and he chuckled again. "Gonna take that as a yes."

"You'll be okay. It's just like living a nightmare."

"You say that like it's normal."

"Boss, normal doesn't apply anymore."

My turn to smile. "Is that why a Raven is like a writing desk?"

Forsyth stuttered in his walk, looking back at me. "Uh...What?"

"Wonderland." I said simply with a shrug.

"Jesus, you had me worried, boss. But yeah, pretty much." He led into the command room, Fae and Ms. Steel were looking at some monitors. This room had a large conference table in the center, surrounded by multiple chairs. One side had multiple monitors and a large screen, it looked exactly like a briefing room should look. Maybe a little plain. Ulid slammed the door open behind us, beelining to a seat at the table, looking like a kid in a candy store. Forsyth and I took other chairs.

"Gentlemen, got an unknown." Fae informed us, her voice a little stronger than I was used to hearing.

"Yes!" Ulid exclaimed. His excitement was palpable. I shot him a look, but he didn't see it, and Forsyth rolled his eyes.

"All I can give you is a location. It's...Not strong but it's there. Like it's spread out." Fae was essentially our intel nerds, and she did a great job. If this was an unknown, that means no one had encountered this before.

"We are joining you tonight." Ms. Steel spoke with an air of finality. Fae looked at her, a look that seemed like a resigned fear. "I wish to see this new entity and Fae is probably the only one who will be able to pinpoint it." Boss lady herself is coming out? I looked at Forsyth, who seemed wholly unphased. Maybe she was wanting to see me in action? Guess I can't blame her for that. "We will deploy with two vehicles, Mr. Forsyth will be riding with Ms. Rosewill and myself. Once we hit the ground, I expect you to run the show." Her green eyes hit me, and I could tell this was an evaluation.

"Yes ma'am." I showed no emotion, this was mission time. Fear is for later, back home or at the bar.

"Intel gathering first, then we go from there. Normal gear should suffice." Ms. Steel continued.

"Understood. Do we have any maps of the AO?" I interject.

"AO?" Fae repeated.

"Sorry, Area of Operations. Where are we going?"

"Oh!" She motioned to a larger monitor, it appeared to be a sporting goods store. "This is the best guess I have."

"Zoom out, please?" She did so. I stood up and got closer, examining the entry and exit routes.

"Here, it's a smart board. You can draw on it." Fae handed me some markers. A quick glance told me they were specifically for this type of board.

"Fancy." I made some circles and arrows after a quick and careful calculation. "Okay team, primary entry is right here."

"Dude, we are just going to take a look at some freaks-"

"And how many have turned out to be hostile?" I cut Ulid's comment short, without so much as turning around or breaking my stride. He paused. "Exfil is here and here." I pointed to two separate routes out of the parking lot. "Ma'am, better to park close or approach on foot?" I looked at Ms. Steel.

"We've never had a problem parking close by." I could tell by her response and her expression that this was more in depth planning than they were used to. I paused and looked around.

"Do…Do you normally deploy without a plan?" I asked cautiously.

"Not to this level, boss." I stared at Forsyth for a moment.

"Then I am either over prepared, or you have all been exceptionally lucky." I turned back to the board. "Ms. Steel, you take this entrance, Ulid and I will enter here. Maintain radio contact at all times, search for the…thing. I don't want any shots fired until we know what we are working with. Watch spacing, watch your buddy. Once inside, I want Ms. Rosewill to do her thing, and we can advance after that. Expect up the center, guns sweeping the walls, or we skirt the walls, guns pointing forward and towards the rear." I turned around after making my sketches. The faces I saw were a mixture of fear, awe, and concern. "Watch your muzzles. I'll make the call once we have an idea of what's going on. Questions?"

Silence. I sigh, knowing that training in the future is going to be very painful.

"Excellent. Load up. We leave in 20." I hand the marker back to Fae, and head towards the armory, ready to deal with Lena.

***

"What did you say to them? I've never seen that boy so quiet." Lena asked softly, as I helped her hand out equipment.

"Nothing. I think my planning scarred him." I grinned.

"Damn, wish I was going out tonight. That boys been grinding my gears since day one."

"Say the word, I'll make it my goal to get him to piss himself." I shot back with a deadpan delivery. She actually laughed this time, a surprisingly pleasant laugh.

"Do it. He could use some reality."

"Done." I smirk at her. She returns it before turning to the wall and then back again.

"Think that's the last bit of gear, Sixx. Here's a scanner just in case." She offered up a burnt orange hard case with a grease pencil marking of SCANNER 3. "Ya know, maybe we will be besties." She offered a menacing grin with a sickly sweet voice that very much did not match her demeanor. I winked in return, a flash of a reaction told me she wasn't expecting that.

"Don't worry, I won't let Ulid touch it. Thanks Lena."

She waved as I turned, leaving the armory. We all had been equipped with essentially the same gear. M4 rifle, black or gray chest rig, a belt for pistols (everyone seemed to have their own preference) and each of those pieces had pouches with magazines, lights, tourniquets, water, snacks, flares, etc. It may sound like a lot, but this was a fairly mild loadout for going into known hostilities. Ms. Steel, Ms. Rosewill opted for a helmet, the rest of us did not. A simple headset to make radio comm easier was all I took. I also admit I was quite jealous of the UMP that Ms. Steel carried.

Quick gear shake down, tested the radios, then I hooked the scanner onto my back with a little help from Forsyth and we were off.

Ch. 2 The White Rabbit

The ride was quiet, I definitely think I scared Ulid. Still not totally sure how, but I'm sure that it will come with time. We took two black SUVs, both a modern Explorer. They were largely unaltered on the outside, with some markings that clearly indicated these were Steel Roses equipment. Probably better that way since we often traveled fully loaded for combat. Limbo hit shortly before we arrived, we were just pulling into the parking lot as the colors faded and the shrill whine hit my ears. Our vehicles had remained operational somehow, but everything else froze in its place. We parked in front, as I planned.

"Don't think I'll get used to this. It's 1400 but it looks like midnight." I grumble.

"We normal people say 2." Ulid quipped back. I glared at him.

"2-1, 2-2. How copy, over?" I called in the radio. It took some persuasion, but I got them to use proper call signs. The first digit was the team number, then the second was each fire team as necessary.

<"I got you."> Forsyth replied, and I sighed. The radio discipline was…Awful. I could only assume Forsyth got lazy after leaving Highway Patrol.

"2-2, entering west door." Ulid and I are 2-2, the other three are 2-1. Ms. Steel was the boss, she got the better call sign.

<"Same.">

Fighting the urge to cuss him out over the radio, I pushed open the door for Ulid to enter and followed him through. We moved quickly, rifles low, as I scanned the area.

Have you ever been inside a store, but it was a black and white photo at a busy hour? That's what this felt like, as if we just stepped into a still picture of life itself. One look told me this was not going to be easy as we had to watch our shots with all the mannequins around. Because those mannequins are definitely vulnerable to 5.56 and they would certainly start spraying blood once the color came back. And there were a bunch. We advanced to an unused checkout counter, parking ourselves behind it and scanned the area. While I hoped Ulid would mirror my actions and keep our firing lanes apart, he just followed me like a moron. I viciously pointed to my eyes and the other direction, which he understood with an eyeroll.

<"Hey, Fae says it's somewhere in the back left, your side. But…Still spread out? Weird.">

"2-2, copy all. All units proceed up center, watch your corners."

I took the lead this time, hoping to contain the chaos a little better. We pushed towards the center, main aisle, and I saw Ms. Steel leading her team, then Forsyth in the middle, followed by Rosewill. Not the best formation, but whatever. We pushed up through the aisle, the dead silence weighing on all of my senses. We all had to weave around the people frozen in time. Even my footsteps seemed quiet and distant, muted by Limbo. As we moved, I could tell that everyone besides

Rosewill had experience, but there was a disconnect on abilities. Like a hodge podge. No one really knew how to operate like a tight-knit team though. This made me nervous, as I was coming from a team that could almost communicate telepathically.

As we neared the back wall, something seemed off, even in this messed up Limbo world. Hairs on the back of my neck were standing up, just as I heard Forsyth hiss out.

"Hey! Over there!" He pointed with his offhand, tother on his rifle.

I stopped, instinctively putting up my fist as a signal to stop, and dropped to a knee, examining. He had pointed towards an area that seemed like offices, tucked in the back corner of the building. It was darker over there, but it wasn't meant for customers so that made sense. My head tilted, it almost seemed like the darkness was moving? I looked at Ms. Steel, and her eyes were locked in the same spot, some of the color draining from her face. I had my rifle low, but ready. I shifted to put a low counter of tennis racket displays between me and the...Mass? Shadow? I couldn't tell. The silence didn't feel quite so silent anymore, like there was a low rumble. A rustling? I still couldn't place it, and it was pissing me off. That was until I heard the scream. Shrill, loud, and from behind me. Fae had lost her nerve, and the sound reverberated in the darkness. I chance a glance, and she's white as a ghost, and she was frozen in her spot. The rustling ceased immediately. The lizard brain I had developed over years of combat started to freak out.

Out of the corner of my eye, I could see Ms. Steel start to fall back. I decided to follow suit with a motion of my hand, but made sure everyone else was behind me, I kept myself between the team and the shadows. The rustle started to return, but it was different. This time...Shuffling? A hundred feet moving around aimlessly?

Okay, THAT noise was a growl. Time to go. I jabbed with my hand in the air, telling everyone to fall back to the cars quickly. When I scanned behind to check where everyone was, Ulid was already at the door, and Forsyth started pulling Fae along. I still didn't understand what was happening, but I knew this was bad. You don't survive as many years in combat as I have without developing a sense of danger, regardless of whether it was from this earthly plane or something else entirely.

The shuffling intensified, it was growing around the wall to my right as I back peddled toward the entrance. Then I saw the wave of darkness move and morph. I could barely make out the individual shapes, but it looked like a massive crowd of people made from shadows, moving around the frozen real, colorless people and displays. Steel and I began a faster retreat towards the door as I identified their play. Old school pincer move. It started on the left of our formation, quickly spread out around the front, and I could pick up sounds and movements trying to encircle us. There had to be dozens, if not hundreds of individual forms.

They moved fast too…Shit, I wasn't going to get to the door! "To the trucks, now!" I finally turned and started at a run, the rest of the team broke into a dead sprint towards the door. Forsyth's smaller frame combined with being a little too much of a gentleman struggled to get the petrified Fae to the door as she was essentially frozen in fear.

I swore under my breath as I could hear the telltale sign of an engine revving and tires screeching. Did Ulid leave us? Sure enough, I could see one of the trucks drive away through the windows of the door and peel off into the distance.

"Go!" I barked at Forsyth. "You drive!" He looked at me, nodded, then bolted through the door. Almost like a linebacker, I scooped Fae up around the middle and pushed full speed toward the door. She was light, but her gear clocked me in the jaw and dug into my shoulder, none of which actually concerned me at this point. Forsyth was outside first and cranked the engine, as I slammed through the door. I hit hard enough that glass shattered, began to fly, then it just froze in time. I pushed through, ducking my eyes away from the shrapnel, seeing that Ms. Steel left the remaining rear door open so I could toss Fae inside like a human projectile. Pretenses, gentlemanly actions, and chivalry were gone now so I threw myself into the vehicle right on top of her getting a nice yelp as I rolled off her onto the seat. "Last man, punch it!"

The engine roared as we tore away. Steel, also sitting in the back, started hoisting Rosewill off the floorboard, and I clambered into the front seat. Now we were outside of the building, I could see the growing gaggle of what looked like people made of thick smoke. There were so many...It looked like a zombie movie but with the essence of people. One broke away from the pack as I got my bearings, a leader? A scout? It was so much faster than the others. It was also darker, with a hint of red eyes. It moved too quickly, it's visible features slightly elongated and completely unnerving. The worst part? The absolute lack of any facial features except those eyes.

"Don't stop! One broke away!" I barked. It was gaining on us, not like we had much chance as we had frozen cars all over the road to dodge. "Steel, can I kill this thing?!"

"I don't know! But...try!"

I rolled down the window, shoving my upper body out, wedging my legs on whatever surface I could get them secure on. It was only 20 feet behind us as Forsyth swerved us through traffic and turns. BANG BANG. Two shots, center mass, it didn't even flinch. "No effect!" I hollered back. BANG BANG BANG. Three more, they hit the shadow and then it just...Absorbed them? How am I supposed to fight this? I looked at my rifle, the tool I had bet my life on for years. How could it fail me now?

No sooner did the thoughts leave my mind, there was a soft, subtle, deep green that engulfed my rifle that faded after just a moment. Something told me to try again.

"Fuck it." I grumble.

I lined up my sights on the shadow, a task way harder than normal as I was still wedged in the window with Forsyth veering sharply and swerving as necessary. BANG BANG. The recoil felt different this time, and by God those rounds hit! The shadow thing screamed and convulsed, clearly caught off guard.

"HA!" I barked. My victory was short lived however, as it recovered quickly and lunged forward, rapidly catching back up to us. Apparently, it was done playing around. I could feel the jolt as it struck the rear tire, yanking my leg free of its secure position. As Forsyth lost control, the truck veered hard and began to spin, and before I could even react, I was thrown at the asphalt. Hard.

> *The Explorer had begun spinning and found a guardrail with its back end. That sudden jerk began to flip the vehicle, and Mr. Sixx went straight down, the Explorer rolling over his head by a fraction of an inch and into a ditch. The sounds of shearing metal and smashed glass were clear, and Jake was isolated from the team with the shadow glaring at him. His rifle had skittered across the pavement.*

I looked up, seeing nothing but sky. I could hear the chaos. My body screamed and my head swam. Everything was plunged into chaos, and I temporarily lost where I was. No rifle. I'm still breathing.

"Fuck..."

Fight on.

I drew my pistol.

> *He was unaware, but it had glowed green for a moment as well. The shadow slowed, staring at the broken car. It seemed as if it was a predator, examining its latest meal.*

"Fuck you." I levelled my pistol one handed, my left arm not seeming to respond. POP POP POP. They weren't great shots, but the thing sure felt it. It screamed, recoiling into itself. POP POP POP POP. Screams. Those hurt.

"Sit your ass down!" I growl towards it. I was halfway through my magazine.

POP POP. It screeched, convulsed, and collapsed to the ground. I took the chance to raise myself to my knees, I could tell I was in rough shape, there was a gash on my thigh. Don't care, fights not over. The shadow wasn't moving, but I leveled my pistol once more. POP- head POP- heart. Before the second round fired, it had begun to fade into nothing. I held my pistol aimed at where the thing was, but it seemed to be gone. I finally lowered my arm.

"Hell of a first mission. Oh shit." As I spoke, it was clear I had cracked some ribs. I turned towards the wreck, I saw Forsyth struggling to his feet and Ms. Steel standing, clutching her stomach and favoring her leg.

"Ma'am?" I choked out.

"What, Jake?" She almost growled back at me.

"This a bad time to ask about health packages?" She stared at me for a solid 5 seconds before dropping her head and looking away. "Understood ma'am, fucking off." Forsyth laughed audibly at that one.

"Jake, you still mobile? I need a hand getting Fae out." He asked through his laugh. I fought to get to my feet, the gash in my thigh screaming, causing my leg to shake violently as I put weight on it.

"Afraid not." I dropped to a knee to look at the injury myself. "She okay?" It was deep. It was my least favorite fix....Time for a tourniquet. No way to know how long it would take for medical to get to me.

"Think she was just knocked out in the wreck. She seems okay." He calls back. Out of the corner of my eye, I see Ms. Steel helping him pull Rosewill out.

"Good deal." I leaned against the guardrail and worked on getting the tourniquet on my leg. I had gotten really good at one handed setups, luckily. "Everyone still breathing?"

"Mostly." Ms. Steel had gotten herself to the same guardrail I was leaning against, I assumed Rosewill had been extracted. I looked up at her. If I had to guess, she had a broken rib or two, smacked her elbow and knee hard and got some cuts from the glass.

"Ma'am, what do we do now?" The tinnitus sound started growing about this point. Faint right now.

"This is my part. You relax, and don't make the docs think you're crazy."

"No ma'am, nothing crazy about fighting crazy shadow demons." I'd like to imagine she grinned, but I couldn't see it.

She actually did...I'm wondering if she has a concussion too.

"Here it comes." I grumble, the tinnitus grew towards crescendo.

"Indeed." She appeared to be working on some kind of device, as I set to take stock of the injuries I could now feel all too well. Dislocated shoulder, probably a few snapped ribs. Internals feel fine for now. Definitely smacked my head. But the worst was the deep gash, no longer bleeding thanks to the tourniquet. But I sure wasn't going anywhere any time soon. In fact...

"Ma'am...? I...May be taking a short nap soon." My vision had dark rings around the edges...Getting hard to think... "May have...Over done..."

Ch. 3 Drink Me

AUGUST 9TH, 2023

Everything felt heavy...Spongey even. Like I was stuck in Jello. I chanced opening my eyes, and it was bright. Medical, definitely. Great. The room began to materialize around me, medical equipment and its beeps and hums. White linens. It was hard to focus.

"Welcome back, kid." Male, somewhere to my side. Looking around, I easily found him. "Take it easy, I have you pretty doped up."

"Who you...?"

"They call me Jerry. And that is all you need to worry yourself with." He looked at the monitors. He seemed older...60s? Gray, receding hairline. Lots of lines on his face. "Ms. Steel put you right into the fire, didn't she?" He spoke softly, and a little slower than normal. It really made him feel like some kind, caring grandfather that everyone loved.

"Where...?"

"Relax kid. I work with Ms. Steel, you're back at the office. You lot like to take work home with you, so I'm your on call trauma doc." He gently patted my arm, it felt like it took a few extra seconds for my brain to recognize the feeling. The last mission slowly came into view in my mind.

"My team?" My voice was clearer now. "Where's my team?" I was trying to sit up, although it proved to be very difficult, even before he put his hand on my shoulder pushing me back down

"I said take it easy, kid. I'll hit you with more of the good stuff." His tone was harsher this time, but more cautionary than threatening. "They are mostly fine, some bumps and bruises. Ms. Steel got the worst, looks like an airbag nailed her ribcage and fractured her arm."

"Rosewill? Forsyth?"

"Nothing a few days and some aspirin won't fix." I finally started to relax. "Swift thinking with the tourniquet. Your past life taught you well." He grins at me before he steps out of the room. My head falls back to the pillow.

AUGUST 10TH, 2023

The next few hours passed slowly, but I was dazed thanks to the meds. I guess that meant I really didn't know how much time had actually passed. I was nearly dead accurate for all my injuries, I'd probably need a crutch for a week or two, but Jerry fixed me up good. He was tough but kind. I slept poorly through the night, I was unable to really find a comfortable position despite the heavy meds trying their best to make my head float away. Eventually, it must have become morning at some point as I woke up shortly before Ms. Steel and Fae arrived with coffee.

"You're my hero." I croaked, fatigue and pain mixing with the meds. I still wasn't all there.

"How are you today, Mr. Sixx?" Fae handed me the cup of coffee, stepped back, and Ms. Steel grabbed a seat and pulled it closer. She still handled herself well, even with only one arm, but I could note the stiffness in her movements.

I squinted at her. "I certainly am." Fae smiled at my broken sentence, Ms. Steel almost did but killed it. I looked between them. "Glad you're both okay. Did y'all figure out what that thing was?" I pause, realization hitting me. "Can...we talk openly here?"

"No one gets past the lobby without knowing what our real purpose is."

So that confirms we are back at the Roses. Not that I didn't trust Jerry, but I didn't know him. "Unfortunately, not a lot was learned. All we can say is there is some form of Shadow hoard, and it can contain some very fast shadows within it. We've taken to calling it a Shadow Swarm for now. Once you took down the leader, the rest vanished." My eyes fell on Fae.

"You look like you want to say something." I watched Fae, there was a look in her eye.

"How did you do it?" She almost whispered.

"Survive? I'm too stubborn to die." I shrugged, my tone a little confused and very sarcastic.

"No-I mean-Your gun." She was stumbling over her words. "It didn't work on them, then it did."

I shrugged again. "It glowed, then I felt like I should try again."

She stared at me. "That's...That's it?" I nodded. The ladies looked at each other, and Ms. Steel nodded again. Fae reached into her purse and pulled out-.

"My M9!" I could feel the smile creep across my face. "Oh, thank god." She handed it to me, I could instantly tell they had unloaded it, simply by weight alone. "Thank you." I looked it over, and sure enough, those letters were etched into the slide "SO OTHERS MAY LIVE - ATLAS - 11-23". On the opposite side, in a curvy font 'We're all mad here...' It was my retirement gift that I had been given on the last day. I still never figured out what magic trick the boss pulled to get my actual service weapon pulled from the armory, but I was beyond thankful. Most folks would have gotten a brand new one, but this one with years of service, holster wear, and more than a few scratches was my baby. She saved my life once or twice.

"Most of your gear was pretty roughed up, Lena did what she could for that pistol." Fae spoke, in an almost fearful tone. "She told me you better not die, she reserved that honor."

I smirked at her. "Like to see her try." I glanced at Ms. Steel, knowing there was more to it. "I assume you want me to try again?"

They both nodded. "Yes please, Mr. Sixx. I would like to see your ability in person." Ms. Steel spoke, as if awaiting a magician to do a trick.

I stared at the pistol, not really sure what to do. I racked the slide, double checking it was empty and aimed at a spot on the wall. Nothing happened. I lowered, raised again. Even imagined the shadow thing coming after us again, nothing. "Sorry ladies…" I tried again, and was intent to keep trying, when Ms. Steel touched my forearm.

"That's enough for today, you need to rest. We can try again later."

I nod. "Hey…"

"Yes, Mr. Sixx?"

"Ulid ever turn up?" There was a pause, likely from the hint of a growl in my voice.

"Yes. This morning." Ms. Steel finally spoke, her voice was possibly even angrier than mine.

I looked at her, apparently an aggressive expression as she cocked an eyebrow. "I'm gonna kick his ass."

"He's been suspended." She said tersely.

"He's gonna have his ass handed to him." Suspension wasn't enough.

"Mr. Sixx-"

"He deserted my team and his CO." I interrupted and Ms. Steel paused. I could see Fae's face get whiter as I spoke. She started looking everywhere but at the people in the room. "Suspension ain't enough."

"This isn't the military." Same terse voice. But I could tell there was an agreement in her tone.

"I'm aware. But this is combat, and that little shit has no discipline."

"I-"

"Ma'am, you recruited me for my background did you not?" I didn't let her finish again. She nodded slowly. "YOU wanted me to lead team 2. Correct?"

The room was silent. "I can make a lot of things disappear and happen to cover our activities, Mr. Sixx." Her tone changed to almost one of defeat, or resignation.

"That's not what I asked." I growled.

She sighed looking at the ground for a moment, before back at me. An understanding appeared in her eyes.

"Don't kill him."

"I second that." Jerry had walked in. The ladies both looked at him, as I suddenly realized how tightly I was gripping my pistol. I truly didn't want to kill him, but desertion...Only thing worse is being an actual traitor. "Good lord, I don't know what you kids are talking about but he needs to breathe." He was looking at the monitor, apparently my blood pressure and temperature were on the rise.

"Sorry doc." I leaned back against the bed, trying to recenter myself, taking a deep breath or two.

"Last mission went...sideways." Fae offered to Jerry, and he cracked up laughing.

"Yeah, I noticed. Ain't worked this hard for a while." He had turned back to the monitor. "Jake, you okay?"

"As well as can be?" My eyes flicked open and I looked at him.

"Your vitals returned to normal fast..." His voice trailed off.

I smirked at him. "I learned a few tricks in the service." Jerry looked at me, an impressed look on his face. Fae cocked her head to the side, confused. "So how long you gonna keep me cooped up here?"

Jerry looks at the monitor and consults a chart. "You seem stable enough." He looks at Ms. Steel. "He can survive a car ride home. However, I'd rather hold him for a day or two first." Jerry sets the chart back down, I got the feeling that Ms. Steel got the final say. Probably over concerns of Limbo issues?

"That will be sufficient." Ms. Steel stood up as she spoke. "You know what to do." She spoke to Jerry who nodded as she left. Fae remained, looking concerned, as Jerry busied himself with equipment in the corner.

"So." I spoke, Fae jumped. "This happen a lot?"

"Kinda…" Fae murmured.

"Not usually this bad." Jerry spoke up without turning. "Some minor injuries are to be expected, but you lot made me earn my pay today."

"Hey, looking out for you. Don't want you to be bored."

"Well, you could at least wear a helmet next time." He had returned to the side of my bed with a gentle smile. "Wasn't that a requirement for you?"

"No comment." I grumble. He had a point, sadly.

"Oh, I love the stubborn ones." He smirked, patted the edge of the bed and left.

"I should go too. Let me know if you need anything, okay?" Fae spoke softly again, her concern was evident. Now, under the sterile lighting of the medical room, I could see most of her faded highlights had vanished from her hair.

"Sure thing kid. And hey, don't worry about me. I've been through worse."

She pauses mid step, turns to me and then looks back at the door. "That…"

"Didn't help?"

She shook her head and left. This part sucked…I knew this was going to be a slow and painful ride until all was good.

AUGUST 11TH, 2023

Jerry got me out of bed and gave me some meds with some crazy words about 'taking things slowly' to which I wholesale ignored. I hated the crutch, but I managed to get used to it fairly quickly. They tried putting me in a wheelchair, but my stubbornness won out. The ladies drove me home in that same MKZ she first came by my place in. It was a mostly quiet ride which was fine by me, my head still wasn't quite right from everything that happened plus the medications. Speaking of, I felt every single bump as they started to wear out. It was not an easy task, but they both assisted me out of the car, the door and on the couch, which I greatly insisted on going to first. None of it was exactly smooth, neither one of them knew exactly how to help, but they did their best. Finally landing on the couch with a heavy sigh, I pushed my legs out in front of me and leaned back.

"You seem oddly calm for nearly dying." Fae spoke very tentatively. Judging by her expression, it was something she had been thinking for a while before finally blurting it out.

"You have no idea how common that's been." I smirked. Fae responded with wide eyes, as Ms. Steel reappears with a glass of water and the bag of meds. "Ma'am, you truly are a terrible gift giver." She didn't respond but handed me the water and set the bag next to me.

"And you have an awful sense of humor." Her tone was *almost* as if scolding a child, but I could hear the amusement in her voice. Much to my surprise, she sat on the recliner across from me. "I expect you to take those as prescribed."

I simply glare at her.

"That wasn't a request."

"Yes ma'am." There was an odd look in her eye, it was hard to place. It felt...soft? I looked between them. "Now, how are you two?"

Fae hung her head, refusing to answer. Ms. Steel didn't flinch. "Twas not the worst I've been through." I believed her. I had no reason not to, considering she's been doing this for a few years now.

"Ms. Rosewill?" I asked her pointedly.

She mumbled something.

"Didn't catch that. Ears don't work like they used to." I speak mostly plain, but there was an air of amusement. I've seen that reaction a few times before.

"I hate field work…" She spoke softly, still staring at the ground.

"I understand." I really did, it wasn't for everyone. "But your intel was helpful. Could have been way worse." She didn't seem to acknowledge me. "Fae?" She finally looked up, nodding slowly.

"I…" She chewed on her words, and I let her work through it. "Thanks." I made a mental note to try and keep her at base as much as possible.

"Any time, kid." I turned back to Ms. Steel. "Yall really don't need to babysit me. I'm sure you have other things to do."

"Fair enough." Ms. Steel stood up. "Please call one of us if you need anything. I expect you to take your medications and keep off your leg. No work until you're healed."

"But mom, what if Jimmy wants to play outside?" I could hear Fae snort and Ms. Steel tried really hard to keep a straight face.

"Then I'll call his mother and both of you will be grounded." She fired back without hesitation and I groaned loudly. "Sleep well, Mr. Sixx."

"Ma'am, ya'll drive safe. See you in the morning."

Ms. Steel shot me a look.

"I'm kidding! Good lord." She shook her head, and they departed. I grinned as the silence settled in. Once again, hard up with meds and bandages. Some things never change.

AUGUST 12TH, 2023

I had just woken up as my phone went off, text from Forsyth. I fixed myself some coffee and hobbled over to the couch to read it.

[Hey, still kicking?]

[Yup, only one leg though.]

[Ha, yeah. Heard you tried donating some bone marrow.]

[Something like that. You good?]

[Bit banged up but good. You hear from Ulid?]

[Nope. Probably for the best.]

[Yeah. Kid shocked me, always been a PITA but man…New low.]

[Yup. You got the receipt? Can we return him?]

[LOL nope. Hey, IDK if Sarah told you but that was actually a pretty dicey mission. She worried about you.]

[aww she DOES care]

[LOL yeah, I get that. Anyway, glad you're good. Think you're a good fit.]

[Thanks, glad to be here. Don't let her worry too much, I've had worse.]

[Yo, I stay outta her way. She scares me.]

[Lmao, yeah that checks. She got a way.]

Forsyth liked that message.

AUGUST 14TH, 2023

I never actually thought I'd be excited to see take out Chinese, but I couldn't turn it down when Ms. Rosewill pulled up at noon today with a bag of food! She still couldn't hide the concern in her eyes, which only cemented the fact that they have become accustomed to minor injuries at worst.

"So, how does your...detection work?"

"Hmm?" She looked up, finishing her bite. "It's...Hard to explain. Almost like a...A feeling. I've been experiencing it since I was a girl, so I've gotten really good at predicting it."

"As a kid? That had to be weird." I leaned back in the couch, cracking open a fortune cookie.

"Yeah..." Her face fell a shocking amount. "My parents put me through therapy...They couldn't understand why I was saying the color disappeared sometimes and that I saw weird things." She shrugged, coming closer to normal but not quite. "They tried to pass it off as imagination but eventually they got worried."

"Damn. I can see it." I glanced at the fortune. *'Smile when you are ready.'* I smirk, finding it humorously timed.

"Yeah...So about 12, I decided to ignore it and keep it to myself. Funny enough, using Limbo helped with my study time a lot."

"Okay that's slick."

"Yeah?" She smiled at me.

"Use your situation to your advantage, it's a big lesson I tried to teach the new guys."

"You mean, PJs?"

"The very same. The newbies are a bit of a blockhead usually, so getting them to think outside the box can literally save their life."

She nods, processing.

"I'm kind of impressed you came up with that plan at such a young age."

"I like to learn and study things..." She said sheepishly.

"Well, I'm glad you have the job you do, Ms. Rosewill." She shrunk into herself a fraction.

"Just...Fae. Fae is fine."

"Fair enough, Fae. I can handle that."

"So, yeah, I can detect it up to 2 weeks or so in advance and I've got a 90% accuracy right now. The scanners help a lot too and bring us up to a 99% of when, but the length is a real wild card. I can only really tell if it's just a little blip or it's going to be something worth sending a team out for."

"Right now, any little bit will help."

She smiled again, and I got the feeling she wasn't used to compliments. At very least, she didn't know how to handle them.

"By the way, I do apologize for manhandling you during the mission. Chivalry may not be dead, but it's not present under fire."

"Oh no it's fine." She looks up at me and smiles sweetly. "I understand, and I'm used to getting manhandled anyway." A single momentary beat happens before her eyes widen like saucers and she immediately hides her face in her hands. I can't stifle the chuckle that escapes me.

"Alright then, good to know." I smirk as I see the redness growing in her face.

"I..." She stammers a little before blurting out "Gotta go back to the office!"

AUGUST 16TH, 2023

"Yo, pegleg!" Forsyth barked as he climbed out of his truck. Not surprising he had an old Ram 2500. He closed the door with a thunk.

"If that sticks, I'll shove my crutch up your ass." We smirk at each other as he joins me on the porch and drops a brown bag with a burger and fries in my lap.

"You'd have to catch me first."

I glare at him as I unwrap the burger.

"You healing up?" His tone shifts as the topic changes.

"Too damn slow." I grunt.

"Yeah, I feel ya. Sarah hasn't said a word about her cast, but I know she wants to rip it off herself." Forsyth took a bite as he finished talking, and one of the pickles shot out the side.

"Nicely done." I quip.

"Thanks, I was aiming for your foot."

"Glad you shoot better. Anyway, she doing okay?"

"Still stressed. Think she feels like this is some kinda professional black eye."

"I can see it. She usually take things so personal?" I look over at him as I take a drink.

"Only the bad things. She's actually really great to work with and is an excellent boss."

"I got that feeling, she's a true professional."

"What gave that away?" He glances at me between bites.

"What doesn't?" I grunt.

Forsyth snorts. "Yeah, fair enough. Mind if I smoke?"

"Porch is fine. Inside, I'll snap your neck."

Unfazed by my threat, he lights up a cigarette, and we sit for a bit enjoying the sunset.

"Hey…she pissed that she got one mission out of me then had to bench me for a month?"

"Nope." He blew out a cloud of smoke into the empty air. "Hard to tell, but I think she's pleased despite the results."

"Cool."

Another comfortable silence.

"Before you ask, we ain't a thing." He suddenly blurts out, and I turn fast to stare at him.

"Fuck you talking about?"

"Sarah and me. Nothing going on."

I shrug. "Okay, what brought that on?"

"I watch people. Some people call it intuitive."

"Ah. Makes sense." I nod. So, he's the quiet, insightful type who doesn't talk much. That could be very valuable.

"Yeah, figured you were about to ask."

"Nah, last thing on my mind is who's sleeping with who."

"Lonely." He jabs under his breath.

"Professional." I correct and glare at him. "Dickhead."

He smirks and takes another drag as another silence settles in. After a while, he finishes it, flicks it out into the gravel and stands.

"You know how to reach me. I don't live too far."

"Thanks, Forsyth."

"Any time, boss."

AUGUST 18TH, 2023

I woke sharply on the couch, my TV having shut off at some point. Jeez, I must have taken a nap. I look to the window as I pick up the sounds of an engine shutting off followed by a door shutting. I could barely make out a flash of red hair from someone approaching my door.

"Open." I bark out as she knocks.

"I suspected you of all people would lock your door."

"I like to live life dangerously." I smirk as she enters, and I pull out my pistol hidden in the couch next to me. She nods with acknowledgement as I return it to its home while she crosses to the kitchen.

"I have purchased some gyros for dinner." She placed the bag on my counter and started setting stuff up one handed.

"Need help?"

"I require you to regain your health."

"Same could be said for your chicken wing, ma'am." I heard silence other than the rustling of food stuff. She appeared shortly handing me a pair of gyros and she took her own, sitting across from me. "You seem to be getting along fine though."

"It's not complex." She said simply. I nod, taking a bite. It was surprisingly good.

"So, injuries a common occurrence?" I was curious to hear it from the horse's mouth, but doubted I'd be able to glean much.

"We are a combat orientated organization, Mr. Sixx." As I expected. "I must say, this mission has definitely been a higher cost than average."

"Was there anything we could have done differently?" I ask, I lacked the experience to truly analyze the outcome.

"Alas, not this time. A new iteration always brings forth uncertainty. I'm fine with replacing one of our vehicles, those are expendable."

Her eyes flick to me from her meal, before returning to her meal. I could pick up the unspoken 'people are not'.

"Makes sense. How are you holding up?"

"I can manage just fine, thank you." I saw a ghost of a smirk on her face. She really was a tough cookie.

"Don't know about that ma'am, you are missing a critical part of your recovery." I motioned at her cast, and she looked at me with an eye of confusion. "You lack signatures, well wishes, and insane drawings on that cast."

She simply sighed, apparently dismissing my comment. I grinned at her.

"I should inform you of some intricacies of Limbo, while we are here." She had just finished half of her meal and wiped her hands on a napkin. "I am positive Fae informed you of some of the aspects we deal with. However, one thing I must stress to you. Limbo does not have laws, nor does it respect your logic. It simply does not care what you understand of the world."

"You know, the Wonderland comments I've made before are a lot more accurate now." I quip between bites.

"Certainly. From all we can understand, it is a fracturing of space time that allows certain entities to operate with freedom. Fortunately, it is usually easy to make that determination as those entities retain their color and autonomy when Limbo opens."

"Yeah, I noticed that. Couldn't tell on the shadow people cause...well...Shadows are absent of color."

"Correct. Some entities have the ability to affect our world. The Siren would be a prime example, they can in fact corrupt normal people over time." She takes a drink, while I nod and process the info.

"So...Unexplained disappearances. Unexplained murders, or even ones that don't seem right..."

"Correct again. Some can kidnap, maim and murder and leave their destruction on our world. Some can cause people's minds and wills to be changed."

"So…This mission's more important than I thought."

"Typically, the vast majority are contained within Limbo and the damage they can inflict is minimal. We must remain aware of all of them, however. Additionally, as I stated before, Limbo has no laws. It affects the world over, however the Appalachians seem to be a known hot spot. This was not the case when I was a girl. Most of Europe was a hot bed, and Limbo reliably opened at noon every Sunday."

"Sounds almost nice."

"The predictability was welcomed, however my parents told stories of the activity being far more intense and dangerous."

"Catch 22." I grumble.

"Precisely. We also had part of a year where the color was not drained. More specifically, seven months. Then it came right back to what we know. Nothing has indicated a reason."

"Guessing we aren't supposed to know." I said softly.

"Perhaps." She picked up her meal again and started to eat once more.

"You've been at this for a while, haven't you?"

"Since a kid." She spoke between chewing and a bite.

"And all this time, it's still hard to nail everything down." I exhale. "This is gonna be a wild ride."

"One might say it's like following the rabbit."

AUGUST 25TH, 2023

The revolving doors of meals and visitors alike kept up at a very predictable pattern. Every other day, typically Forsyth, Fae, then Ms. Steel. I'd be a liar if I said I wasn't looking forward to it. I was doing my best to stay sane this time. This morning, I had just sat down with my cup of coffee, muttering a few choice words at the pain in my leg. That's when I could hear it, a small faint whistle that grew quickly to the shrill whine once more. Fae was right, she texted out an alert that something was coming this morning. This would be the second time since my injury, but the first was only a blip. I went ahead and paused the TV, as I knew it wouldn't work when it hit anyway. And then, the colors faded. I laid my head back on the couch and sighed into the silence of the air around me.

A few moments passed before I felt an oddness about the room. I picked up my head to scan the room, but it didn't take any effort to see a shadow standing in front of the TV. It just stood there. It was different from the swarm boss, but I couldn't place it. Slowly, I reached over to where my pistol was, and just as slowly it reached out a hand as if to say it wasn't necessary. I paused, staring at where its head was, poised to lunge for it if needed but something in the air told me it would be fine.

Memories of the Siren are still in my head, so I wasn't leaving much to chance.

As if reading that last thought, the strangest thing happened. Despite Limbo still being well established, a soft, gentle wind blew through my room and played with my hair. It felt as if the earth was telling me it was okay, not to worry. The shadow tilted its head slightly. I focused more on it, and it certainly seemed as if it was a human, made of dense dark black smoke. It was nearly solid, but the glow of the TV partially bled through. Its head turned towards the window, and another smokey form phased through the window. This one was much different, it seemed to have a hint of brown and what appeared to be leaves and twigs barely visible but swirling around its form. It looked more like a fox than anything else. It approached the figure, rubbing against its legs before turning to me and sniffing my outstretched foot. It gently put its foot on mine, as the shrill whine started to take away these odd images and replace them with color.

"Now what the hell was that about?" I mutter to myself as normalcy returns.

AUGUST 27TH, 2023

The absolute slog of healing. I've reached the depths of every streaming service known to mankind, the delivery guy was on first name basis with me, and I hated seeing the same walls. Day after day. I was going crazy! Despite the Roses sending someone every other day, I was definitely getting cabin fever over here. I ditched the crutch yesterday, my leg was still really tender, but I was mobile enough. I'd kill for a drink, but I wasn't about to mess around with drugs and alcohol. I checked my watch, it was about 0900 on a Sunday. I made two cups of coffee and went to the couch, setting one in front of me and the other in front of the recliner. Sure enough, I could hear the faint sound of crunching gravel and the purr of that Lincoln.

"Doors open, ma'am!" I called out from the couch as she approached. I heard the pausing of footsteps before she recovered and entered. She closed the door, turning to face me. Today she wore a ponytail, black leather jacket and jeans. Must be a bit chilly out. She stared at me. "I'm psychic." I quipped, short and dry.

"Have I really become that predictable in less than a fortnight?" She shakes her head, crosses to the recliner and sits down, I eye the cup telling her it's hers without words.

"Ma'am, no one says fortnight anymore."

She sighs, takes the cup and smells it. "I see you're feeling spritely."

"Well, I've been sitting here staring at the wall...Soooo...Yeah. I may be a little angsty."

"How's your leg?"

"Usable."

"That's not an answer."

"Surely it is?" She stared at me. "Still tender but weight bearing. Not that I've tried running laps or anything."

She nods as she takes a sip. "Good. Guess just a few more weeks?"

"Damn I hope less. Getting really tired of this."

"Thought you were enjoying your time off?" I glared at her, the only hint of playfulness was a glint in her eye. "Rich, coming from the one who claimed he was retired." I glared...uh...harder? She smirked.

"Look, I was expecting to be able to walk. I'm tired of games and videos." I grumbled.

"Oh, I bet." She leaned back in her chair, nursing the coffee.

I paused. "Ma'am?"

She tilted her head, eyebrow raised in acknowledgement.

"Don't take this as a complaint, but you have four teams to run. Surely you have your work cut out for you?"

"Kicking me out so soon?" She did not move to leave. "Can't I monitor my latest investment?" Hmm. Maybe Forsyth was right, she wasn't used to this much injury.

"Phones work just as well?" I threw back at her.

"Well, if you don't care for the company." She started to get up.

"Hey now, I didn't say that." She called my bluff. I enjoyed these mental tennis matches, even though I rarely came out on top.

"Oh?" She paused.

"Just...trying to understand. Get a read on the people I'm working with."

She looked at me intently. "You were a First Sergeant, weren't you?"

"You have more of my record than I do." I grumble again, a little annoyed at that fact.

"I can see why." She leaned back into her chair. "However, I don't intend to be easy to read."

"Well, you got that damn well under control." Again, she was on me before I could even make an advance.

Her face was attempting to goad me into continuing, which I was intent on not doing so. She took another sip of her coffee, the air of victory floating around her. We sat in a comfortable silence for a few moments.

"Ma'am, any updates from the office?"

"Been pretty quiet. Some small Limbo strikes here and there but nothing substantial. Fae seems to expect something in about a week or two, but nothing solid."

"Glad I ain't missed anything then."

"Quiet overall." She clarified and paused, chewing on a thought. "Ulid came back."

My nostrils flared but I tried to keep it together.

"He's actually scared witless. Asks daily when you're coming back." She said, softer this time.

"Good." My voice was a little more of a primal growl than I intended.

She pauses again, looking at me. "I hope you intend to honor your promise."

I look back at her. "You really think me that ruthless?"

"I saw the look in your eye."

"Yeah, fair, I heard I have a glare. You charged me with leading that team. I doubt you'll want to be there when I set him straight, but I'll do what I can to make him a team player."

She looked at her cup. "Doesn't really make me feel better."

"I will not kill him, ma'am. I promised you that."

She looked up at me.

"I understand our situation. I also understand combat and how youngins can react. I only need him to fear God, not see him," I tried to clarify again, I think my performance in the field made even her wonder just what I was capable of.

She was chewing on her thoughts. "I suppose I am unfamiliar with your techniques."

"I know you ain't got a reason, but I'm gonna ask you to trust me. This is far from my first rodeo." A beat, I tilt my head to the side. "First one with shadow people though…"

I could see a little lightness return to her eyes. "Unique, isn't it?"

"Not the word I would use, but yes ma'am."

"What would you use?"

"Fuckin' fucked." She smirked. "With some fuckin's on the side."

"Eloquent."

"You didn't hire me for my words, ma'am."

"Quite right." She set her cup down and stood up. "I need to take this." She pulled her phone out as she crossed to the door and stepped outside. I couldn't make out enough words to figure out the conversation, but it sounded relatively important. After a few, she came back inside, collecting her cup but not sitting. "Afraid I will have to leave you alone again, paperwork awaits." She downs the rest of her coffee.

"That's the life of the boss. Thanks for coming by." I raised my drink in a sort of salute to her.

"Certainly. I'll ask Jerry to come check on you in the next day or two." She speaks as she walks to the kitchen, and cleans her cup, setting it by the maker.

"I would have gotten that. Ain't got much better to do."

As she returned to the living room, "Until Jerry says you're good, I expect you to stay off that leg."

"Okay, but what if I just really don't want to?"

"I shall not repeat myself, Mr. Sixx." She checked my meds on my end table before straightening up. "Expect Jerry shortly, perhaps I'll see you at the office soon."

"Have a good one. Don't get a papercut!"

She shook her head again at me. "Rest up, Mr. Sixx." She left, and I listened to the car leaving the driveway. Back to the boredom I suppose.

Ch. 4 Eat me

AUGUST 29TH, 2023

"Interesting…" Jerry had been doing a checkup for the past ten minutes, checking vitals and looking over everything. He sat back on the chair he dragged over and sort of glared at me. "If there was a procedure to remove stubbornness, I'd make you go through it."

"Hey I have been behaving!" I actually had been trying. Plus, the alternating visits from Fae and Ms. Steel helped a lot to keep me at bay.

"Hmm…" He looked at my leg then back at his clipboard. "Ah, I see now. That does make sense." He nods to himself, pauses, and pulls out his phone. "Ah good evening, ma'am. Yes, I am here with him now….Certainly. Not quite as fast as I hoped. I would say no earlier than the 10th…Yes, next month…."

"Next month??"

Jerry put up a finger to shush me, which just irritated me more.

"We shall see. I'll wrap up and head out." He hung up.

"That bad?"

"No, just slower than normal. I have a theory but you can't just will yourself to heal I'm afraid." He started putting everything away.

"So, I'm stuck here til the 10th?"

"Yup."

"Don't tell me, desk duty."

"You're a smart kid." Jerry smiled at me, which only made me groan and lay my head back on the couch. "It'll be over soon enough. At least you're still getting paid?"

"Yeah yeah. Just sucks."

"I'm sure." He flipped the flap of his bag closed. "Well, I'm off. Enjoy your forced vacation."

"You know I won't."

He gave a soft chuckle as he left.

SEPTEMBER 8TH, 2023

As the days dragged on, the visits luckily continued as scheduled. I really appreciated the silent company of Forsyth, the borderline awkward Fae and the friendly business of Ms. Steel. They really did keep me grounded. I had a long chat with an old buddy who was still in the service, he made merciless fun of me getting injured on the first mission out, but it was a good reminder of days gone by.

Still not officially cleared to walk, I ignored it most days. I wasn't quite ready to run again, but it was able to handle walking around the house and taking care of long overdue chores, thankfully.

SEPTEMBER 10TH, 2023

Ms. Steel met me at the office door, her eyes narrowed. Scrutinizing. I dare say, even judging. "Where's your crutch?"

"Morning, ma'am! Oh yes, it's great to be back, thank you."

She was blocking the door, and a small piece of me wondered how easily I could have moved her if I so chose. Another part of me figured she wouldn't let it be as easy as I thought. Catch 22.

"If you break your stitches, I'm going to have Jerry keep you sedated until they fully heal." Her arms were crossed. I could tell she was not amused, and quite possibly completely serious.

"They'll hold, not to worry." I grinned at her.

"You better bring it with you tomorrow."

"It's the darndest thing, it broke just last night. When I was using it, of course." I grinned as her nostrils flared, finally relenting, and stepping aside so I could enter.

"Welcome back." She spoke softly, almost reluctantly.

"Thank you, ma'am."

She was not waiting for my response and was already halfway across the room. "Yeah, suppose that's about right." I mutter to myself and follow her deeper into the building, making my way back to the team room at a much slower pace. As I entered, it was clear it had been empty for a while. Lights were off, no smell of coffee, nothing. Suppose meeting Ulid on my first day back would lead to some issues, but I did half expect to see Forsyth. Might as well get coffee started.

Shortly after I had the pot brewing there was a knock on the door. I turned to look, but it didn't open.

"It's open!" I called out, leaning against the counter.

"Jake? You're back already??" Fae peeked around the door, her eyes lighting up. "I thought you had another week?" She entered, followed by another young lady behind her.

"I was bored."

"How are you?"

"Eh, I've had worse. Leg's still a bit tender but the rest is fine."

"I'm glad." She paused, hesitated and bounced forward for a hug. It was brief, but was tight, and reminded me that my ribs were still a little sore too. "Sorry...I was just worried." She muttered as she let go.

"Takes more than that to take me down. Who's your friend?" I had noticed another figure with her lingering in the doorway, I assumed my existence threw off Fae's plan.

"Oh! Amelia Lancer, meet Jake Sixx. Team 2 lead."

"Pleasure to meet you." I offered her my hand, sizing her up as I did. Medium height, medium build. Athlete of some kind, nervous as hell though. Dark brown hair, just past her shoulders, and a practical outfit. Her eyes were wide, a hint of being lost and unsure about coming here but determined to stick it out. I liked the look in her eyes.

"You too." She shook my hand, a firm enough handshake but a hint of timidness.

"New guy?" I asked, she nodded. "Cool, full fire team now if Ulid shows his dumbass head." She looked at Fae, a mixture of confusion and alarm. "Don't worry about it. Coffee?" I pointed at the machine behind me.

"No thank you, I'm a tea fan."

"Heathen." I grunt, she looks at me like I just cussed her out. "Ah, yeah, sorry. Usually, I wait until the second day to be an ass. Where you from?"

"You guys flew me in from California."

"Rog, how long you been dealing with Limbo?"

Fae took a seat nearby, listening as we talked.

"I can remember maybe...Four times. It's all a blur though."

"Good deal. Any fighting experience?"

"Kinda. I did some boxing in high school. Does archery count?"

"I mean yeah, if you can actually use a bow that can deliver some hurt."

"I'd say a 50 pound compound can do the trick." There was a hint of smugness. I did not know the metrics here for being considered impressive though.

"Sounds solid to me, make sure you check in with Lena, and she can make sure you have the right stuff."

"Who?" Her brow furrowed.

"Oh, just a sweet teddy bear of a woman. You'll love her." I smirk and toss a side eye glance at Fae.

"Mr. Sixx..." Fae's turn to scold me, that's a first. It also lacked any real punch and just made me smirk again. "She is...Passionate and gruff. Just be kind and patient."

"Yeah, and don't make eye contact." I gave an absolute deadpan delivery here. "No sudden moves, don't wear red. You know, that stuff." I maintained my expression as she looked between the two of us, confused and concerned. I finally break into a smile. "Come on kid, I'll protect you." I saw Fae shake her head as I led Lancer to the armory. Out in the hall, I stirred my coffee a little as we walked. I kept my slow pace because my leg was still mending. I could tell I had a soft limp as we moved.

"Are you okay?" Lancer asked softly.

"Yeah, just got a little roughed up in the last go."

"Is...Is that common?" She asked even more hesitantly than before.

"Combat of any kind could get you injured. But you have me. You'll be fine." I gave her a soft smile over my shoulder. "I'm unkillable."

I opened the door to the armory before she could fully process my words. I spoke before Lena could bark. "Morning, Lena, did you miss me?"

"You're still alive?!" She tried to sound angry, but I could tell there was a relief in her voice, hidden deep. Very deep.

"Sorry to tell you, but yeah. Still breathing."

"Damn, next time I'll cut the brake lines." She had actually stopped what she was doing to talk.

"You sure you know what those are?" That got a glare, as I walked up to the counter, leaning against it more to keep weight off my bad leg than anything else.

"You drive that F250 yeah?" She almost sounded like a viper.

"So, this here is Amelia, a new member of team 2. She is an archer." I motioned to Lancer who was lurking by the door, clearly unnerved by the conversation I was intent to end before I signed up for something. Lena sighed, spinning up for her usual spiel.

"We can offer you a plain M4 and some mags with a basic chest rig. Pistols, swords, bows are on your own dime." She pointed to a closet with the same screwdriver. "Arrows are in there. Ordnance on the back wall." She glared at me. "I won't be giving out the ordnance 'toys'." So, I made quite the impression, it would seem. "I can clean whatever you bring me. Backlog ain't short. Everyone gets comms, one scanner per team and I only issue those to team leads. They are worth more than you are."

"Polished, I am impressed. Thought I was special at first." I said dryly.

"Oh, you're special alright. Now shut up before I balance that hole in your leg out."

"Uh... Thank you." Lancer squeezed out.

Lena aimed a threatening screwdriver at Lancer then me, before back to her as she talked. "If you kick this guy's ass, I'll buy you dinner." Lancer's eyes went wide.

"Say the word."

"And get the wrath of Sarah for breaking her new favorite toy? How dumb do you think I am??" She brandished the screwdriver like a sword at this point.

I never flinched, but Lancer looked concerned. I simply grinned at Lena.

"Well, I see my job is done here, let's finish the tour. See you around, Lena."

"God, I hope not."

***

The next few days were a pleasant, if sometimes mundane, return to form. I got to know Frank Sire a bit more, he was a very friendly man who used to be an actor before joining the Roses. He was amusing but honestly, a lot to handle when he was around.

Forsyth, Lancer and I had begun doing some light training, which usually ended up with me teaching, trying to demonstrate, and getting yelled at for not taking it easy. A lot of the training I directed was combat based first, medical and survival a close second. I was forced to triage the skills we all needed for this with little understanding of Limbo and even less time.

Lancer was a killer shot with the bow and had some decent cardio but was lacking in just about every other combat skill. What she lacked in ability, she made up for in tenacity and drive. Forsyth was certainly learned, and working with him was great. He and I had matching and complimentary skill sets, so Lancer got the best of two worlds. The lone wolf mentality in Forsyth seemed to be slowly disintegrating too. One morning he even went so far as to bring in some doughnuts.

Ch. 5
The Spade Gardner

SEPTEMBER 13TH, 2023

It was getting near the end of shift. Despite not being cleared for duty, I still came in during our shift to show support. I wasn't keen on the night shift, and it was nearing the beginning of normal people's work hours by now. I had settled to work on the coffee machine. Finally, it finished up. I grabbed my cup, turned around and the door opened. I was not expecting the face I saw, it was Ulid. He froze, eyes wide, as I slowly set my coffee down. I stared back, waiting for him to make a move.

"Good...Morning...Sir." His voice was strained and horrified.

"Good start. Sit." I motioned at the table, collecting my coffee and sitting across from him. "I promised Ms. Steel I wouldn't kill you." Ulid's eyes were a mix of fear and a shred of defiance.

"Yeah?"

"Yes." We stared at each other in silence. "You understand what you did was treason, right?"

"Treason?!" He exclaimed loudly.

"I didn't stutter." I didn't even flinch at his outburst. I really would have enjoyed lunging across the table, though. "We are a combat team. Military or not. That means when we hit the field, I need to trust you to have my back. I will do the same for you."

"But-"

"Do not interrupt me. You destroyed the little trust and faith I had in you." I could still see him wanting to lash out. "You left us to die. You left your CO to die."

"You got away-"

"The fuck did I just say?"

"I....Not to interrupt." His voice lost the last bit of defiance it had. Apparently my disturbingly calm mannerisms finally did him in.

"Then shut the fuck up, boy. Your actions cost me two months on the bench and broke the commander's arm." I took a breath, I could feel my pulse rising. "If you work with me, I will drag your ass out of hell no matter my cost. If you work against me, I will cast you into it myself and leave you there." My tone hit home, as his eyes changed once more. It looked almost like a resignation. "I expect that my team trusts each other, and we will train and fight until that is so. I will not accept leaving a man behind or being left behind. Is that understood?" He nods. "Words."

"Yes."

"It happens again, you won't see another sunrise." I stood up from the table, collecting my coffee and walked out immediately, without waiting for a response. I stopped outside the door, taking a sip of coffee before walking towards the lobby area. I glanced at my watch, 0657.

She should be here any second now. And sure enough, the lobby door chimed as she unlocked it and entered. "Ma'am."

She looked back at me, hesitating as she was not expecting to see me at all. "Shouldn't you be asleep?"

"Negative. End of shift debrief."

She stared at me. "We could do this after you sleep…"

"Sure." I dismissed her statement.

"Yeah, okay. Come with me." Had to be a record, got her shaking her head at me before 0700. I followed her to her office and took the chair on the other side of her desk. She placed her coat and bag in the corner and made herself comfortable. Her office was simple, some photos and certificates, licenses on the walls, and a strange painting of an ocean scene on one of the walls.

"Ma'am, shift was quiet. Single blip, no deployments."

Her head tilted, processing how that was applicable. "Good. No funny business?"

"No ma'am." I took another drink and shrugged.

Ms. Steel nodded and cocked an eyebrow. "Well anyway, this all sounds like an email."

"Sure, but then I wouldn't get to bother you first thing, ma'am."

She sighed.

"Oh, Ulid's back." She looked at me sharply, the tone in the room changing immediately. "He's still breathing. Don't worry."

"How'd it go?"

"We will see. I plan on abusing him during training."

"Excuse me?" Both eyebrows went up this time.

"It's not hazing, just gonna put him through the most demanding training I can." I smirked. "I'm not an animal."

"Just be careful."

"I will." I grin at her.

She paused and took a deep breath. "You're probably the only one here that makes my hair start to turn gray."

"Ma'am, not even Ulid?" I feigned being hurt.

"He's an idiot, you're a handful." I grinned as she talked. "Maybe an idiot too." I feigned another hurtful look.

"Ma'am, how could you? My delicate sensibilities..."

She simply glared at me.

"Understood, shall I leave you to the daily chores? Team 3 is already here and getting warmed up."

"Yes please. Thank you."

"Yes, ma'am."

SEPTEMBER 15TH, 2023

I evaded it for as long as I could, but Ms. Steel herself dragged me to the doctor. I had mostly healed, but he wanted to do a follow up, nonetheless. I sat on the cold table as he came in and paused, looking at me.

"This isn't a funeral." Jerry said with a small grin.

"Sorry doc."

"Yeah yeah, I get it. Looks like you've been in a room like this more than most." He sits down on his chair. "Military life isn't easy on a body, and your job is one of the worst. Most of these I'm not worried about, easily manageable with our current ops. These two..." He showed me an MRI of my brain and a document about my Pernicious Anemia.

"Yeah, well. Setting off an IED sometimes has lasting effects."

"Agreed, but there's something different about this spot here." He pointed to the MRI. I couldn't tell you what he saw, but I trusted he saw something. "I'd like to monitor you while you're here as that doesn't seem naturally forming. Don't worry, you aren't the only one like this. I suspect Limbo has something to do with it." He tossed the scan on his desk and leaned back in his chair.

"Yeah, we don't know how it works, do we?"

"Correct. Everyone here does have some form of anomaly. Mundane birthmark, to shadows on the brain and everything in between."

"Weird."

"Very. I pulled your data from before and after the TBIs, I'd like you to retest in a few months to make sure all your marbles are in order."

> *A TBI is the acronym for a Traumatic Brain Injury. It encompasses most things that involve sudden or severe*

impact to the skull. Concussions are often the most common.

I chuckled at that. "Dunno about that one, doc."

He grins and nods. "So, this other concern…"

"I have to take a shot every week. Usually Sunday night, and I have two in a small hard case for my kit. I've become adept at it." I was waiting for this question and ran through it a few times mentally by now.

"Slow down, killer. I don't doubt you, just need to know what I'm working with. It is quite the rarity." He pulls out a small hard case from his desk, not unlike the one I carry in the field. "Here. Autoinjector. If you need it in the field, you'll want something easy." He hands me the case and I take it, popping it open. It was bigger than my normal stuff, but not enough to be concerned. It really resembled an EpiPen.

"Thanks doc."

"I'm here to help, believe it or not." He collected his papers as he gave me a soft, knowing look.

"I'll keep that in mind."

"I would say it's safe to assume it's affected your overall health?"

"Not really. I can get a little winded before the next shot. Oh! Uh, healing from injuries isn't exactly fast…As you noticed."

"Mmhmm. Good. I'm done torturing you for now, you're free to move about the cabin."

SEPTEMBER 16TH, 2023

Today may be a record. I hadn't even fully entered the lobby before I saw Ms. Steel glaring at me.

"You have a new job to do." She spoke simply, turned and walked deeper into the facility. I hurried after her, thinking we were going to her office before she turned into a side office I hadn't really noticed before. Inside there was a pair of desks, nothing out of place for a normal office section. Fae sat at one of them, busy clacking away on a keyboard and only pausing to look up as we approached.

I looked at Ms. Steel, then the desks and dread began seeping in. Was she chaining me to a desk?

"Oh, good morning!" Fae chirped.

"Good morning to you too. I believe we have found someone to utilize this desk, finally."

"Yeah?" Fae smiled widely. "Oh good! Mr. Sixx, you're going to help out?"

"Apparently so." I was full of apprehension as to this new tasker.

"Fret not, Mr. Sixx. I suspected someone of your caliber could make good work of a semi secluded space. Plus, Fae has been chasing down something interesting for a few weeks and could use some assistance."

I look between the two ladies. "So..."

"I assure you, I fully intend to put you into harm's way again as soon as you are able."

"Fair enough." I nod quickly, happy with the answer and assuming she could read my mind. A sudden thought appears and I look at her. "So, resume first sergeant duties?"

"One could say as such. Fae?"

"On it!" Fae jumps up as Sarah leaves. "Okay, so I have been tracking the location of some new kind of entity."

"Another one already??"

"Not unheard of, but a little abnormal, sure." She grinned, I suspected she was excited to chase down a puzzle. "Okay, so..." She leaned over and busied herself with the computer and the wall lit up with a projector. "See the dots?"

"Yeah, kind of all over the place, aren't they?" I looked over the map, it was essentially a third of the state of North Carolina, the whole triangle of western NC. Some dots even ventured into Tennessee. There were probably 50 or so dots of various colors.

"Yes. These are all different mystery events that have been confirmed in the area. Red dots are murders, yellow is injuries that shouldn't be possible, and orange are people that lost their minds, even for a few minutes." She pointed at a corresponding color as she moved. "I'm trying to isolate the what and where, but it's proving difficult."

"I can see that, it's almost like a unicorn puked on the screen." I speak softly, sitting on my new desk. "Are these confirmed to fit the bill or just suspected?"

"Oh, the suspected ones fill the screen. One of us has reached out or gathered some form of proof that backed up the story."

"Shit." I grunt.

"It's been keeping me busy." She smiled sweetly, the girl loves her puzzles it seems.

"So, what's the dope?"

"Uh..."

"What do you need from me? I'm no puzzle master."

"Oh! A fresh set of eyes and tactical advice. Limbo has been too short lately-"

The door opened and Ms. Steel reappeared.

"Got a new one for you, Fae." She walked in and handed her a folder before looking at the screen.

"Oh, thank you!" Fae opens the folder and nearly dives in.

"Seems like it hasn't gotten any clearer. Every report just muddies the picture." Ms. Steel spoke softly.

"Hold on…" I step closer, my fresh eyes picking out a slightly denser batch of dots. "What about this?"

Both ladies step closer, Fae stepping very close, but I could tell she was fixated on where I was pointing.

"Wait…" She grabs a ruler and runs back to the screen.

"Could that be a Graal pattern, Fae?"

Fae starts measuring and muttering incoherently to herself.

"Don't mind her, Mr. Sixx. This is her system."

"No worries, there was a kid that wasn't much different a ways back. Parachute packer, kid talked to himself the whole time but there was no one I'd rather on my gear."

"Glad to hear it."

"Aha!" Fae jumped in. "Yes! This matches a Graal hunting pattern." She pauses, I guess she was disappointed that it wasn't so new after all. "But that is way more psycho than physical attacks…" Her excitement immediately returned.

"Uh…FNG in the room." I speak softly, reminding her I am mostly clueless.

"Oh! Yes. Graal are killers. Mean things, they can fire brutally effective spikes at their victims. They usually don't mess with their victims minds, just kill or maim…"

"What about the rumor overlay?"

"Untrustworthy. Many people claim they see things in the mountains, however it is usually a manifestation of something else or some substance that inspires it." Ms. Steel spoke up, half absently as she analyzed the map.

"Exactly." Fae replied and then huffed. "Still too much ground to cover. We need more intel."

"What about probing patrols?" I offer.

"Pardon?" Ms. Steel looked at me.

"Okay, so take your best guess and station a team there when Limbo hits. Like right here." I grab a pen off Fae's desk and point to a spot that looked like a strong concentration with a lot of possible hiding spots. "Limbo opens, they scan the area. It's slow, kinda painful, but it's better than sitting around waiting."

The ladies look at each other, thinking. Finally, Ms. Steel breaks the silence.

"Change the schedule, Fae. Two teams per shift when Limbo is likely. Deploy a team to start searching, leave one on standby."

"Will do. I'll start working on a search pattern!"

"Good work, you two." Ms. Steel nods, then makes for the door.

"Thanks, ma'am."

"Yeah, thanks Sarah!" Fae returns to her computer. "Oh hey, can you look at the schedule and reassign teams?"

"Yeah, no problem." I take the folder from Fae's hands and slap it on my desk as I take a seat and wake up the computer.

SEPTEMBER 20TH, 2023

"Alright boys, here's the sich." I sat on my desk, the projector lit up on the wall.

"Sich? Ain't heard that since some cartoon in the early 2000s!" Sire smirked.

"Shut up, I'm old." I used the laser pointer I found in some box somewhere to circle the hot spot Fae and I isolated. "That is a possible Graal. I assume you know what they are?"

"Oh yeah, nasty pieces of work, man." Castanza Growled. "Fought one a few months ago."

"So be smart about hunting it. Limbo should hit in...?" I look at Fae.

"Expect five hours." She spoke, breaking her silent observation.

"Draw straws, rock paper scissors, whatever. One of you guys stay here, one deploys and start a search. Fae?" She narrowed the map, but it was still a solid 25 square miles. "Start here, move north, report back."

"That's a big area, Hermano." Castanza said again.

"If it were easy, my broken ass would go alone." I goaded him.

"A'ight, I gotcha. Sire, you good sitting ready?"

"Yeah, no problem. I'm working on something anyways."

"If you say anything about a script or a movie, I'll personally kick your ass." I grumble.

"No way! Writing my autobiography." Sire smiled, Castanza and I groaned in harmony.

"That...Was impressive..." Fae contributed.

"Go kick some ass today, boys." I wave them off.

SEPTEMBER 29TH, 2023

We had a little luck with the dense openings of Limbo, however still no joy in finding the lair. It certainly struck way more often than normal right now, but I guess that's part of its charm. Being unpredictable...I stayed in the command center for every patrol, and it was entirely uneventful. Sire and Forsyth (Who was once again in charge of team 2) were happy with that, but Castanza shared my frustration. We got another report of a serious injury at the hands of this damned Graal, and I couldn't do anything about it. This time it was a young backpacking couple. The official story was that one of them slipped and fell off a trail and got their leg skewered by a perfectly placed tree branch. Yeah, sure. I saw the photos, and that wasn't perfect chance.

Lancer had taken to her role shockingly well. She was no longer the scared little bird that first showed up, and she took to her new role in life well. Ulid was still scared of me, which I suspected wouldn't change until something big happened and I had just the idea. I only needed to get healed up before I could do it. In the meantime, I tried to teach them how to fight and survive the best I could, and Forsyth instilled Limbo skills into each of them. Each training session usually seemed to add some straggler from another team to the roster. I couldn't complain, we were all on the same side after all.

Still, not being able to deploy really bothered me. I felt like some kind of base bunny, sitting comfortably in the rear.

OCTOBER 1ST, 2023

Another month. Another day on crippled status. I was happy to be able to come back to the office at first, but the bench was starting to really wear me down.

OCTOBER 3RD, 2023

I grabbed the mic from the desk. "1-1, say again?" The reception was rough, but I swear I heard something.

<"1-1, Graal confirmed!">

"Fae!" I threw a notepad at her as she had fallen asleep. She jerked awake with a start. "Control copies, 1-1, SITREP?"

"Holy shit, they found it?" Fae said simply.

"Looks like it. Sounds like they are engaged."

<"Control, this is a big one!"> The radio died for a moment. <"Six feet tall, standard Graal appearance. Hey, watch it!"> Silence again.

I held the microphone, listening intently. I absolutely hated not being able to help. The seconds ticked by.

"Are they okay?" Fae whispered.

"Sire can handle it." I say back to her. The more seconds ticking by, the worse I worry.

<"Control, 1-1. Target escaped, one wounded. We can RTB on our own.">

"1-1, control copies. SITREP when able."

<"Control, 1-1 actual. 2 got a little messed up, first aid applied, ambulatory.">

"Control copies, RTB gents. We'll get it next time." I dropped the mic, frustrated.

"I'll call Jerry." Fae muttered as she left the room.

"Fuck this damn leg." I grumbled. I was sick of being trapped here.

***

I met Sire's team at the door, and one of his team had gotten pretty roughed up. It was a middle aged woman, and she looked like she narrowly avoided a much worse fate.

"Whoa, easy there Vicky." Jerry rushed over to her, as another of Sire's team helped her in the door. "Got a good one, didn't you?"

"How bad is it?" She grunted.

"Looks like you'll be fine but it's gonna smart for a while. Come on." Jerry led them back to the medical bay. Judging by how she moved and her injuries, it seemed like she had taken a spike, but it had missed everything vital and gave her some really bad road rash on her abdomen. She had been very lucky.

"Sire, you good?" I ask him.

"Yeah. Those things are fast." He leaned against the wall, I could see the sweat stained onto his face. "But we're okay. Close calls are great for the adrenaline!" He smiled.

"Go clean up, I already let Ms. Steel know you're here."

"Your kindness and proactiveness is renowned, good sir!" He beamed and clapped my shoulder, to which I glared at him. That only seemed to aid his smile and his team departed.

OCTOBER 7TH, 2023

We had worked on a bunch of weapons training today. Lancer was far more efficient with a bow than a rifle, and she was able to do some real damage so I made her a deal. I wouldn't make her carry an M4, but I did expect her to have a sidearm just in case. Sure would make an odd loadout, but I couldn't deny her skill, plus having a nearly silent but lethal ranged attack would give us an upper hand in some circumstances. They were on shift tonight, and we had them set up for a patrol. I was certainly nervous, I did not like the amount of firepower they possessed, plus Sire had a rough go with it the other night.

Limbo waits for no man though, and I sat alone in the command center tonight, the microphone laying in my lap and my legs kicked up on an empty chair next to me. Limbo had been open for about an hour now, and all was silent. A tiny movement caught my eye though, and I looked over just in time for that little brown, smoky fox to poke it's head around the door. It paused as I saw it, before sauntering over and hopping up onto the chair I was using as a leg rest. It didn't disturb the cushion, I couldn't feel its weight, it just sort of was there.

"Hello again." I said softly, and it tilted its head at me. "I guess you're not like the other entities huh? Or is this part of your play?"

It tilted its head in the other direction before circling, then curling into a ball next to my feet.

"Alright, well, fair enough."

We sat like this for about an hour before the fox just kind of fizzled and blew away.

OCTOBER 13TH, 2023

Finally, the day had come! Jerry had put me through the ringer this morning, but he cleared me for combat duty! I was apparently a little excited and it was bothering Lena. Maybe she was allergic to happiness? Either way, I had offered to help her out in the armory for a bit today in a show of good faith. This only really got me an earful of every single members bad habits with their equipment and at least two rags thrown in my face. I had just caught the third one that I didn't even know why it was thrown.

"Keep it up, I'll make you regret it."

"Please, cripple man. Just try not to collapse." She threw back without hesitation.

"I'll have you know-"

"Oh, for fucks sake!" She tossed a wrench onto her bench that clattered loudly. "I'm calling you out. Training room." She growled and pushed me roughly out of the armory, shutting and locking the door behind her.

"Really? While I'm still 'cripple man'?" I smirk, not really caring about the risk of injury as I just got cleared anyway. I proved I could handle way worse before, but that was four years ago.

"Oh, weren't you cleared for duty? You're not scared, are you?"

I ended up following her to the gym for what was likely a terrible idea. As Lena opened the door, she rang some loud bell and stepped onto the mat.

"Sarah's gonna be pissed when you go right back to the hospital after I'm done with you."

"I'm only worried about zapping myself on that electric hair of yours." I tossed my jacket in the corner.

"You're gonna pay for that. Get on the mat."

"Rules?" I ask as I kick my shoes off.

"I won't kill you." She growled.

"You can surely try." I stepped on the mat as the door opened. Sire, Forsyth, Lancer and Fae entered.

"Jake what are you doing?!" Fae barked.

"New guy and Lena?? Oh, this should be good!" Sire chuckled, Forsyth was quiet.

Lena and I had started to circle each other. I made no show of defense, I was simply walking and watching. And she matched me.

"Don't tell me you're one of those 'I don't hit women' types."

"All's fair." I said simply, and she snarled, not taking the bait. "Talk a big game to just walk around in cir-" She lunged forward. I stepped backwards quickly and she went in front of me, I jabbed my good leg out to catch her foot. It caught, but she had already twisted like a cat in midair and hooked my arm, trying to force me off balance.

With a thud, we both smack the mat. We landed in a way that neither of us took the full force, but she had got herself in position to take my back. I kicked my legs out and slammed her torso with mine, crushing her and knocking the wind out of her chest which got me the chance to twist and straddle her. Before I could do anything, she thrusted forward, flinging me up and over, and I rolled away from her.

"Not bad, not bad." I smirked at her. Someone hit the music, and 'Devil is a Barmaid' started playing.

"Beer on the loser tonight!" Pretty sure that was Sire. I took a step forward, and that's all she needed. She lunged again, this time it was smarter. She grabbed at my thigh, but I had planted hard. She yanked, and nothing happened until I took a step into her, hooking her leg with mine and taking her balance, following her down to the mat. She squirreled her way out from under me before I could latch onto anything and we rolled away from each other. We were both panting at this point.

"Hey!" The door slammed open. Ms. Steel was in the doorway, looking angry.

"Mom's home." I hissed at Lena.

"You're really going to get yourself another injury right after going back on combat status!?"

"Just some friendly training, ma'am." I wiped a bit of sweat from my brow. I heard Lena grunt, it sounds like she wasn't done.

"Bullshit. Back to work, both of you." She crossed her arms, standing in front of the doorway.

I turned and offered Lena my hand, not knowing if she would take it. "You've got some fancy footwork."

"Wish I could say the same." She paused, looked at my hand, and finally shook it. "Adequate."

I smirked, shook her hand and let her go. "Fair enough. Just wait til mom lets me play for real."

"I heard that." Ms. Steel spoke up, apparently her hearing was as sharp as her wit.

I think I caught a hint of a smirk on Lena's face as we left the mat and got back to work.

OCTOBER 14TH, 2023

Today was going to be a good day. For me. I finally got cleared for combat and training started at a bright and crisp 0500. The sun wasn't even out yet. I took the team on a nice run, totaling about 3 miles overall with hills and valleys, making sure that they were good and gassed before the sun was even up. Luckily, my leg was holding up just fine, however I certainly felt the two months of sitting on my ass. Ulid kept trying to fall behind to which I ensured he didn't with some…Choice words of encouragement. Forsyth kept up pretty good, Lancer was actually doing way better than I expected.

I let everyone clean off the sweat before we went to hand to hand combatives in the gym, and I intentionally paired off with Ulid. He never caught on, but I was making a game of drawing him in and absolutely smoking him over and over again, until his anger snapped.

"Fuck you!" He barked. I just smirked, which pissed him off even more. "I'll kill you, old man!" I raised my hand and with one finger, beckoned him forward. He took the bait, charged, and I hooked him around the middle with my arm, tripped him with my leg, wrapped around his back, and had him pinned on the mat with my arm wrapped tight around his throat. The remainder of his yelling was incomprehensible as he flailed trying to get at me. Forsyth, Lancer, Sire and Lena had appeared on the outskirts to watch, and I couldn't help but note the almost invisible smirk on Forsyth's face. Pretty sure he wanted to do the same for years. Shortly, as his struggle started to constrict his own airpipe, it turned from a struggle of attack to a struggle of survival. His movements changed to sharper, more desperate attempts to get to me but he had no chance.

"Hey…Uh…You gonna let him up?" Sire spoke up, his voice filled with concern.

"Yup." I said simply without moving. I could hear the strained gasp as Ulid's voice stopped trying to yell. I leaned down so I could essentially whisper in his ear. "You're fighting yourself right now. Focus." I didn't release any pressure, he had enough air to stay in the fight, but he was gonna have a bad headache later. "Stop struggling. Find a way out." The flailing slowed, and I could see him try to think. "Focus, boy. Don't let the fear of death cloud your mind." I could feel him force a breath against the constraint I was applying. Finally, I could feel Ulid's chin digging into my arm.

"Good. You need that wiggle room."

"Fugyu." He struggled to choke out so I tightened briefly for a half second and he growled.

"You can insult, you can find a way out." I said softly again. He was getting a little more oxygen now, and I could feel the wheels turning in his head. Finally, he bucks his hips into me, throwing me a little off balance. I let it happen but maintained my overall grip. It was enough.

Ulid clawed at my side, managing to get a hand hold on my thigh and wrench himself around so that he was on his side and preventing my chokehold. He gasped for air, and then threw an elbow into my gut, which I was ready for.

"That's it! Finish the fight, boy!" He throws another, stronger this time. I could see his eyes, enraged and terrified. I let him take some ground, but I ultimately kept control over his head.

After a few more moments of this, I finally set him free, and he scampers away like an animal released from a cage. He was covered in sweat, his face red and those terrified eyes came back with a nice helping of anger. I calmly got to my feet as his eyes darted around the room wildly.

"You learn something today?"

"Yeah, you're a fucking psycho." He growled, his voice rough and inflamed.

"You think anything in Limbo is gonna be as nice as that?"

"Nice?!" He gasps out. I simply nod.

"I want you to understand something. If you draw breath, you can still finish the fight. Sometimes, the cavalry ain't coming and your back is against the wall." I step forward, offering my hand in a peace offering. He glares at it.

"Seriously?" He growls again.

"We are on the same side, after all." I paused, a small smirk crept in. "If I wanted you dead, you would be."

"Fuck you. Not comforting." He looks away, and back to my hand which is unwavering and patient. He takes a small step forward. "How'd you learn all that?"

"Military." I spoke simply.

"Hell no, that was shit out of an action movie!" Sire added. "I would know!" I shake my head, not turning my attention from Ulid. Finally, he reaches forward and takes my hand.

"I still hate you."

"I know." We shake and break apart, he was still glaring at me.

"Can...Can you teach me?"

"Which part?" I ask with a soft grin.

"All of it." He says softly.

"Yeah..." Lancer added in, making me jump a tiny bit.

"Shit, I'm in too." Sire piled on, and I felt Forsyth clap a hand on my shoulder.

"I'll help if you need it. I recognized some of that."

I looked at them all in turn.

"Well...Don't seem like I've got a choice." They all reacted in their own way, ranging from a nod to a big grin. "Ulid, hit the showers. I kicked your ass enough today. Who's next?"

OCTOBER 16TH, 2023

"Man, your boy ain't useless no more." Vic Castanza spoke with a smirk. I never asked his background, but something told me not to. He had a very thick Hispanic accent and carried himself like he had seen some stuff. I once asked if he had served and got a very short 'nah' with no further explanation. That was when I decided I didn't want to know any more. Frankly, he led Team 3 well and took care of his people, and that's what mattered.

"He's been kicking his ass for weeks." Sire said with a grin. "Pretty sure he has the taste of the gym mats memorized!"

Castanza, Sire, Lena and I had congregated just outside of the armory to jaw jack. Lena broke into a wicked smile.

"Yesterday was glorious, he threw the kid like a sack of potatoes." She said, savoring each word. I simply shrugged.

"Training can be exciting." I said simply.

"I've seen training, that's something else, boss." Castanza added, a hint of respect mixed in with the knowing look of his eye.

"Speaking of, you better be ready." Lena poked my chest, that wicked grin never leaving her face.

"For what? You want the Ulid treatment again?" I return a grin.

"Please, not here. Don't want blood on the armory door!" Sire chuckled, stirring his drink. "Plus, may scare the kids."

"Better learn now, man." Castanza threw back. I nod in approval as Sire shrugs.

"Alright you two, not all of us are trained killers."

"Oh? Who said I was trained?" Castanza bristles a little, but I could see the look in his eye. He was looking for a reaction.

"Hey I didn't mean anything by that."

"Yeah, sure thing, Hollywood." Castanza cracks into a grin, Sire sighs and shakes his head.

"I'll get you one day."

"Bullshit." Castanza grunts.

"Who's on tonight?" I ask.

"You, boss." Castanza grunts, and I reply with a groan.

"Yup. Yup, checks."

"Fae said that she was tracking something too, so have fun!" Sire clapped my arm and I returned a glare. "Oh stop, I'm working on a training plan for tomorrow, so I'll be here."

"Appreciate that."

"No problem! Was thinking...Stage Presence...How to scare your enemies with just your voice!" I lean back, my head thunking heavily against the wall as Castanza covers his face with a hand. "I'm kidding! You two are no fun."

"Gosh look at the time, guess I gotta head to the briefing room." I pushed off the wall and started walking off as Sire chuckled softly.

"You three are worse than old women." Lena groans, throwing her hand in the air and turning down the hall.

"You off to recharge that hair of yours?" I called after her and was greeted with a middle finger in return. The three of us chuckled.

OCTOBER 19TH, 2023

I had gathered the team leads up, per request of Ms. Steel and Fae. While I am glad the radio discipline was starting to get better, I of course had to hit them all with that lecture first.

"Clear, concise, correct. Use your damned callsigns. Questions?" I leaned against the wall as they sat in the seats around the table. Ms. Steel had taken a seat at the head of the table, listening.

They all nodded in agreement, Sire and Anne Greene were taking notes, but Castanza just listened. Greene was a recent hire and took over team 4. She was the best person for the job, and sadly her credentials were a fitness instructor who was an avid paintball player. Beggars can't be choosers, but Greene was very responsive to everything and quick to adapt.

"I would like to adopt actual names for each team, as I suspect it will help build morale and teamwork. For now, we are going to go with this. Sire: Pretty. Castanza: Pathway. Greene: Project. I take Passport." There may have been a little word play on my part.

"Pretty? Me?" Sire started. "You...You get me!" He beamed, and Castanza and I sighed in unison again.

"Feel like you need your own, boss." Castanza spoke up, looking between me and Ms. Steel. "We got control, Sarah over here is Rose. You kinda like...The Lieutenant in this shit."

"I'm no Lieutenant." I growl.

"Let's keep with the P theme and go with Prophet!" Sire chimed in.

"Prophet?" I look at him incredulously.

"Hey I kinda like it." Castanza grinned.

"Easy to say and remember." Greene added. "Just like you have been wanting, sir."

"I don't need my own callsign." I sigh.

"Big boss?" Castanza asked Ms. Steel who looked at me and shrugged.

"You're on board with this??" I ask her.

"It seems to annoy you, so indeed." She delivers dryly, and I sigh.

"Okay. Fine. Prophet it is. Don't whine to me when you lot get confused later."

"Copy that, Prophet Actual!" Sire spoke loudly, fighting a laugh. I immediately chucked the smart board marker into his chest which got a few more laughs.

"Alright simmer down. Any updates on your people? How's Vicky?"

"She's fine, a little slow but she's back up. Her pride is still hurt though."

"Fair, she need more time?"

"Nah, she's pissed and wants to rip that thing to bits." Sire grinned.

"Good. Any other issues I need to know about?" I paused, no one spoke up. "Nothing heard. Have a great Limbo fightin' afternoon."

***

End of shift. I had returned to the gym to retrieve my bag before heading home. After I had walked in, I was smacked by a pair of sparring gloves and turned fast to see where they came from. Lena was standing there with a glare, pointing at the mat. I smirk.

"No audience today to show off for." I taunted her.

"Good. I intend to embarrass you. Don't want you crying to mommy."

Her voice was almost a growl as I put the gloves on, but I could see a twinkle in her eye. The next ten minutes or so had us trying hard to find an opening and make the other tap out. While I was very skilled over years of training, it was rare I got to fight someone like her. Small framed, fast, slippery and tenacious. I imagined it was like fighting an eel. Finally, I managed to get her neck tucked in tightly behind my knee and squeezed. Tap tap tap, that was it! I bounced up, both of us covered in sweat by now, and offered her a hand up.

"Okay, that was good."

"Fucker." She grumbled, catching her breath and finally taking my hand. She lightly got to her feet and glared for a second before she jumped, a sneak attack. Dirty move, and we were onto round 2. She was too quick, popping my knee free, swinging around my back and dragging me down to the mat hard. I managed to rotate and face her, but she still landed hard on my chest.

Then she surprised me. Her forearm pressed against my neck, just enough to let me know she was there, and she leaned forward and kissed me deeply. My eyes shot open in shock as she pulled back.

"Damn. If only you were my type."

Without another word, she bounced to her feet and headed to the showers. My mind was spinning as she opened the door.

"The hell does that mean?!" I called after her, hearing her cackle as the door shut. Needless to say, the ride home was a very confusing one.

OCTOBER 22ND, 2023

"Been a long time since I went hunting." Forsyth muttered from the passenger seat.

"Never been." Ulid added with an almost sad tone. "Sounds boring though."

The four of us had taken one of the trucks out on patrol. We narrowed the Graal's lair down even farther and we were on deck to chase it down some more. I had the wheel, Forsyth was shotgun, with Lancer and Ulid in the backseat. It felt good to be back in the saddle once more. Lena was merciless when I pulled a helmet out of the armory, and no amount of death glare made her stop. I learned my lesson from the last battle and decided being cool wasn't worth another concussion. Make your jokes, you crazy lady. My eggs are scrambled enough, leave my newfound love for helmets alone.

"That's not a bad thing." Lancer glanced over at Ulid. "Sometimes boring is nice."

"Boring is safe." I added.

"Heh, yeah. Boring means everything is going to plan." Forsyth grabbed the soda from the cupholder and took a sip.

"Seriously, carbonated drinks before you hit the field…" I grumble.

"Ain't killed me yet."

"Moron."

"Hey, don't be jealous of my iron stomach." Forsyth glanced at me, and we both looked at Ulid who had been working his way through a carbonated energy drink. "On second thought, you might be onto something." Forsyth admitted as Ulid caught him looking.

"What?" He asked.

"Don't worry about it kid." I sigh. "Alright, recap. Point Alpha is a suspected lair. Forsyth and Ulid, you two get the flashbangs?"

"Good to go, boss." Forsyth spoke simply.

"Target Alpha is the Graal, Bravo is the lair. Of course, Alpha is primary so let's hope we find it."

"Blowing the lair should disrupt it's operations enough that it'll piss off for a while." Forsyth contributed. "These things move fast, but they can only attack behind them. But they got range, so be smart."

We had been on the road for a while and had finally pulled into the park. We had a short window this morning, so we didn't have time to spare. Luckily, it was a weekday and the place was deserted. We all unloaded from the truck, rifles slung, Lancer had her bow strung across her back. I fidgeted with my helmet as we made our way down the trail, getting used to it.

"Hey, boss." Ulid spoke up from behind me.

"Sup?"

"You know that it's not a truck, right?"

"What?" I looked back at him.

"The Explorer. It's an SUV." I couldn't gauge if he was being genuine or a prick, but lately it's been a lot more the former.

"Old habits. It's close enough."

"True. Oh boy, here it comes." I heard the whine start up as he spoke and it rapidly increased until Limbo broke.

"Weapons ready. We have a quarter mile to point Alpha." I listened to the soft rustling of equipment as we transitioned from a nature hike to an armed patrol. We proceeded quietly up the trail, I was pleased to see how much better they worked since our first fight. Lancer led the way through the forest, her keen archery eyes had proven to be extra valuable during training, so I wanted to see what she was capable of. I was right behind to support her, Ulid was between me and Forsyth as my trust was still damaged.

As we got closer, there was a strange form of corruption affecting the area. At first, I didn't notice it, but as we got closer and closer, I noticed the trees and plants seemed to be shifting between healthy and unhealthy. It reminded me of a broken video game I tried to play that had two textures assigned and both were fighting to be visible.

"Ulid, ever see this before?" I asked softly.

"No, not at all." He said even softer.

"It's a Graal." Forsyth spoke just loud enough for me to hear. "Bet my truck on it."

"Eyes peeled then. We may have found its home." I checked my watch, we had 18 minutes before Limbo was supposed to close. I keyed my mic. "Control, Prophet. Confirm closing time unchanged."

<"Prophet, affirm. 18 minutes left.">

I clicked my mic twice as acknowledgement.

After a little more walking, Lancer stops and motions for my attention. She pointed at a cave, where the corruption certainly seemed to be at its worst. I nod at Lancer and turn.

"Forsyth, Ulid, you're up. Kill it."

They both nod and advance as Lancer and I monitor the area, forming a perimeter. We were extremely fortunate that a simple flash bang seemed to have a tremendous effect on Limbo lairs. They approached quietly, and I heard the ring come off the first flash, then the second, followed by the tinkling of metal cans on rock. A few short seconds and I heard a pair of detonations.

"Perimeter. Let's see if it comes home to see what happened." I spoke just loudly enough for everyone to hear me. The corruption seemed to freak out worse than it had been, before the unhealthy 'textures' began to fade away. I checked my watch. Four minutes, ten seconds. "Control, Prophet. Made it to point Alpha. Target Bravo confirmed and destroyed. Holding for Alpha."

<"Control copies, good work.">

I scan the horizon, a noise in the distance setting me on high alert. Nothing should be moving, but I swear I just heard a heavy footstep. There it was again. My lizard brain kicked in and yelled that I was being stalked. I slowly lowered myself to a crouch, rifle out. Another foot step. My eyes flicked to my watch, 80 seconds left. I scanned around the area once more, and another footstep. I could also pick up a series of noises that sounded like a chittering of a giant bug? Another step, and I picked out a small movement about 150 feet away. Something big and brown. I squinted trying to get a clearer view, as the shrill whine began to sound.

"Get down!" Lancer yelped. Instinctively, I flattened myself to the ground with a thud as a spike goes flying over my head, right where I was a second before.

"Contact!" I barked out, trying to line up my sights but Limbo had begun to close, and I couldn't get a good view. "Son of a bitch!" I yell. The color regained its composure, and the sound of nature filled my ears. "Shit! We had him!"

"You good?" Forsyth called from his place as he started making his way over.

"Damn Graal was right there! If I had a few more seconds..." I pointed into the woods where the spike had come from. Lancer was pale as a ghost as she joined us, followed by Ulid.

"Yeah, that happens." Forsyth spoke matter-of-factly.

I shook my head and slung my rifle. "Pisses me off." I growl. "But Lancer, thanks. Saved my bacon today." I playfully punched her shoulder. She looked at me blankly, her face still pale.

"You did good. Both of you." Forsyth spoke to the younger members in turn.

"Lancer?" I turned to face her. "Lancer!"

"Huh?" She snapped back to reality, eyes alarmed at my loud attempts to get her attention.

"You good?"

"Y-Yeah." She spoke weakly.

"Any fight you can walk away from was a good fight, kid. Let's go home."

"Control, Passport. Spotted Alpha but couldn't take it. Heading home." Forsyth handled the radios as we began to walk back to the truck.

<"Control copies. Safe travels.">

"Lancer?"

"Yeah, yeah. I'm coming."

I ended up walking beside her on the walk back to the truck. I was definitely worried about her, but at least she got her first taste of combat today.

"Seriously, you did well today." I spoke softly, letting the boys go off ahead.

"That...Was terrifying." Her voice was hollow.

"First time usually is. But, you did exactly what you were supposed to. You kept alert, you called out an attack, and you covered your buddies."

"Is...Is...It...?"

"Nah, you get used to it."

We walked in silence for a moment, her head low.

"How did you...?"

"I kept at it. Lots of training. This is a vacation compared to my old life."

"So, are we screwed?"

"Not at all." I grinned at her. "You have me, and I'm unkillable."

"But I'm not..."

"Oh no, you are. My invincibility covers those near me." I was trying to lighten the mood, but it wasn't working well. We walked in silence for a bit. "Hey, it's natural to be scared."

"You're not. They aren't." She motioned to Forsyth and Ulid walking ahead of us, Ulid just let out a bit of a chuckle for something.

"Been around a while. But if you think any of us never get scared, you're wrong. It's absolutely natural, and if you didn't respond this way, frankly, I'd be more worried."

Lancer looked at me for a bit before returning to the ground in front of her. "I don't want to be scared."

"Find a way to use it. Heighten your senses instead of letting it control you."

"That sounds impossible."

"Only if you deem it so."

She nods softly. "Yeah..."

***

We made our way back to base, but I did make a stop at an ice cream shop and buy everyone a scoop. The boys laughed about it, but I did it for Lancer. As goofy of an idea as it may be, the laughter, sugar, and jokes about me being a soccer dad actually got her to crack a tiny hint of a smile, so it was worth it.

OCTOBER 24TH, 2023

I really should not be surprised. As my team's training continued, we ended up taking more and more people in and helping them learn. It wasn't long before we had established a daily training program with various instructors and topics that changed every week.

This is exactly what I did before. Why should I be so surprised when they started calling me dad? Again? Lena had worked hard on creating a new type of weapon to fight these entities. We called it the Dreadnought, a metal spike that extended into a barbed spear like thing. I couldn't tell you the materials, but Lena was convinced it would cut any entity down and slay them, even the shadow ones. We had the prototype complete and developed a few to issue out to the teams. It wasn't tested yet, but it worked amazingly against our test dummies. We all had quite a bit of watermelon the last few days. Next step? Training.

"Boys and girls, I present to you the key to our salvation. BEHOLD!" Sire held up the sleek Dreadnought. "The Dreadnought! So named for the fear it will strike in your enemies!"

"What a ham." I whispered to Ms. Steel She had her arms crossed watching, I had my back against the wall, one leg bent against it. She smirked. We had gotten a lot more comfortable in the past few weeks, working closely on improving our people's abilities.

"Are you surprised?" She whispered back.

"Nah. Almost jealous."

"You??" She looked at me, a smile with fake shock on her face.

"Yeah, you right." We grin at each other before returning to watching the scene unfold.

"To deploy this wondrous machine, you hit this button." He did so and the Dreadnought extended, the barbs deploying. Some of the younger members were in awe. "Our own Lena assures me it will vanquish your enemies in the Limbo! Now, step up and take the training stick. Let's get started!"

"At least they take to him. It's goofy but it works." I speak softly to her as people start pairing off to train.

"He does have a way." She nods. "Even if it may be…Out there."

"If it's dumb, and it works, it's not dumb. Too bad he wasn't more famous, wouldn't have to worry about funding ever again."

"We manage quite well, thank you." Was that a hint of indignation in her voice?

"No complaints here, ma'am. Though the chair in my office squeaks something fierce."

"Sounds like something you can handle."

"Ouch, ma'am." I saw a soft grin as we continued watching the training. After a few spars I checked my watch. "We got what, three days before we can test it?"

"That's what Fae said."

"Hua. What team you want on the line?"

"You have to ask?"

"5th?"

"Why did I hire you?" She says with a sigh.

"It's my wit and charm, ma'am."

"I think I will join you. I want to see firsthand if these things are worth the cost."

"They that expensive?" She just looked at me, the answer clear on her face. "A'ight fair enough. Was wondering why we only got a handful."

"I almost get the feeling something odd may happen." I glance at her strange comment.

"Why's that, ma'am?"

"I cannot articulate that."

"Gut feeling."

"Yes, I believe so."

"Fair enough. We can play it safe."

She pauses. "Just like that?"

"I always trust the gut of my people."

She simply nods. "I appreciate that, Jake."

"Anytime, Ma'am." I glance at her. "Quite informal of you."

She swats my arm.

"That's more like it."

She straightens up and heads towards the door.

"Am I supposed to follow?"

She simply glared at me out of the corner of her eye but never broke her stride. Taking it as a yes, I followed after her, until we reached her office. As was the typical song and dance, I entered and took the chair across from her desk, expecting her to bring something up or ask for my evaluation of one of the members. I think she's done this about four or five times now. What I was not expecting, however, was when she pulled a bottle of whiskey out of the cabinet, poured two drinks and wordlessly handed me one.

"Ma'am?"

"Since I can't get you to stop calling me that," She sat on her desk, taking a sip, her tone warm. "I wanted to thank you."

"For?" I took a sip myself, it burned the whole way down, but it was a surprisingly pleasant one.

"It seems you were the missing piece to make these teams cohesive."

I nod, temporarily lost for words. "Guess this old dog still has some tricks, eh?"

"Say what you will, but I mean the sentiment." The warmth was quickly replaced with a minor frustration.

"Well...Thank you." I set my drink on the arm of the chair. "You had a good setup to begin with, I didn't do much."

"Please. It was a hodge podge at best, and I know I don't have the ability to form a cohesion with this wide variety of personalities."

"I guess I just have a magnetic personality." I smirk, she sighs and rolls her eyes, taking a bigger sip this time.

"I suppose, in a rather sophomoric way, that is what I'm trying to say."

I pause, my eyes flick to her. "I was just being an ass."

"I'm not." I met her gaze, and we both took a sip, nearly in unison.

"I've never been much on kind words, so thank you. Sarah." Using her first name felt almost painful. She was the commander...My throat almost constricted when I tried to say it. Likely part of the internal struggle for these foreign thoughts and feelings I've been catching about her.

"Same, but you're welcome." I could see her eyes show her amusement as she saw my inner turmoil.

We sat together for a moment in a comfortable silence.

"Where are you from? No one seems to know much about you, and I can't pick out an accent."

She grinned. "Wouldn't you like to know."

"There's not a thing about me you don't know, you won't even give me that?" I playfully jab back.

"Me family moved here when I was a lass." I was NOT ready for the sudden introduction of an Irish accent. She grinned at my expression. "I was three. Moved to Ohio, of all places."

"Well, god damn." I blurted out, she grinned again, a little bit of a blush showing up. "Where are they now?"

Blush faded and her face fell. "Underneath matching gravestones."

"Fuck, I'm sorry."

"It's fine. They died when I was about 17. They led the Roses for years, but an entity took them both in one night."

"Shit…That's awful."

"It's why I'm here, pushing us forward."

I nod, letting her continue.

"That way I can honor them and finish the job." She stared at her drink.

"I understand the investment. I'd suspect they would be pleased."

"They…" She hesitated. "I hope they are. Wherever they may be."

I hold out my glass to hers in toast. "Wherever they may be." She clinked my glass with what can only be described as a melancholy smile.

Ch. 6 Cheshire

OCTOBER 31ST, 2023

We got our marching orders. Entity should appear around 2100 hours tonight, location was downtown in a warehouse. Forsyth decided to go and catch the flu, so he was home and we took Sire into the briefing.

There was an eerie air tonight. I had heard in the past that sometimes warriors felt something like this. A...Finality? Heaviness? A feeling that told me the story was about to end, and the conclusion wasn't written. I had written it off. No way, you couldn't know this was your last mission. Those guys were full of it.

But here I was, alone in my office, sitting at my desk. Feeling...Feeling like this was it. There was no reason to think this, everything was normal. Limbo was coming in a few hours, nothing abnormal on the scanners, so why can I not shake this feeling??

I pulled out a notepad from the drawer and grabbed a pen. What would it hurt...?

To whoever picks up this note.

God that's terrible.

Dear Ms. Steel.

If you found this, then it needs no explanation...

Okay, that's better. After all, it would be her that found this. I spent the next hour writing. It helped feel like I was at least providing someone with closure, but the feeling didn't leave. This wasn't some eloquent declaration of love, or anything weird. It was simply stating thanks for giving me a chance to fight again. I folded it up and put it on my keyboard. If nothing happened, I would be good. Trash it when I get back. If not...Well, at least I had some form of will? I guess? I headed to the armory to get dressed and await whatever happened next.

***

There was no warning.

The colors drained from the world and immediately I was hit by a large and heavy...something and was sent sliding into a wall, the wind knocked out of my chest. By the time I can even understand reality, I saw Ulid's body laying limp in front of me, he was clearly the thing that slammed against me as Limbo activated.

I need my rifle. I spotted it about 5 feet away, and I scampered over to it. I glanced over at Ulid, he was still not moving but I thought

I could see him breathing. I hoped he was only knocked out. I saw Lancer standing frozen to the spot in the distance.

Scream. Sire. I whipped around to see what was attacking us, and it was a massive beast, the size of a bus. It had two, long black tails, each ending in a vicious, yellow spike. It had the body, tail and claws of a scorpion, but the head of a dragon. It was covered in a deep black velvet scale skin. One of the tails had Sire skewered through the gut, his weapon dropped on the ground as he clutched at the spike, struggling in vain to escape. As the second tail surged forward, Sire's scream was cut short, his body went limp and the thing threw him away with a sick thud. I had no time to react by the time I was able to understand what I saw in front of me.

"No!" I could hear Sarah's scream, filled with anger.

"Control, Prophet Actual! We need back up, NOW!"

<"Copy Prophet, I'll get another team en route.">

"Now, Fae!" I barked back.

The beast roared. Lancer, pale as a ghost, finally moved and hunkered down behind a stack of crates. I've seen it before, she was freezing up. I was glad she could at least get to cover, but she locked up again and was most likely useless at this point.

The radio, and Fae, were quiet for a while. I scampered away to a low wall near where Lancer was. I could hear the panic in Fae's voice when she came back on the radio.

<"Team Three is deploying now, ETA 9 minutes, over.">

"We don't have that fucking long!" I barked at the radio, not keying it this time. I scanned the area, Sarah was ducked in an alcove near the entrance. Ulid was still in a heap on the ground, and Sire...Well...I looked at the beast then between Sarah and Ulid.

"Sarah, cover me!" She looked at me, lost for a moment before engaging. I shot out from cover, sliding to another low wall I could use. I narrowly missed the tail, as I saw the spike flying through the air at a spot I was in only a moment ago.

<"I'm sorry, they are moving as fast as they can!"> I ignored Fae's call, turning around the corner and firing into the beast.

"Amelia, I need you to focus up!" Nothing. She was whimpering, cowered in the fetal position behind her crates. Her bow was on the ground, just lying there. "Not making any hits, Sarah!"

"Same here!" Sarah called back.

I swore under my breath and was beginning to shift into a retreat mindset. I heard one of those evil tails slam against the wall I was using as cover, narrowly missing being its next victim, again.

"AMELIA!" I screamed at her. Nothing. I bounded through the open, sliding next to her and grabbing her collar. "HEY!" She wasn't home. I slapped her across the face, and still nothing. "Fuck!" I gave her one more good shake before giving up for now.

The beast screamed and turned its attention towards Sarah.

"Lancer is locked up!" I called out.

I had to make a move. I pulled a grenade and tossed it at the thing, the grenade clinking to a stop underneath its gut. This situation has gone to hell. I need to get Sarah and the team out of here. BOOM. The grenade popped, I sprinted to Sarah's cover, and the beast shrieked. It felt that one at least. I peeked out around her cover to see that it wasn't enough. I had barely even made a dent and just pissed it off. We were down three shooters and our weapons were ineffective.

Options?

Only one.

I looked at Sarah's back, she had a pair of Dreadnoughts strapped there.

Technically two options. I pulled one off her kit.

"Thank you for giving me the chance to go out on my own terms." I spoke curtly. Without waiting for a reply, I sprinted around the far side of the cover. I was still worried about everyone, but I had just enough of a chance to leap onto the beast's back. I sprinted like a bat out of hell, holding my fire and hoping Sarah would distract it, which she luckily did. Close enough, I leapt, climbing onto its back, slinging my rifle around on to my own. Scampering up the rough shell, I noted it had some kind of horn on the side of its head. That was my target.

It was now it recognized I was here, and its head turned to face me. I was fortunate it couldn't fully turn around and managed to avoid the gnashing teeth as it started snapping at me. I narrowly dodged the tail and grabbed that horn, yanking its big, ugly head around. The deep orange of its eye swiveled and I knew it was focusing on me, and me alone. Hopefully, Sarah used this chance to get everyone out of here, if nothing else. Without hesitation, I pulled my arm back, the Dreadnought extended.

But the beast was faster.

Before I could drop my arm, a long yellow spike exploded out of my chest. The pain was indescribable, I immediately lost my breath. I couldn't wait, I drove the Dreadnought into that damned orange eye as hard as I could as a second spike exploded out of my abdomen. It screamed, as a light yellow blood erupted out of its eye, and it rapidly flailed until it collapsed. I was pitched forward about 15 feet, landing in a heap. Luckily the Dreadnought worked. It flailed itself onto the ground, it appeared as if I was able to stab deep enough that it made contact with some form of brain.

Sure was getting dark...and cold...

Mr. Sixx was bleeding profusely and rapidly turning pale. The stab wounds from the monster's tail were very much fatal, and his consciousness was rapidly deteriorating. Ms. Steel had run up to him, and did her best to stem the flow, but it was futile.

"Jake!" *She screamed at him.* "Don't you dare!"

She pushed on his chest, but it was but a pebble in a river. Tears began to roll down her cheeks as he stopped moving. They had both become covered in his blood within the few seconds it still tried pumping. She screamed. Be glad, dear reader, you could not hear it. There is something...ethereal...when a well put together woman absolutely loses her control and submits to her pain.

As her scream faded, the darkness of the room seemed to grow deeper. A peculiar sound, not unlike metal being sheared open filled the room, and a being appeared out of the darkness. She seemed to just float into existence, as if the pure black was a pool of water.

"Ah, I see I am too late."

She spoke, her voice haunting...But somehow assuring. She was pale, wrapped in a dark cloak that obscured her figure, with large black wings. She floated in the air though, as if not needing them. She seemed to just levitate, approaching the pair. Ms. Steel was simply too distraught to realize, until she saw the beings feet, pale and bare, set down beside them.

"This simply won't do."

She kneeled next to Mr. Sixx's...Well...Corpse it seemed. Ms. Steel eyes the being with apprehension, and fear.

"Who...Who are you?" *She chokes out.*

The being ignores her, looking at the beast that had slain Mr. Sixx. "I see." *She looks at Ms. Steel finally. This being acted like a stereotypical angel would, however she was most certainly not so in appearance.* "Would you be Sarah Rose Steel?"

Ms. Steel nodded. Her eyes were red, face wet with tears. One hand was clutching his, one resting on his chest, absolutely drenched in his blood.

"Your efforts are noted. But there is much left to do." She looked back at Mr. Sixx. "He will need your help to reconcile what is about to happen."

Ms. Steel stammered "W-What..?"

She smiled. "I am Liliana. I am known as the Keeper of the Void." She reached out and touched Mr. Sixx's chest.

"No..." Ms. Steel whimpered, before finding herself. "Don't touch him!" She grabbed Liliana's wrist, to which she simply smiled.

"Funny, it seems you wish him alive, yet your actions speak otherwise." Her voice was almost poetic.

"He's already gone!"

"If I had a world of my own, everything would be nonsense." Liliana brushed away Ms. Steel's hand with ease. "Nothing would be what it is, because everything would be what it isn't." She placed her hand flat upon Mr. Sixx's chest. "And contrary wise, what is, it wouldn't be. And what it wouldn't be, it would. You see?" Liliana seemed to be almost toying with Ms. Steel, looking up at her with a smile as she finished her lines. "Save your strength, my dear. I know not of how he will react." Ms. Steel didn't have time to react herself, as a black void erupted inside his massive wounds, emanating from her hand.

I thought the Limbo was hard to breathe in. But now, I couldn't see...feel...was I even really thinking? Where am I? Hell, am I even...me? I can't see anything, it's pitch black but I just...I can't feel anything, I can't even touch my own hands together?

Where am I?

"Good evening, Jake." That voice is...Haunting...But...Melodic? I try to speak, to ask what is happening but nothing happens. "Do not panic, please. I am here to help."

Oh yeah?! I've heard that before!

"I'm sure you have, I assure you I mean every word."

.......The fuck.....?

"My name is Liliana. Allow me to help you make sense of this place."

The darkness began to shift and morph, a kaleidoscope of colors and shapes. It began to slow and I could finally make sense of what I saw. I was in a briefing room...An eerie reflection of one from my past. The same worn table, but only two chairs. A cloaked woman sat in one, with what appeared to be some kind of folded wings attached to her back. They had a look of black leather, and I almost felt like they were bat wings. It was one of those things that I felt I should be concerned about, but I just wasn't.

I wish I could say this was the weirdest thing I had seen, but it felt like another regular work week. She smiled at me, as if she heard my thoughts, which she probably did. So, I didn't wait for her to ask, and I took a seat across from her. She lowered her hood, a relatively plain face with pale skin and dark hair. Her eyes seemed to be steel gray, not unlike that of a battleship.

"Well...You clearly have my attention, miss."

She put her elbows on the table, clasping her hands. "Welcome to the Void, Jake."

"Please excuse me, but I do not know how to respond."

"No one does." She leaned back. "This place is unique. I can say it is one of the last truly neutral places left in time and space. Souls come here before they get sorted to their final destination."

I click my tongue. "So that scorpion thing got me for real, didn't it?"

She nodded.

"Guess those old farts were right." I let my head drift to my chest.

"Sure. However, this isn't the final chapter."

I look up at her. "What's that supposed to mean?" I was afraid of the answer.

"Souls that have been corrupted, damaged, or lost have to be dealt with."

"Which one am I?"

She chuckled. "I wish you'd not think so little of yourself, Jake. Or should I call you Atlas?"

I glare at her. "You ain't earned that privilege, ma'am."

"Fair enough." She waved her hand like she was swatting a fly, a smile on her pale lips. "Let me explain something to you. These souls I mention, they are sent to a place that you mortals typically think of as Hell. It's not your typical Christian fare, we genuinely attempt to fix them, free them from what curse that has befallen them." Out of thin air, she produced a glass of water and slid it across the table to me. I eyed it suspiciously. "It's not simply never ending torture, you see. The problem with that is, sometimes they make attempts to escape. Thus, your Limbo."

I just stared at her, trying to understand. One gnawing fact has enraptured me. This is all well and good, but my fight is over.

"What's wrong?"

"I died."

"And?"

"I fucking DIED. I failed. Now Sarah and the team are out there without me."

"Partially true."

"PARTIALLY?!" I fling the water against the wall. "Explain!"

"Huh. You waited longer than most."

"I'm not here to play games!" I stood this time, my chair sliding roughly and loudly backwards.

"Fine." She leaned forward again. "I can offer you a return to your world."

"Why? How?"

"I want to seal Limbo up and return the wayward souls to their rightful spot."

"Again, why?"

She sighs. "Are you familiar with Cleopatra?"

"Like...ancient Egypt?"

"Yes."

"Wasn't she some super pretty ruler?"

"Essentially, and not as pretty as the history books want you to believe..." I almost felt like I hit a sore spot, somehow. "Anyway, unimportant. When I was alive, I was a temple Priestess at the time. The highest you could attain. When Cleopatra passed away...something...snatched her soul. To this day, I'm not certain if it stole it, corrupted it, or attached to it, but that entity is the cause of Limbo. It was the first to escape which left a rift that others have tried to use. Some were successful, mind you." She leaned back in her chair, I couldn't understand how she could do that without crushing her wings. I saw a small smirk, I assume in response to the thought I just had.

"So, it's your fault." I growl, and she flicked a glare back at me, which was intense for a brief second.

"Charming. No, but it did skewer me with a spike. And it was a very slow death."

"Oh, sorry to hear that." I felt a sudden kinship, however fleeting.

"I'm over it. I woke up in the void, and the first voice to greet me was that of the god Ra."

"Ra? Don't tell me he's a Marine."

"Look it up later. He charged me to capture and or kill the thing that stole her soul in exchange for rebirth." The parallels forming here were not lost on me, to which she smiled. "And luckily, you are smarter than you look but this isn't quite the same. I accepted, hunted her down, and was poisoned. I died again. Ra didn't meet me this time, and I don't know why."

"Is he not the forgiving sort?"

"Perhaps. Yet I haven't had a chance to ask. I am essentially the master of the void here, and I can visit your world during Limbo."

"I sense a catch coming."

She leaned forward on the table, conjuring a green martini out of nowhere in her outstretched hand. She took a sip before eyeing me.

"I can grant you a return to your body. With at least two less holes."

"In exchange for hunting this Cleopatra down?"

"Yes...." Why does it feel like there's more? She took another sip of her drink. "But I must possess your body."

I stared back at her. How could she be so cavalier about this? "Sorry. What?"

She grinned. "Not like that, I'll be a passenger following you on your mission. I can even assist you in battle and give you wonderful commentary to boot."

"It's already wild in my head, I don't need more voices."

"I gathered...but that's the option. You carry on, leaving your team behind, or you accept my offer and continue fighting." She leaned back in her seat. There was an air of victory that reminded me of Sarah. Shit. Sarah. The rest of the team...Sire...If I die too, she would be devastated. Team 2 would basically be done...not to mention I think she's become soft on me...I leaned against the table and hung my head.

"What happens if I choose the void?"

"That part I don't know. I understand you may return to the abyss of time to be reincarnated, maybe something akin to a Christian heaven. But alas, I know not."

"So, nothing says I won't come right back into this mess but no longer armed with information and experience. Maybe totally alone too."

She raises her glass, as if toasting me before taking another sip. "Yup."

"Well. Fuck." I look up at her. "How invasive would you be?"

"Try as I might, I won't be able to ignore your thoughts and experiences, similar to how it is here. Anything you think, I'll hear. I'll be quiet when you have any...moments...with Sarah." She playfully jabbed, to which I simply glared back at her. "What?? You think I want the 24 hour live stream of some grunt??" She smirked.

"Fine. And what kind of help are we talking?"

"You'll see. Expect some benefits the next time you fight. I can maintain your defenses and benefits pretty much indefinitely, but injuries can take it out of me. The worse the hit, the harder I have to work."

"Can we heal others?"

She tilted her head to the side. "I suppose it's possible. But I warn you, it is very taxing."

I lean back in my chair. The unknown, or back in the fight with some extra bonus and burden? Wait. "You can only revive me if you possess me. And you cannot exist in the real world. Or....my world."

She sets her drink down, her face betraying a sorrow she tried to conceal.

"So, it's like that."

"It's unfortunate. But yes. If we succeed, you'll return here with the choice to move on or help me from here."

Fuck.

"So, I guess I decide in how I get fucked? I die now, go onto the great beyond. Or, I fight to end Limbo and get sent to the beyond as my reward."

She smirks. "You do get a second chance. That's more than just about every other soul. One more chance to do what's right and provide closure for yourself and those you love."

I stood, pacing for a moment. "Fine. Do it."

"Certainly, but do try to contain your excitement."

I glared back at her, a smile stretching across her pale face.

"I will help you as best I can. I hope together we can end this thing and put Limbo to rest."

***

I gasp, my eyes shooting open. I can feel the ground, the cool air, but I feel a weight around me and a much heavier one on my chest, my arms are tight to my sides...?

"Jake?!" Sarah's voice. The tightness loosens, and I briefly see a flash of her face before she engulfs me again.

"Ma'am, please don't kill me again." I croak out, my body feeling almost foreign.

"Shut the fuck up!" I could tell she had been crying and had just started again. Doubt I could pull myself away if I tried, so I put my one free hand on her back. I really couldn't see much through the mask of red hair, which did not help the disorientation. "She did it...she brought you back..." she croaked again.

"She did."

Should I tell her everything?

~A good relationship is based on truth.~

Oh...oh this is gonna be fun. I can feel you grinning.

~Just sayin...~

Let me process everything.

~Hey, I'm along for the ride. You do you.~

Sarah finally pulled back, her face pale and her eyes red. We were both covered in blood, but I was in one piece.

"Are you okay?" I asked softly. She looked at me, shook her head and sat on her feet.

"How could I be? Sire is gone, Ulid is hurt bad and you...."

I touched her forearm. "I'm fine."

"I watched you die..."

"Oh, I did. But I got better." She glared at me. "Not a good time for jokes?"

"No!" She barked.

"Understood. I'm fine though." She finally let me sit up, wiping the tears from her face. I felt the urge to do so for her, but I'd just be smearing blood all over her. My blood...

Liliana, anything we can do about Sire?"

~Afraid not. It took all I could to find you and bring you back, he's been gone for too long. I'm sorry.~

Shit.

~Were you close?~

Not really, but he was a fellow team lead. Still hurts.

I start standing, Sarah attempts to help me but realizes it's unnecessary and awkwardly pulls her hands back.

"Seriously, I'm fine."

She half stared, half glared at me as I scanned the area. The beast was certainly dead, it laid in a heap with its blood forming a large pool around its head. Lancer had finally come to and was assisting with Ulid. Sire was gone, his body lying about 20 feet away. I could see his eyes, empty and hollow, staring at the ceiling. It's not lost on me, how close I came to being in the same way. Well, I was.

~You're not though.~

Doesn't change the facts.

~Facts are, you have a mission to complete and you're still alive.~

Yeah.

Sarah and I walked over to Ulid, I took a knee next to him.

"How are you?"

I could tell he was in a lot of pain. He didn't want to talk and he grimaced badly every time he moved.

"Relax. Let me look you over."

I could tell he tried his best to relax as I prepared. I pulled out my kit and used the antiseptic wipes to clean off my hands the best I could and put on the gloves. It didn't take long to determine he likely had about 3 cracked ribs, a dislocated ankle and quite possibly a minor concussion.

"I need this damn Limbo to end so we can get him to Jerry. Everyone keep your eyes peeled for more attacks."

"It's being persistent, is there anything we can do to assist?" Sarah asked.

"Watch him closely. Basically, it sounds like he has a cracked rib that may have punctured his lung. The rest I can't do much about. Let him be comfortable, don't let him move too much."

Sarah nods, placing her hand on his shoulder.

"Stay strong, Ulid. We'll get you out of here." I could see the confusion in his eyes. He knew how I felt about him, there was a mixture of fear and pleading in his eyes. We had made strides since his desertion, but I knew I still terrified him. "I'm going to look at Sire."

"What can you do?" Sarah asked, confusion and shock in her voice.

I stood, turned and started walking. "Not a damn thing." I spoke heavily. Each step felt heavier as I approached. Without the blood, he almost looked like he was taking a nap. I kneeled next to his body. "I'm sorry friend. Ad astra." I placed my hand on his face, closing his eyes. This...could have been me. It WAS me.

~There's nothing left to do.~

I'm aware, Liliana. Let me do my job.

~You're not a mortician.~

I'm a warrior. I'm a PJ. Everyone comes home today.

~So others may live?~

So others may live.

She went quiet, I sensed an air of respect in my head as I looked over Sire quickly. It was around this time that team Three barged in through the door. I let them work and secure the room as I secured Sire for transport.

"Control, Prophet Actual. Team three on site. One casualty, will need litter. One KIA. Get Jerry ready."

There was a pause. <"Control copies."> Her voice was almost hollow. <"Limbo closure in about 45 minutes.">

"Prophet Actual copy all. Will be RTB shortly."

There was no response.

"Fae...I need you to stay alert. We are not out of this shit yet."

Silence.

"Fae!"

<"Yeah...Yeah I got you."> I could hear her pushing through tears. <"I don't detect any other hostiles at this time.">

"Prophet actual, copy all."

A hand touched my shoulder. Team Three leader, Vic Castanza. "You good, Hermano?"

"Think you know that answer, Vic."

"Si." The silence lingered for a moment. "He was a good one."

"Yeah. Y'all clean us up?"

"We good. Ready to head back."

"Copy." I started to collect Sire's body.

"Yo we can handle that."

"No. I've got it." He looked at me as I steadied Sire's weight in my arms, a look of respect across his eyes. He backed off and let me lead.

~I've never seen this part before.~

Please, let me take care of this.

~No, I mean, I'm impressed. I'll shut up now.~

NOVEMBER 1ST, 2023

The rest of the day passed in a haze. I carried him to the vehicles, and back into the office as Limbo finally broke. My arms burned with his weight, but I wasn't going to let him down. Again. People blurred around taking care of the injured, I left Sire with Jerry and went back to the team room. I sat in one of the chairs, covered in the carnage of the last battle. I didn't bother turning on the lights or making coffee, just walked in and sat down.

That was me.

That should have been me.

~I disagree.~

Who asked?

~Don't need asking. You realize I could have selected either of you?~

Then why not him? Everyone loves him. He was a strong team lead.

~And how do you think he would have responded in your shoes?~

What do you mean?

~Do you think he would have sacrificed himself for the rest of the team? Carried your corpse, personally, all the way home?~

I...

~Come on, sergeant. You know how to read people.~

No. No I don't think he would.

~He would have cracked, just like Amelia. Team would be smoked and Sarah dead. Then who would lead the charge against Limbo?~

I sighed.

~Never minding all that, who has been the instructor for the whole group? Teaching these guys how to fight?~

Fat lot of good it did.

~You can't hold yourself responsible for this. It was an ambush, you were down two people before you could even draw your weapons.~

I sighed again.

~Thought so.~

"Mr. Sixx?" Lancer's voice. A sharp reminder of the world as I tuned back into reality. She was standing at the door with a terribly sheepish look. "Are you...okay?" She was taking in my presence, still covered in carnage.

"Yeah, yeah I'm fine. How are you?"

"I...I have no idea."

"Grab a seat." She hesitates but does so. "Don't feel ashamed of freezing." Her eyes went wide.

"B-but I let you all down."

"It's handled. That was an absolute mess, I'm not surprised you froze."

"But-"

"Stop. Don't go down that path." I stopped her, shaking my head.

~You should follow your own advice.~

"Path?" Lancer asked, puzzled.

"You learned something about yourself. You also have the experience of an absolute worst case scenario."

~You really are dad, aren't you?~

I shook my head again, Liliana's commentary making my head crowded.

"But...I'm scared." She looked down. "I am so scared..."

"You should be."

"What??" She turned to me sharply, shock written clearly across her features.

"You think fear didn't try to claim me too? My god, the thing had two spikes for tails! That's pure nightmare fuel!" I grinned at her and could see she tried to see the humor I was weakly offering. "Truth is, you're in a combat unit. People get hurt, people die. It may even be you on that list. Let your fear fuel you, not control you."

"But how?"

"Time and experience. Trust yourself, trust your team." I put a hand on her shoulder. "I will bring you home. I will protect you to the best of my ability." She was staring at her feet again, a tear fell between them.

"I can't do this." She muttered

"I don't believe that."

"I'm just a college girl, I'm not a warrior."

"You're still here, aren't you?"

"What...?" She finally looked up at me.

"If you weren't a warrior, you'd be gone already. Run off, quit. But you're here talking to me to get better."

"I'm apologizing for what I failed to do."

"That's what I'm saying, you're here facing your choices." She looked up at me, it was clear she was waging a losing war against her emotions.

"You...Don't want me to go?"

"No. I don't." She stares at me, looking for the lie. There was none to be found.

"I...Don't know."

"You don't need to decide tonight. Sleep on it, but just know, I'm here for you. I fully expect you to return and fight alongside me again."

There was a hint of a smile. "Okay...Can we talk again...like...tomorrow?"

"Come find me, text me or call. Anytime."

"Okay, I can do that." She pauses, then stands. "Thank you."

"Anytime, kid." As she left, I noticed that Sarah had slipped in at some point and watched the exchange. They exchanged greetings as

Lancer left. I watched her leave and my eyes fell on Sarah, who returned the look.

~You going to say anything?~

Why don't you mind your own shit?

~She wants to talk, she's worried about you.~

No kidding?

"You look like shit."

"You say the kindest things, Ma'am."

She walked across the room, taking the seat that Lancer vacated. "How long have you been sitting here like this?"

"Don't think it's been long."

"We've been back for about 4 hours."

I pause, nodding my head slowly.

~You disassociated, didn't you?~

You blame me?

"About that then." I muttered.

"Go home. Shower. Relax." She directed.

"Can't, not til I hear Ulid's alright."

"He's fine. You were right, but he's gonna be down for a bit."

"And you?"

"Unharmed."

"Not what I asked, ma'am."

She paused, staring at me. "No one has been killed in the line of duty before. Not under my command." Her voice was heavy.

"Then you're lucky."

"Excuse me?"

"Not everyone makes it home alive. Get that through your head right now. He won't be the last, especially if this is only ramping up." She glared at me.

"How can you say that?" There was an incredible tone in her voice, as if I told her something completely vulgar.

"Anything else is living a lie."

"We made it this far!" She was actually getting angry. I suspect I tripped a defense mechanism.

~Yeah, you did. Did you need to upset her?~

She needs to know, she needs to be ready for the next one.

~Seriously?? Let her recover.~

There should be two body bags.

Liliana went silent.

"We made it this far by pure dumb luck. Things are not going to get better, they will only get worse."

"How could they be worse??" She stood up. "We lost Sire and almost lost you!"

"You did." I look up at her, remaining as calm as I can. "Do you understand that this is dumb luck that I'm still breathing?" She was at a loss for words. "You, the commander of this unit, need to understand that you will have more killed in action. You need to understand you cannot stop it, and you will feel powerless. You must trust your people to continue the mission, despite this knowledge."

"How can you say this?!" Anger was bubbling in her eyes. "What made you so callous??"

I stood up, my calm and patience failing. "I fucking lived it, Sarah. I still see every face when I sleep." She stopped dead. "Two friends died in the line of duty. I was unable to save eight more that died because I couldn't bring them home fast enough." I took a step into her. "So, heed my damned warning so you're not haunted like I am. Be ready." With that, I turned and left the room before she could respond.

~That was dramatic.~

Fuck off.

~Oh...You're serious.~

~I'm sorry.~

I continued into the changing room, removing my gear and sorting the salvageable and not, everything was on autopilot. Even Lena quietly came in, collected my equipment and left silently. I showered, changed and left. No words left my mouth, Liliana was silent, and I wasn't even thinking much.

> *I am keenly aware of the jarring shift in tone in Mr. Sixx's Dialogue. His earned callsign comes into full display during times like this. Despite whatever he may be feeling or going through, he immediately changes gears to support his people and those around him. Sadly, it is not without consequences, ones that are tamed by certain vices.*

NOVEMBER 2ND, 2023

I didn't sleep much that night. Few hours maybe? Giving up, I headed into the office pretty early. I made a mental note to restock at the liquor store after I got off for the day. The office was pretty light, Team 3 was still on call when I arrived. Vic and I exchanged friendly insults as I proceeded to my room, to make some extra strong coffee.

~I get the feeling you're making some choices.~

Who the hell starts a conversation like that?

~Well? Aren't you?~

Maybe I am.

~Why deceive me? You can't hide your thoughts, regardless.~

Yeah, trust me, I know. Makes thinking a real challenge.

~I had no idea you were so damn difficult.~

I warned you it wasn't fun in my head.

~It really sucks.~

Tell me about it.

~How are you?~

You, of all people should know.

~Trying to fight the demons, keeping bad memories at bay, plotting how to lose yourself in helping others?~

I didn't ask you to fuckin' say it.

~Ohhhhh, you're gonna distance yourself from Sarah, aren't you? Probably everyone else too?~

Kindly fuck off.

Coffee pot was done. I poured it, straight black, and took a sip before it had cooled at all. It stung.

~And what was the point of that?~

Don't expect you to understand.

~So, what, all that 'don't blame yourself' shit was not applicable to you?~

I don't know how, but I will find a way to shove this mug down your throat.

~Empty threats.~

Fuck. Off.

~Seriously. Listen to your own advice.~

Still waiting for you to fuck off.

~Fine. Punish yourself all you want, but don't torture those around you.~

I won't.

~Self-loathing will not help things.~

I don't need a mother.

~Clearly, you do.~

I fought the urge to throw the cup of coffee against the wall.

You're gonna piss me off.

~I told you I'd give you commentary.~

Fair enough.

I looked at the door, as I leaned against the counter. I should check on her. Didn't exactly leave things happily last night,

~You should.~

Piss off.

~I'm really seeing this whole 'Atlas' thing.~

You still ain't earned it.

~I saved your life, didn't I?~

And?

~Stubborn ass...~

I turned around, making a second cup. I knew she wouldn't like it, but it was a peace offering. After I poured it, I walked over to her office. The building was still quiet as I coasted through the corridors, juggling the two cups. Not surprising, it wasn't even 0500. I rounded the last corner, noticing her door was ajar which wasn't terribly new, and eased it open. The desk lamp was still lit, and she had fallen asleep at her desk, her red hair splayed everywhere. The most concerning part was the bottle of nearly empty whiskey.

Well fuck.

~Is she okay?!~

Yeah, she's breathing.

I set the coffee down in front of her and turned back out to collect some water and anything I could find with salt. Apparently, she didn't take my advice lightly.

"Hey, what's up?" New guy from Team four, I couldn't recall his name. Idle chatter, passing through the hall, and I respond on autopilot.

"Taking care of business."

"Fair enough. See ya."

I secured a few items from our break room and Team 3s, plus I liberated one of Ulid's Gatorades from the fridge before heading back to Sarah's office.

I eased around the door again, gently shutting it behind me. She stirred as it latched, barely moving with a loud grunt.

"Morning, ma'am."

She grunted again. It was clear, she needed a first sergeant right now more than anything else.

~Knew it.~

Knew what?

~You really gonna stiff her?~

What's that mean?

~She likes you! A lot! And you're about to shut her out, aren't you?~

How about you once again, go fuck yourself?

~Dick!~

Been called worse by better.

~Don't be like that, not to her.~

I will do what is necessary to keep these people alive. Her included.

~You're an idiot. What's the point of being alive if you don't LIVE?~

That is what I am enabling.

~At what cost?? How many lives do you think I can give you?~

Doesn't matter.

~Jesus!!~

Sarah raised her head finally, the smell of the coffee finally reaching her brain.

"Tough night?"

"Something like that." She spoke thickly, eyeing the drinks and snacks I placed in front of her. She didn't say anything, just took the coffee in both hands.

"How are you?"

She shot me a look that told me everything I needed to know.

"It's still early. No one but the guys on call are here." I gave her the usual brief, she simply nodded. "You want to slip home?"

"No. Got shit to do."

"I can handle it. So can Fae."

"No." She turned and woke up her computer.

"Right." I took a sip of my own coffee. "If you need anything, let me know. I'm gonna get ready to play chaplain today." She didn't say anything, so I took my leave. As I closed the door, I heard her mutter 'thank you'. I paused in shutting the door to acknowledge I heard her before closing it all the way.

~Dick.~

Yeah yeah, tell someone who cares.

I made my way to the med bay to check on Ulid.

~You haven't told her about our arrangement either.~

Well, aren't you observant?

~Seriously?~

It's better this way.

~I certainly believe that you believe that.~

I smirked as I entered the med bay. The smirk vanished quickly as I saw Ulid's torn up body. That was one hell of an impact, he's lucky he didn't get ripped in half. I lingered for a while, checked his chart and his vitals. Nothing I could do at this point but wait. I touched his leg.

"Hang in there, kid."

After a few moments, I turned and headed out. I was only going to start feeling useless if I lingered any more.

The day passed slowly. Team mates came in, I consoled as many as I could. Team one was devastated, one of the youngest blamed me. He even threw a punch, which ended in him tasting a wall. The day after someone falls is always a wild ride, and the atmosphere felt it today. I was glad Liliana let me work in silence for the most part, I suspected she got tired of berating my choices. I had not seen Fae yet, and I had a bad feeling she was rough. Sarah didn't emerge from her office, but I made sure to crack the door and roll a bottle of water every hour. No response was made, so I didn't know if she was even still awake.

After about 1100 in the morning, I finally knocked on her door.

"Ma'am, I hate to ask this, but have we notified next of kin?"

I could hear a muffled swear.

"May I?" Silence, which I took as a yes and entered. Somehow, she almost looked worse, more tired. I closed the door behind me.

"I have not."

"Give me the address, I'll handle it."

"I should go."

"In this state, ma'am?"

She glared at me hard, then took out her phone and looked at herself using the camera. The glare faded.

"If you insist, I suggest you clean up and let me drive you. I'll stay quiet unless you need my help. I can handle this on my own, though."

"Give me 30 minutes."

"Understood, ma'am. I'll wait for you in the lobby. I'll make you another cup of bean water too."

She simply nodded, I turned and departed. I went to the team room, worked on a new pot of coffee and brought both cups to the lobby. Sure enough, damn near on the dot, she showed up looking like her usual self. For the most part. She couldn't hide her eyes. I silently offered her the coffee. "My car or yours?"

"We can take mine." She handed me the keys.

"I'll try, but might be too fancy for my blood." My humor was lost on her today.

We got in the car and started driving without another word. After a while, I broke the silence. "Who are we going to see?"

"Francine. His older sister. Only living relative he told me he had."

"Copy. Know what to say?"

"Nope." Her voice was soft.

"Fair enough. Just let me know how I can help." I let the silence settle in. She didn't respond, just stared out the window. We had a ways to go, Francine wasn't even in this state.

After about twenty minutes she finally spoke. "How do you carry on?"

"Pardon?"

"How do you keep going after losing someone like this?"

"Don't let it control you."

"Easily said." She grumbled, almost inaudibly.

"Sure. Okay, how's this? It is foolish to mourn those who died. Instead, rejoice they had ever lived amongst you." She let my words drift in the cabin.

"I...Hate that. But...I don't."

"The duality of woman." I deliver dryly, once again, the humor fell flat.

"It's...As if to say honor them and their existence. Let their achievements reign supreme and have them live on." I nod, allowing her to continue. "Even if they are no longer amongst us, they can still live on." She falls silent again, contemplating.

"Basically."

"But how do you get past the pain?"

"You won't like my answer." My turn to grumble almost inaudibly.

She looked at me, finally peeling away from the window.

"Lots of alcohol." I finally state flatly.

"That's it? Get drunk?"

"Pain fades with time, ma'am. Alcohol can expedite it. And you know, saying it out loud certainly makes me feel worse about my life choices."

"That can't be it."

"If it were easy, we wouldn't be talking."

"Suppose that's fair." Silence fell again. It was a bit before I broke it.

"I'm sorry if I was rough the other night. I know my words were far from kind."

"You're right."

"I'm trying to keep you from falling into a pit of despair. I can't do your job, ma'am. Don't think anyone else can."

She looked at me again. She was chewing her words, I could feel it.

"It was then I decided to be your first sergeant. I don't need a title, but I'll handle your people's issues. I'll keep you moving forward, keep you straight. I have ample duct tape after all."

She was chewing her words again. "What's in it for you?"

~Ohhhh she is fishing. I'm going to laugh when you fuck this up.~

"The end of Limbo."

"That's it?"

"Would you rather me say the fate of the world?"

~You do realize she can tell you are trying SO HARD not to look at her, right? You're not as slick as you think.~

Not helping. Besides, I'm driving. Looking forward is responsible.

~Not helping you, maybe.~

"Okay, sergeant." She looked forward to the road. I could tell her tone was off, and I couldn't tell if it was disappointment, or victory.

"Yes ma'am."

~You are the biggest idiot, I swear.~

Say what you want. Times like these are when a dumb airman comes home, mentally torn up, and marries a stripper. She's vulnerable. She doesn't need a lover, she needs support. Anything else is irresponsible and taking advantage of her.

The ride fell into silence again.

***

The rest of the trip was tough. Francine had an absolute melt down, and I had to step in to get her inside on the couch. Sarah did well, all things considered. None of this was easy, notification was probably the worst part of the job. The family didn't sign up for this loss, half the time they never expected it to be an actual consequence. Sarah passed out on the way home and slept the whole way, and I didn't dare bother her. Probably the most sleep she had in nearly 36 hours if I had to guess. This was fine, as I finally had a chance to process everything. It felt like I hadn't stopped moving or carrying everyone's load since that night. What does this even mean for me?

~You end Limbo with my help.~

Sure, got it. But if we win, that's it. Game over, lights out.

~Unfortunately...~

This is why I'm pushing her out. I'll be gone any day.

~Not even going to warn her? Don't you think that may even be worse when you just vanish without warning??~

Don't know. Never been much good at this stuff. Hell...I can't even grasp that I'm still here. All of this...just...It's too much.

~You're not wrong. Luckily, I've had centuries to grapple with it.~

Show off.

NOVEMBER 3RD, 2023

We finally got back to the office. As we entered, we could hear a commotion in the team hallway, and I decided to investigate, Sarah following behind me still waking up. It was pretty early in the morning. At this point, my eyes were burning letting me know I was nearing that 24 hour awake point.

"Is that it?" Youngster from Team 4. "Why? What for? How do we even know that's true?"

"You can't tell me you think it's good." A youngster from Team 3.

"But how do we know?!"

"The trail of bodies not tell you something?"

"What if that's only happening because we are fighting them!? Look, I ain't willing to die for no reason here!"

We rounded the corner and it was a large gaggle of different people.

"Limbo has killed people that have no idea it even exists." Sarah spoke. "Almost everything has been aggressive and willing to kill at a moment's notice."

"Why though?" Fae this time, her face pale and terrified.

"That's what we are trying to figure out, isn't it?" Lancer, timidly tossing in her two cents.

"And how long has this been going on? What if we are making it worse?" A middle aged man from Team 1. "And why did HE come back?!" He jabbed a finger at me, and it felt as if it was a knife stabbed in my chest. Why did I?

"Yeah! How do we know it's even him!" Team 3 youngster again. "False prophet! Wolf in sheep's clothing!"

"How the hell is he better than Frank?!"

A door slammed. Forsyth had walked into the hall, his face ensnared with anger. "This isn't about who's better, George!" I had never heard him speak with such force. It was impressive, and it commanded the entire hallway. "You, in particular, need to shut the fuck up! How many of you clowns got sold on being a hero?" He paused, looking up and down the hall. "Do you understand that it takes sacrifice?! Do you think this is some fucking game where you can bank on going home at the end of the day?!" His face was turning red by this point, and when he wasn't speaking you could hear a pin drop. "This is a COMBAT team! The next bullet may have your name on it!" He walked towards the middle of the gaggle. "Nothing is fair and you need to get that in your heads RIGHT NOW! Whether we deserve him or Sire doesn't fucking matter, do you understand that this man" he pointed at me as well "Has probably slept 3 hours since Sire died and has been busting his ass to take care of all of you ever since?! Hell, half of you probably owe him your damn life, and you don't even know it!" I didn't know how to respond at this point, I was in shock. "So quit your cowardice whining and get the hell back to work!" Forsyth turned on his heel and immediately went back into the team room and slammed the door again. There was an air of shock and disbelief that settled in the hallway.

"You heard the man. Get a move on!" Fae? That was...shocking. Folks started moving around now, some into team rooms and some out of the hall, passing me and Sarah as they went. Most simply nodded or didn't speak, but Fae walked over and stood next to me. After a few moments, it was just the three of us left in the hall, and Fae turned to me. "You okay?"

I looked between them both. "Not really. But that ain't stopped me before."

Fae tilted her head. "I don't understand?"

"Means he's as good as he can be, Fae." I nod at Sarah's comment, appreciating that she spoke for me at this moment. "How accurate is that three hours?" She turned towards me.

"No comment ma'am."

"Jake." Her eyes bored into mine.

I stare back at her, giving her nothing.

"Go home. You need to sleep."

"I'm fine, the troops-"

"I can handle it."

"Ma'am-"

"I can handle it." Sarah repeated herself, a little more force this time.

"Understood, ma'am." I felt a little defeated after everything that transpired, but she didn't enjoy the win this time. I was glad. "Call me if anything pops up."

"I'm sure we will survive the next few hours without your cape rustling." Sarah gave a hint of a smirk. I nodded, unable to muster the humor.

~She understands. Let's rest that head, warrior. You earned it.~

NOVEMBER 4TH, 2023

I slept...Kind of. Collective 4-5 hours maybe? It was fitful, flashes of faces and mistakes haunting me. I spent the rest of the time working on chores, cleaning, making a woefully inadequate meal and just generally existing.

Finally, I sat on the porch, staring at the sun fading below the horizon. I felt exhausted, hollow. So much so, I almost missed the arrival of a gray Dodge Ram. It was Forsyth's truck, and he hopped out and walked over. No words were spoken as he sat next to me on the porch. We sat in silence for a good while. No one spoke until the sun had fully vanished behind a mountain which cast the area in a beautiful partial light.

"Hit different this time." I finally break the silence.

"No shit, boss."

"That why you're here?"

He grunted.

"Been here before, but not like this."

"Ain't nothing like Limbo."

"No shit, bud." I repeat his words back to him.

A silence fell again.

"Sire is the first to die in like...ten years. So many people come here and think it's like a video game." He paused. "Sadly, they needed the reminder. We got too comfortable."

"Yeah...But that's a high price to pay."

"Complacency can cost way more. Y'all were lucky as hell."

"Fuck, yeah, you're right." I hung my head. "What if the Dreadnought didn't work?"

"We may have lost you all."

"Yeah." I picked my head up. "Can't play the what if game, though."

"Yup." Silence fell, he lit up a cigarette and wordlessly offered me one. I declined and he put his lighter and pack away. "Momma said this habit would kill me." He looked at the cigarette. "Suspect something far worse is gonna get me first."

"You hear about that too?" He looked at me, eyebrow raised. "Heard from some old vets that their buddy swore up and down this was his last battle, he could just feel it. They were right way more often than you'd think, just some kinda...weird feel in the air I guess."

Pause.

"It true?" He asked, I could hear the hesitation in his voice.

Pause.

"Yeah." I admitted. Suddenly, I felt the color drain from my face.

"What's wrong?"

"I fucking wrote a letter and left it on my desk, it's still there."

"Will?"

"That...and more." He smirked, I saw out of the corner of my eye.

"I'm sure she will enjoy the read."

"Fuuuuuck." I toss my head back and lean back on my chair.

"Ha, can't be that bad, can it?"

"Guess not...just more complicated than I was hoping..." I spoke towards the ceiling.

"Fair enough, good luck man."

"Gonna need it." I saw him look at me out of the corner of my eye and I saw a smirk. He's that quiet clever type, he knew what I implied. We sat in silence for a while longer.

"So, after paying the ultimate price...Now what?" I asked softly, contemplating.

"What do you mean?"

"I died that night. I paid the price, the world called my bluff and cashed it in."

He took a long drag off his smoke. "And?"

My head snapped towards him. "Fuck you mean, 'and'?"

"Still here, aren't you?"

"Yeah...?"

"Chalk it up to luck. That bullet wasn't meant for you and you got lucky."

"Every other time, that's what I did. This one though...Seems different. Seems...Borrowed?"

"Look, boss. Whatever it may feel like, it is what it is. You're breathing. You're still in this fight. Call a spade a spade."

"Don't get me wrong, I get that. I'm still here, I won't be giving up. Just can't help the strange feeling."

~Why not just talk to him real? Tell him the truth? Doubt you could talk to someone better.~

And scare him more? I promise you, he's going to report at least some of this to Sarah.

~And??~

I can't. This is my burden, and once it's known that I have to trade my life for the end of Limbo, people are gonna flip.

~You don't know that. You don't need to do this alone.~

"I can't claim to understand that feeling boss, you're the only human that's been to the other side and came back." He looked at me for a moment. "That thing ever tell you why?"

~Tell him!~

"Only that my job wasn't over."

~UGH!~

"Ominous."

"Yup."

We sat in silence for a while, I could feel Liliana's frustration in my head. It was getting late, and I saw Forsyth's phone light up.

"Duty calls, boss. Limbo coming up, tomorrow night."

"We on call?"

"Of course."

"We're still down a body. I suspect Lancer might be a wild card too."

"I'll get someone." He stands up. "Probably should hit the hay, see you tomorrow."

"You too." I remain sitting as he starts to walk off. "Hey…Thanks Bill."

"Didn't do anything, boss." I nod at him as he got in his truck and departs. I watch as his truck leaves and just rest for a bit. Again, another shrill whine as Limbo spins up, must be another blip. Once it hits and the color vanishes, that fox appears once more, walking along the railing of my porch.

~Who's your friend?~ Lil asks, almost a wonder like tone in her voice.

Dunno. I see it on rare occasion, think this is the second time.

~He's cute. She? Hmm…~

What ya thinking?

~Friendly visitors like this are rare. It just says hi?~

Yup.

~Huh.~

Silence settles in again as Limbo breaks, and the color comes back. I found it oddly soothing. Almost like something out there in Limbo didn't mind my existence.

NOVEMBER 5TH, 2023

Another mediocre night of sleep. I made it in the office on autopilot it felt like, and Forsyth had the coffee already running. I made my cup and proceeded to the briefing. I slipped into my office and snagged the note I had written a few days ago. As I got to the briefing room, Forsyth was there, as was Fae and Sarah, everyone chewing the fat. There was a sudden hush as I walked in, but it quickly recovered. I'm not blind, I knew what that was.

~Can you blame them?~

Nope. Can't.

~They are WORRIED about you, you lug head.~

Yup.

I grabbed a seat, enjoying the coffee. It was still early, and the conversation returned. It sounded like Fae was considering buying a new car and they were discussing some of the newer options. I felt Sarah's eyes lingering on me but opted not to engage. After a few moments, the door opened and Lancer entered, taking a seat across from me. Her eyes were terrified, but a mixture of determination was there, just below the surface.

"Glad you're still here, kid." I grunted out, soft enough to not disrupt the others' conversation. She whipped her head towards me, gave me a curt nod, and returned to watching the others talk.

"Let's get started." Sarah broke the din.

I looked at Forsyth. "Nobody else available?"

"I took the slot." Sarah spoke, and I couldn't tell if she was daring me to call her bluff or not. I looked at her, head tilted. Let's see where this goes.

"Glad to have you, ma'am." Still couldn't tell that expression...So be it.

The mission was pretty simple, an unknown entity in a park. Suspected siren, praying on some teenagers. We proceeded as normal, and the return to routine felt good. There was an air of apprehension, as was normal right after a terrible mission. We wrapped up the brief and went to get geared up. My body operated as if a machine programmed to do a specialized task. I pulled my rifle, checked the chamber, popped it open and put some extra oil. Close it up, repeat with my pistol. Gear, on. Magazines, loaded. Everything installed in their proper spots, water filled, snacks in the pocket just in case. Everything was as it was, except one thing.

This was the first time back in the saddle since Sire died.

***

"Control, Prophet actual on scene."

<"Copy Prophet, expect Limbo in about fourteen minutes.">

"Prophet, copy." We sat in the van, Forsyth behind the wheel, me riding shotgun and the ladies in the back. I hacked a timer on my watch to keep tabs and leaned back in my seat, eyes shut. "Place your bets? Siren, nothing, or something brand new?"

"Siren." Forsyth grunted. "Always a damn siren." I smirked at his tone.

"I hope it's nothing." Lancer spoke, her voice a mix of apprehension and forced determination.

"I ain't taking that bet, Lancer. Murphy likes to cast his vote." I could hear the smirk on Forsyth's voice.

"Murphy?" Lancer asks.

"You never heard of Murphy's law?"

"No…"

"Ha, anything that can go wrong, will."

"That's a positive outlook." Sarah interjected.

"No ma'am, it's a realistic one. In combat, always plan for Murphy." I added as I shifted my kit a little, still getting used to the Dreadnought tucked into my vest. After last time, I won't be leaving home without one now. It gave me some comfort, at least.

"Guess that makes sense…" Lancer spoke up, softly.

"The unexpected shit is what gets you." Forsyth spoke up. "Constant vigilance."

"Mhmm." I grunted and nodded. "Final checks, ya'll. Lock and load." I checked my watch, four minutes left but the start and end were never dead on. Sure enough, it started about two and a half minutes early this time. "Time to go to work."

The team went quiet as we deployed from the van, weapons drawn but not at the ready. We started to move out in a wide patrol formation, on the hunt.

~Wait, I can see something…Siren for sure. Look for a cluster of trees off to your right.~

If I turn my head, can you tell me where to go?

~Yes…There! Go that way!~

I motioned to the team to change direction and beeline towards the trees. I can make out some bodies in the distance, looks like a group of three. They were colorless, but they were not completely still. They were pretty young, two boys and one girl playing frisbee in the park. The stakes were now evident.

~Watch the tree line…~

Naturally.

I motion to spread out the team, and we start moving with intent. I sent Lancer to flank the teens, Forsyth and Sarah in the middle, and myself on the dangerous flank closer to the trees. Yet again, I find myself thanking Reggie for teaching me his OIT in the woods.

> *Senior Airman Reggie Lightfoot, a Choctaw who he once served with. An OIT is an 'old Indian trick' that the two joked about a lot during their service any time something just worked out for the best. Sometimes it was unique skills that Mr. Lightfoot had that no one else did. Mr. Lightfoot taught Mr. Sixx his namesake skill on a bet. SrA Lightfoot was unfortunately killed in combat in 2017, a scar that haunts Mr. Sixx to this day. On rare occasions, Mr. Sixx gets the feeling that SrA Lightfoot is still guiding him from beyond.*

I walk nearly silent through the trees, stalking my prey. I could just make out Sarah's silhouette in the distance, positive she lost track of me at this point.

<"Eyes on vics. Count three, all ensnared."> Forsyth over the radio. I clicked the mic twice in acknowledgement.

There. A spot in the trees, the darkness complete. It was an outcropping of three large trees that made an almost complete doorway out of bark.

~Bingo. That's the liar. Be careful, I feel like there's two in there.~

I clicked my mic three times, trying to signal them I found the spot, and unhooked a grenade from my belt. I let my rifle dangle silently from my neck as I crept closer, pulling the grenade out.

~Look to your right!~

No sooner than I heard what she said, a shrill screech burst out of the trees to my right. I was spotted. "Contact!" Still holding the grenade with one hand, I pulled my pistol and aimed at the trees. I was separated now. Foolish mistake. Especially since I still had no visual on anyone.

<"Where are you??"> Lancer.

"Right here!" I yanked the pin, threw the grenade into the patch of black and started withdrawing, aiming for a wide berth between me and the scream. The grenade blew, summoning an unearthly scream from that direction now. No point in playing games, I dart forward through the trees, aiming for the opening I knew they all were at. "I'm busting through trees, don't shoot!"

Twenty yards from the tree line-I stopped dead with something clutching my shoulder. The sudden stop and reversal of direction made my stomach flip, as I got thrown back into the trees, bouncing hard off another.

~I got this.~

Confused, dazed, and a sharp pain radiating through my arm, I didn't know what she meant and was disoriented.

~Just trust me.~

Let's go.

As I looked at my painful arm, I noticed a deep black seep into my veins. It was...cold? I think?

"What the fuck?"

Another scream, it's pissed.

~Trust me, I need ten more seconds.~

I struggle to my feet, the siren appearing in the trees, walking softly in the leaves. It was almost angelic in appearance. Long golden hair, soft white-gold lingerie covering her slender frame, her bare feet stopping before me. A look of confusion? The only thing that truly stood out as a warning was the deep, black and red eyes that stood out of place.

~NOW!~

It was as if my body got dumped into ice water, my nerves lit up like a Christmas tree, but it wasn't painful, not really.

> *Mr. Sixx rose in the air a few inches as everything he wore morphed, changed, into a set of black armor. This was not a simple paint job, the black was an absence of light. It was as if the armor was eating the little light remaining. The plates were smooth, as if made of glass. It was not symmetrical, not even close, but it was still sleek, portraying the agility he still possessed. His Dreadnought remained attached to his chest, his rifle morphed into a pair of long, slightly curved blades that matched his armor. His helmet morphed into the same matching material as the rest of his new armor. This was Liliana's gift.*

"What the..." I felt my full weight return as my feet contacted the ground. Everything felt foreign, but...There was an air of power I had not felt before. The siren had frozen in place, her mouth ajar. Movement behind her, Sarah was approaching the trees, looking for me. "Lil, giant swords in a bunch of trees?" It would be a challenge to use a long blade in such confined quarters.

~Oh, my bad, let me just do everything for you.~

I charge forward, blades behind me, throwing my armored shoulder directly into the Sirens chest. The shear force and speed were alarming, even to me, as we both came hurtling out of the trees landing in separate heaps. I could hear the confused yelps of the team and recovered quickly to face them.

"Don't shoot me! Kill that thing!"

The siren took the opportunity and hit me in the back, hard. I hit the ground, rolled and bounced back up, spitting out grass. I heard the report of Forsyth shooting, followed by Sarah joining in. The siren screamed again and threw something at its feet. It became transparent as it hit, and the evil grin appeared as their bullets no longer made contact was…Unnerving.

"That's new!" Forsyth barked.

"Since when can they shift phases?!" Sarah yelped.

~Guess we're up again.~

Will these things work?

~Oh yeah.~

"My turn." I advance on the siren at a walk. The evil grin grew wider, past the point it should be able to. It growled.

"You…." it spoke, the same sound that came from inside my skull again. "I've heard of you…"

I didn't give her anything, but I stopped short and prepared my blades. The way they seemed to eat at the light was almost mesmerizing.

"Granted the power of the gods and yet you still wish to play with these rats?"

"Who you calling rat, bitch?!" Forsyth roared.

"Forsyth, let him handle it!" Sarah shot back at him.

"All you got left is words?" It was my turn to coo out a taunt. "Almost sounds like you're scared of a fair fight."

"You have no idea what you're playing with, my dear." Her confidence was exceptionally high. Which of us knew the truth? Which knew the lie?

~Don't listen to her. She is not invulnerable to me.~

"Tell you what…Join us. Join us and when we pull this world into our vision, you'll be a god."

Us?

~Us?~

Shit…Cleopatra.

~Fuck.~

"Us?"

The smile widened even farther, she was running out of face. "The wondrous queen of all…" She took a step forward, her hand outstretched.

I've had enough.

~Same. Waste her.~

Without warning, I lunged forward, swinging both blades in an arc aimed at her torso. The smile widened even farther until the first blade hit, then the second, and tore clean through her torso. The siren's face was a mask frozen in shock as the pieces fell to the ground in a heap and slowly faded out of existence.

After I was sure she was gone, I turned to face the team. Each of them had a varying degree of shock and awe.

"That was wicked, boss!" Forsyth was the quickest to change to full awe, his face a big smile. "You just cut her down!"

Lancer, silent and white, approached and stared at the armor without speaking, seemingly fascinated by it.

"How long have you had this…ability?" Sarah spoke, hesitantly.

"Just found out today. When Liliana brought me back, she promised to help." I raised my swords slightly. "Think this will do nicely."

She approached, her eyes narrowed almost imperceptibly, but the moment was broken as Lancer placed her hand on one of the plates on my arm.

"This...What is it?"

"No idea."

"The way it plays with the light...It feels unnatural."

"Tell me about it." I grunt.

"Does it hurt?"

"Not at all. It feels like I'm swimming in mint ice cream."

Forsyth choked on a laugh as Lancer looked at me sideways.

"Control, Passport. Two sirens dispatched." Forsyth called over the radio, laughter still in his voice.

<"Control copies. Limbo is going to hang around for a while.">

"Copy, any ETA?"

Silence.

"Control, Prophet. ETA on Limbo?" Forsyth looked focused but there was another problem. I didn't hear him on my headset.

"Control, Prophet actual." The radios weren't going out. "Comm out." I spoke to Sarah.

"Excuse me?"

"Radios are dead, ma'am."

She pulled hers from her gear and looked at it, tried messing with it before putting it back.

~Something's coming...~

What?

~Something big...~

"Perimeter. Now." We were on the edge of a field, trees behind us and a field to the front. Lancer stuck to a tree on the edge, Forsyth went deeper in and Sarah took a large boulder to my right. I hunkered down in the middle, and we all went dead silent.

What's going on?

~Fuck.~

Lil?!

~Fuck, she's coming.~

Cleo??

~Yes...~

Over the horizon, a flock of golden birds appeared in the trees. They flew around the field, silently, before fluttering down to where the Siren died. They hovered and moved, shifting into the form of a woman. Dark hair, cut to her shoulders with olive skin. She wore a golden dress, low cut with a long slit up the side. I had no reason to believe it, but it seemed very similar to the material my armor was made of. The dress admittedly fit her very well, and she moved with the air of control. Power. She looked down on the spot the Siren died, knelt down and examined it. It was hard to see what exactly she was doing, but we all remained frozen in place.

~Do not engage her. Not now.~

We have her outnumbered.

~NO!~ Liliana nearly screamed in my head. ~Please, I need you to trust me again.~

Alright...

Cleopatra straightened up, looking around the field. She was looking for something...Us...

"Liliana, my sweet. I see you found another willing sheep for me to sacrifice."

~She's trying to draw us out. Don't bite.~

"Do they know what happened last time?" She...giggled?? "I do enjoy these toys you bring me. Fret not, I shall find them soon enough." Her eyes fell on our patch of woods, but she didn't seem to have noticed us. "You fight a foolish battle. Enjoy this pitiful victory. It'll likely be your last!" I saw a wicked smile cover her face. "I have a friend I'd like you to meet, in fact. Next time, though." She took a deep breath, smelling the air around her. "Ohh...You choose a warrior this time. This should be fun." Her body dissolved into the birds once more, and they silently flew off from where they came. We all stayed in our spots for a little longer, before I rose. I motioned for them all to remain, and I quietly walked to the end of the forest.

Care to explain?

~Not really.~

Will you?

~Later. I promise. You are not the first, but I suspect you are the strongest.~

Yeah, not very comforting.

~Sorry…I…I need to process.~

"I think we are safe."

Rustling branches greeted my ears as the team pulled themselves from their hiding spots.

"Why didn't we attack?" Forsyth stood next to me, us both looking out where Cleopatra came from.

"Gut told me to stay quiet."

~May feel a little weird for a second.~

Liliana was right, it felt like something was being extracted from my veins as the armor and blades faded back into my usual equipment.

"She was unarmed and we had numbers." Forsyth looked at me confused.

"You really think something like that wasn't able to wreck our shit?" I glanced at him, eyebrow raised.

"Concurred. Good call." Sarah spoke up from my other side, as Lancer joined us as well. "Something felt…extremely dangerous."

I nod. "Sometimes you gotta play the long game."

"So, Murphy doesn't throw his vote?" Lancer offered softly.

I looked at her, and grinned. "You're damn right." She grinned back.

<"Jake! Sarah! Anyone!"> Faes voice blurted into the comms.

"Control, Rose. Glad to hear from you." Sarah took this call.

<"Sarah?! Oh, thank God! You went dark for like 5 minutes!">

"Yeah...We will explain when we get back. RTB now."

<"Okay...Okay see you soon.">

I looked back once more and noticed something on the ground where the Siren fell. As I stooped to pick it up, Sarah appeared at my shoulder.

"That would be a relic." She said softly. I turned it over in my hand, and it looked like a pocket watch, but it seemed off. The hands kept jumping unnaturally.

"Rare?"

"Very. We have only acquired a dozen or so in the past ten years." She spoke again, watching me closely but making no move to take it.

"Now what?"

"To the victor goes the spoils. We have had very little luck in utilizing these items."

"Yall coming? I'm hungry." Forsyth called out.

"Yeah, you choose today." I met Sarah's gaze for a moment before tucking the watch into a pocket of my vest. "Besides, if we let Lancer choose again..."

"I'm not sure quinoa is actually food." Forsyth grumbled, I grunted in acknowledgement.

"Quinoa is a wise choice, Amelia. It has many health benefits." Sarah added in.

"Yes mom, we know." I quipped shortly, that got a wave of chuckles.

***

The ride back was quiet. Everyone was processing. We briefed Fae on what happened, her eyes wide with the new implications of everything. I could tell Sarah was very much interested in these new abilities I had, and I certainly assumed she knew more than I was letting on. It seems disruption of our radios is a new thing, and we would have to come to expect that down the line.

I hung back with Fae to discuss the relic, but ultimately, they were wild cards. Every single one seemed an embodiment of Limbo itself. It did what it wanted, when it wanted, and we got no say. Well, got a neat little timepiece now, who knows if it'll come in handy one day.

Ch. 7 Alice

NOVEMBER 6TH, 2023

It was well past midnight by the time I got back home. I put the truck in park, stared out the windshield for a moment, taking it in. This was all getting crazy.

"Much too young to feel this old…" I mutter as I climbed out of the truck.

~Are you though?~

"You say such sweet things." I shut the door, pausing to look out over the hood, trying to take a moment of peace for myself. Well, best I could do under the circumstances I suppose.

Without any warning, there was a throbbing in the base of my skull, I was immersed in a swimming darkness. What happened? Where am I? I tried to yell as a tightness engulfed my neck, but I couldn't push out the noise. I felt my feet leave the ground as my vision started to make sense.

> *Mr. Sixx had been sucker punched in the base of his skull, leading to his confusion. Cleopatra's form was in front of him, clutching his neck and lifting him off his*

feet exhibiting quite a significant amount of physical strength.

"My my...You DID find yourself a pretty toy this time."
~FUCK! WHAT HAPPENED?!~
I clawed at the woman's arm that had a stranglehold on my neck, ignoring the pain in my skull as the lizard brain took over.
"Oh stop, I don't intend to kill you." Before I could kick my legs up, her freehand crushed an item.
~No no CLOSE YOUR EYES!~
She was too late. As the thing in her hand disintegrated, Limbo burst forth. Before I could even comprehend Limbo's start, or the large dog/cat-like beast in front of me with eyes that shone a vibrant purple, pulling me forward into some form of abyss. It was a kaleidoscope of colors, purple dominant as I got pulled along until it stopped suddenly, and I was in a room. Maybe? Floor, but no walls I could tell, and a single light above me that only illuminated the immediate area. I was in a wooden chair and could not make out the area outside of my lighted bubble.
Lil? What the hell is this?
Silence.
Lil?!
Guess I'm on my own.
Footsteps in the distance. Not far. I strained my eyes to see what approached but until the first step crossed into my circle of light, I could see nothing. What I saw caught me off guard. It was an old man, maybe...70-80? Old, slow, but not necessarily frail. He carried a folding chair and a file folder.

"Well, hello." He opened the chair, sat down and promptly opened his folder, reviewing it. We sat in silence, I was analyzing him as much as he was reviewing the folder. I could only assume it was about me.

"Mr. Sixx. Or, Sergeant? What should I refer to you as?" His voice was almost kind.

"Sixx is fine." I spoke curtly, but not aggressively. I suspected I knew what this was.

"Mmhmm, sure, sure." He looked down briefly. "Military man. But early retirement?"

"Yessir."

"How unfortunate. It seems you were medically disqualified." He paused reading more. "Never married, no kids, most of your family has passed on." He stroked his chin. "How fascinating."

Don't give him anything. Lock it down, stay centered.

He looked up at me. "Suppose I can see some of this. You are not very talkative." He smiled at me. "How come?"

"Words are cheap."

"Are they?" He lowered the folder. "Why's that?"

I look back at him.

"Really, you have nothing to fear. We are just having a conversation."

"I just said words are cheap."

"You did." He opened the folder again. "I guess words would be...Inadequate. Perhaps, useless. Past their prime?"

I stared, locking down my emotions. He was digging for something.

"Let's retire this lonely venture. I long for the company of genuine conversation." He looked back down at the folder. "I hope you realize the futility in your efforts to remain alone. Your martyrdom won't assist you here, Atlas."

"You-"

"Ain't earned that right, yes yes." He waved a hand as if shooing a fly. He closed the folder. "You haven't earned the right to stop this either. Do you really feel worthy of stopping that which is inevitable, Sixx?"

Stay. Centered. Flip the script.

"And just what is supposedly coming?"

He smirked. "Cleopatra. She has decided to change this world into her image, one that makes sense to us." He leans back in his chair. "Your world is too...Chaotic. Too colorful. Too many rules." He shook his head. "And too many damned quote, heroes. She has targeted you, and you really think you have a chance here, don't you?"

"I'm not a hero. Never claimed to be."

He chuckled. "Oh please. Let's hear from some forgotten friends. Shall we, hero?"

He looked out into the blackness, I could pick out multiple footsteps, and one stepped into the light. I knew her...She was a cute, very sweet blonde I knew years ago. A light green sun dress graced her small frame...I remember that being the dress I left her at the airport with. I'm ashamed I can't recall her name.

"You told me you were going to separate. Eight years ago. I put my whole life on hold waiting for that deployment to end. You PROMISED me." Her expression started sad but quickly turned angry.

"I'm sorry-"

"Sorry doesn't cut it! A promise is a promise, and you BROKE yours!"

"I-"

"You chose that damned job over me, I held you when you came back! I let you cry when you couldn't handle losing Bishop!! You know what? I'm glad I called you over there and left you! It's what you DESERVED! So much for being my hero!"

Every word was a white hot dart, slamming into my soul.

Steps. Another female stepped into the light…Fuck. She wore a green flight suit, helmet still on her head. She walked with a limp from the complex fracture to her femur, her helmet was smashed on one side.

"Remember me?" She said softly, but not devoid of venom.

"Too well, ma'am."

"You were too late." Her words cut like a dagger.

"I can't be at every crash."

"You could have moved faster."

"That's not possible!"

"You call yourself Atlas, and yet you dropped my world."

"That's not fair!" No. Stop. Back to your center. Deep breath.

A middle aged man stepped forward, dressed in a once sharp business suit. He was covered in blood from a major head wound.

"And what about me? You saw the concussion but missed my internal injuries. Your CPR ruptured my lung and put a rib through my heart killing me. Why?"

"I-No!" I stood up from the chair. My fists were balled but I couldn't tell what to do.

Next, my mother stepped forward, dressed in nothing more than a hospital gown.

"My last year you spent over half of it deployed."

"How was I to know you'd die?!"

"Your own MOTHER was left ALONE!"

"No, stop STOP! This isn't real!!"

"Real? You wanna talk real, sarnt?"

"No…."

Reggie Lightfoot stepped forward.

"Reality is what happens when you fuck up." He was still dressed in his uniform, all his gear. He had four red holes in his chest, blood flowing from each.

"And you keep fucking up."

"NO!"

"Yeah. You do. You just did with the siren. Getting separated and then an enemy between you and your team? You wanna die, man?" He shook his head.

"This is BULLSHIT!" I could feel my nails digging into my own hand, I saw the old man circling in the background. "Stop this! You wanna fight me, let's go! Stop playing with these ghosts!"

"Oh but Mr. Sixx, you stand in the ashes of the souls you sent to another realm. Surely you can ask them if it would even be worth fighting? I doubt you are worth our time."

Another foot came forward, matching Reggie in nearly every way. John. He looked fine, but I knew damn well he had a hole in the base of his skull.

"You made the call. Took us both out. Rookie mistake, no? Didn't he yell at us about that a lot?"

"He did, shame he still hasn't learned." Reggie replied in a plain tone. You would think the two were talking about the weather.

"Reggie, come on!"

"Don't yell at him for your mistakes, old man." Another stepped forward. I didn't recognize him-Oh no...We never found him. "Left me the fuck behind, didn't you?"

"Another team found you!"

"Yeah, but YOU didn't. Maybe if you weren't such a sack of shit, I'd be alive?"

I was speechless as three more faces came out, I was surrounded in a circle by all the people I couldn't save. I didn't know what to do.

"Tell ya what!" I recognized Sire's voice before I saw him. "You always wondered why you and not me. I'm here with a killer idea..." He pulled his sidearm and approached. "Wanna trade and find out?" He offered me his pistol. "Let's be real, Sarah would have never taken you on anyway. Step aside, let her see what a real man is like. One not so fuckin' washed up."

"FUCK OFF!" I was angry. At them, the old man, myself. "EVERYONE FUCK OFF!" The old man entered the circle, smiling. I grabbed Sire's gun, levelling at the old man, but as I did so he turned into... Me...?

"My boy, would you really think it that easy?" He used my voice. I hated it. "Go on, pull the trigger." It was here I realized I hated myself the most in that room. The one common denominator.

"Why are you doing this?" I whispered.

"What do you mean? It's just you here. Just me."

"STOP THIS!"

"Why? I could just take this body, not like you deserve it. You got the first one killed and now you let someone drive you along like a marionette." The pistol shook in my hand as he raised his hands as if playing with said marionette. "Dance, puppet boy." I-He laughed and dropped his hands. "I admit, you're tougher than I thought." He turned and started to walk out of the light. "But not tough enough. This won't end well for you, kid." He left. I was alone in the circle of light, surrounded by empty with nothing but Sires pistol in my hand. I could feel the cold sweat. As the stillness grew, I swear I could hear them whispering just out of sight.

I fell to my knees.

What...What am I even doing?

I look down at my hands. They have caused so much destruction and seen so much blood. Had they even really been of any use? Can they even be useful anymore?

~Jake??~

...

My hands...Are they even mine?

~What?? What are you talking about?~

Should... Should I even be here?

I should be dead. I died. I saw my own blood, and the spikes...I saw it. No, I felt it. I can still feel it...The pain...

What does it even matter? I'm powerless to stop this. I'm just a vessel, a pawn....

~Jake!~

I'm a failure...

Nothing is going to stop Cleopatra if she can do this to someone.

This isn't me, this isn't mine! THAT'S NOT MY BLOOD! Skin...No...NO! I need to get it out! GET OUT OF ME!

~JAKE STOP!~

Nonononono OUT! I can get it out. I pulled out my knife.

Can I bring back Sire?! It SHOULD HAVE BEEN HIm!

~JAKE! STOP IT!~

It's stopping me, it's in my blood! I nee to DRAIN IT! DRAINITOUT! FIGHT!

~I will NOT let this happen!~ I throw the knife across the floor?! NO! getoutGET OUT!

THIS ISN'T MY SKIN! I WILL NOT LOSE! THROW THE TABLE!

Mr. Sixx has become enveloped in a severe panic attack. Liliana prevented him from cutting his own wrist but was not able to stop him from throwing a table. His eyes were that of a rabid dog.

"Get it OUT!" I bellow, slamming my fists into the wall. That fucking voice!
I CAN'T TAKEITANY MORE! ITSTOOLOUD!
~Jake please, listen to me!~
NONONONOSTOP! nOT MY LIFE! nOT MY BODY!
NONE OF THIS IS FUCKING REAL!
"Help...Please"
THATS MY VOICE! YOU CAN'T HAVE IT!
Impact. Can't breathe.

Mr. Sixx had not seen Sarah enter but suddenly was aware of her presence. In his psychotic state, he attacked her, which she deftly countered and delivered a decisive blow to his throat.

The room came back into focus.
Sarah. Her face white with fear? Anger? Both?
I was sweating, panting, and choking for air. My heart was in my throat, and I could feel my pulse pounding in my chest. My throat stung.
"Sarah...?" She stared at me. I was in my living room...
"What the hell was that?" She almost spat, definitely a mix of fear and anger. Her voice was sickly cool and low. I looked around the room. I could feel my skin soaked in a cold, clammy sweat.
"What happened?" The words were strangled in my now swollen throat. Her face showed more concern now. I looked at her. I felt

weak. She grabbed and turned a chair around for me to sit in, but she remained standing. I sat down, leaning forward.

"You tell me." Her voice was a little calmer now, but still on edge.

"I..." I paused. Hindsight is getting really clear right now. "Ma'am, I should have told you before."

"What?"

"Liliana...She's in my head."

~Finally. About time you fill her in, I told you.~

"Please stop."

"I didn't say anything, Jake. What do you mean?"

"She's how I came back."

"...What?" Sarah's voice was soft, as the shock set in. "You didn't tell me you were...Possessed??" She took a step back. Her expression is more fearful than before. As raw as I was mentally, it hurt to see her look at me in such a way, but I can't say I blame her. I hung my head.

"I'm sorry. I thought I could handle it."

~Typical man.~

"Please stop judging me! I'm doing the best I can without your god damn commentary." I could feel Sarah staring at me as I barked at the voice in my head.

"I'm not judging you...You're serious, aren't you?" A flicker in her eyes as she connects the dots.

I nod.

~You need to tell her. If no one else.~

"I fucking know, okay?" I take a breath.

"Jake, you're starting to scare me."

"Fine." I push up, leaning back in my chair. "Liliana brought me back to life to fight Cleopatra. She is how I know everything I do, but in order to keep me alive she has to possess me. Which means everything I see and think, so does she. It's fucking crowded in my head, and apparently, I snapped because I can't deal with this." I stared at Sarah, I could feel a tear rolling down my face. "I couldn't leave you and the Roses to deal with this shit without me. It was this or embrace the great beyond. I should have told you and I apologize." I was direct, talking without pause because I knew I wouldn't be able to restart if I did.

Sarah just stared, processing. "You're right, you should have." I hung my head again. "I don't feel so bad about hitting you."

"You shouldn't. I hate me too, I get it." I grumble.

"I didn't say that." Her voice went quite soft here, throwing me off.

"You can." I look up at her. "I wouldn't blame you."

She took a hesitant step towards me. "Are you truly in control? Have you...Changed?"

"Until today, nothing new."

~I didn't know I could control you at all. That's a first. I'm sorry, but I had to.~

"No, it's fine. Thank you."

"For?"

"Sorry...That was to Liliana."

"What did she do?"

"She threw the knife from my hand. Neither of us knew that was an option. I didn't ask for help...I was...Not here."

Sarah kneeled in front of me, bringing herself to my level. "Why were you doing that? Where were you, mentally?"

I stared at the floor again. "It's not mine. It's not me."

~It is!~

"It's not! I should have stayed dead."

"Is that what you really want, Jake?" Sarah's soft voice broke through my haze.

Another tear was beginning to form. "I..."

"You just told me you couldn't leave us to fight alone."

~Look at her, you idiot!~

"I don't know, Sarah. I don't know how to handle this…"

~Look at her or I'll make you!~

"Fine." I forced myself to look Sarah in the eye. It was as if something snapped again, but back into place. A well of emotion exploded. She reached forward, placing a hand on my shoulder, and that was it for me. The tears came, hard. She embraced me, without saying a word. "Cleo's friend…" I stammered out. "It'll remind you of every failure. I saw them all."

"What do you mean?" She didn't break away, didn't even move.

"Whatever her pet is…It pulls your memories…Feeds off your pain…" I struggled to get the words out through my emotional war. "In Limbo."

"That's the friend she mentioned?" Sarah spoke softly still, almost a warmth in her tone. I simply nodded against her neck as she kept me held tight. We remained this way for a bit.

"I'm sorry." I start to pull away, realizing her knee was buried into the hard floor. She held fast, and I jerked slightly as I hit the wall of her embrace. "Your knee."

"It's fine."

"You're uncomfortable."

~She's a woman, she's used to that.~

I sigh at Liliana's response, but Sarah does not move. I surrender and enjoy the next few minutes of closeness, of human kindness. Something that has been very foreign to me for many years. My life had been categorically violent with very little compassion. I had chosen this path, and it is all I have ever known. Eventually she breaks away, slowly. She pulls a chair over and sits across from me.

"So." I pause, scared of her response. "What will you do with me now?"

"You have a job to do." She said simply. I stared at her for a moment.

"Even with all these new catches?"

"You're a risk, yes. But one with far too much value to be sidelined." She pauses. "Withholding information is something I cannot tolerate."

"Understood."

"So don't do it again." She added, but much softer this time. "How are you?"

"Like my soul was ripped open and laid in a salt field." I grunted. "Being hit with every failure, face to face…"

"It would be a lot." She added. I simply nodded in response. "Take the time you need, okay?"

"Unnecessary." I grunt.

"Mr. Sixx." Her tone turns scolding.

"I need to get back on the horse, ma'am."

She sighs, seeing the resolution set in my eyes.

"Fine. Try to relax tonight." She speaks as if she was about to leave but does not stand immediately. She finally does after a few moments. "I am a call away, if you need anything."

I stand with her as we walk back towards the door. We pause at the entry.

"Understood. We need to get this intel back to the teams."

She places a hand on my shoulder once more, this time a new softness…Warmth even. "I will handle it. I shall call Fae on the ride back. Rest, soldier, you need it."

I sigh, matching her stare before giving in and looking away.

"Yeah, alright."

She takes the opportunity and leans forward, giving me a very soft kiss on the cheek.

"Sleep well, Jake." She said softly as she started towards her car. Her boldness, the unexpected action, rooted me to the spot.

~Wake up, Casanova.~

Shut the hell up.

~Told you so.~

I sigh as I watch Sarah get into her car, turn it on and leave. Judging by the night sky, it had become very late at this point, and my eyes hurt like hell from everything. I closed the door with a thunk and locked it up.

NOVEMBER 7TH, 2023

"Unseelie." Fae reported back, she had moved quickly. It was her, Sarah, and the team leads in the room. Lena had snuck in the back too. "Without going too deep into it, they are evil fairies. It fits the ticket, they play tricks and mind games in order to cause harm to their victims. They often operate at night, which is probably more applicably Limbo for our case."

"That's a new one." Castanza speaks up. "How bad?"

"Bad." I growl. All eyes spin to me. I was still pretty raw, but I had a grip on myself. "Imagine you're put face to face with the worst of your failures." Castanza lets out a low whistle. "It's..." I pause, the words failing to appear.

"Cleopatra is our number one threat." Sarah saved me from the awkward silence. "We are now aware she has relics that can summon and dispel Limbo at her will. We also know that she has an Unseelie at her command."

"Only defense against the Unseelie is to not look in its eyes. Which is even harder since they like to pop Limbo and already be in position." I add.

"Sadly, we lack Limbo control like Cleo does." Fae finished off.

"So, what do we do?" Marianne Campbell, the new lead of Team 1, asked about the room. She was a little older with a pretty calm demeanor. She had spent a few years as a blue collar worker after being a teacher wouldn't pay the bills. She was surprisingly tough but lacked the tactical skills for teamwork like this.

"We find a way, cover each other, and end the threat." I say simply. She glared at me, so I added a little more detail. "We keep fighting. Find a weakness to exploit and that's where we focus. Right now, that means everyone here is a target."

~Those Limbo stones she uses are limited, she can't keep that play up forever. Unseelies are vulnerable to attacks like everything else, they just disable your ability to fight and wreck you from the inside out.~

"She cannot keep up Limbo control forever. And I bet we can stab and shoot the thing if we can evade its mental corruption." I added after a pause.

"Everyone be on high alert until we can get more intel." Sarah orders. It was here that I happened to notice Sarah's peculiar expression. I didn't recognize it, but it wasn't a happy one. I lean against the table, looking at them all before addressing the room.

"You need to stress to your teams that we no longer have reliable Limbo prediction. I highly recommend a force tracker, check in routinely with each other so we can keep close tabs. I know it's not ideal, but this is no small threat."

"I concur. Please keep close tabs on your teams." Sarah said directly once more.

"Questions?" I asked the room at large.

"How long this shit gonna be?" Castanza spoke with a voice that said he didn't want to know.

"Until Cleo is a corpse. Or at least that Unseelie." I pause for more, nothing comes. "Dismissed."

I push off the table, crossing my arms as everyone leaves. Lena and I locked eyes for a second. Her eyes flick towards Sarah and we both nod, before she turns and joins the egressing gaggle. Sarah starts to go to the door, but I try to stop her.

"Ma'am." I spoke softly, not trying to draw attention.

"Yes, Jake?" She pauses her walk and looks towards me.

"A word?"

"Would this be a briefing room or my office type of word?" She matched my soft tone.

"Gut tells me your office."

She nods curtly and waits for the gaggle to leave and head towards her office. Nothing is said as we walk, and I follow her in and close the door. Same ol' routine, she grabs her seat as I close the door and take the one across from her.

"Well?"

"I saw that expression."

"I'm afraid I have many expressions, and you will need to be more specific."

I lean back in my chair with a sigh. "What's your connection with an Unseelie?"

"Who's to say there is one?" She still evaded some of my mind reading ability, but I could tell when her defenses locked down.

"You're not as stoic as you may think."

"You are surely mistaken."

"Yet you have not said I'm wrong."

Silence. She had no response? This was abnormal.

"What would you do in my shoes?" I pressed. She took a deep breath and sat still for a moment, and I was sure I saw a darkness cross her eyes.

"When is your shift over?"

"You tell me, ma'am."

"Let us go to your place. I find myself in need of fresh air and refreshment." She stands, I nod and take out my phone, rapidly dialing Forsyth's number. He picks up quickly.

"You have the office."

<"Shit, what did I do to deserve this?">

"Taking care of some important business with the boss."

<"Ah, copy that. Good luck.">

I hung up and led the way out of the office. "Yours or mine?"

"I do not mind."

I nod and lead her through the lobby and out the door to the parking lot and we hop into my truck. She was silent as a church mouse the whole time, and it reminded me of the trip to see Francine where she stared out the window the whole time. Finally, we arrived and I parked my truck out front and led her inside.

"The usual?" I ask her as I cross to the kitchen.

"Please."

Her tone was a new one, I couldn't place it. I fixed her a drink and one for myself before I head back over to the couch. She was lingering by the window, and I handed her the drink as I passed. I took a seat and waited for her. She would speak in due time. In the meantime, I got back up and started the fire in my fireplace. It had started to get chilly inside and it was definitely the season for cold nights. She stayed silent the whole time as I managed to get the flames to start flicking up the chimney. Satisfied, I returned to my seat, noticing she had started watching me at some point.

"My parents started the Steel Roses." She spoke softly, her voice heavy. "When we moved here. Back in Ireland, they were high ranking officials in a Limbo organization back there. Tasked with stemming the spread here in the states." She paused, taking a drink before finally coming and sitting on the recliner across from me. She had already hit the half way point on that glass and it wasn't exactly a small one. "So that's what we did. In an effort to keep me safe, they enrolled me at an American private school."

"Normally I'd make a crack about etiquette class, but I suspect that was real in your case?" I speak hesitantly, testing the water.

"It certainly was. It was a form of...Family tradition I suppose." She turned away and looked out the window again. "They formed the Steel Roses, in honor of my middle name." Her voice dropped again at this line. "I was not aware until far later, but that was their motivation. To give me a life free of Limbos threats. A normal life." She paused once more and I could see the hint of a tear trying to form in her eye. She took a deep breath and continued. "When I was 17, as I alluded to before, they were working on eliminating an Unseelie." She paused again, finishing her glass.

"Do you want a refill?" I asked softly, to which she simply nodded. I hopped up, grabbed the bottle and brought it back before topping her off.

"They..." Her head drooped.

"They weren't successful." I added.

"If only it were that simple." Her voice wavered this time.

"Look, you don't owe me any explanation. If this is too much-"

"No. No..." She started strong on that statement but fell quickly. "I...I finally feel that..." She took another drink, fully embracing the 'liquid courage' that liquor could provide. "I can be honest with someone. Someone who has experienced a similar trauma." She paused again.

The look on her face made it clear that her mask was slipping and she had not been this vulnerable in a very long time. In a word, I felt honored. I would have to remember to tell her that later, but I dared not interrupt her rhythm.

"I was not there, for obvious reasons. Alas, I remember when Gregoir came and picked me up from school. Middle of the day. Took me to the house." She opened her mouth to talk but the words apparently got lodged in her throat, and she coughed slightly. She was once again down to half a glass, and this wasn't exactly a light whiskey. She took another sip and a deep breath.

"The Unseelie made my father kill my mother. When Limbo closed, he went into a blind rage. Injured another member of his team before turning his pistol on himself." Her words filled the air with a lead weight. She stared at her glass, perched between her hands on her lap, her crossed legs still showing her refinement despite the visceral rawness of her soul being laid bare upon my table.

"Fuck." I mutter. She nods softly, still not looking at me. "Guess that explains how you knew how to handle me when I came back from that."

"Indeed." Her voice sounded like it came from another room entirely. "I need not pity." She added, almost in a rush.

"Pity?" I asked, shocked. "Shit, Sarah. I'm sitting here thinking about how damned awed I am that you could take that much whiskey, give me that brutal of a backstory, and still not be a blubbering mess."

She looked up at me, those green eyes piercing right through me. I suspected this was another evaluation, a personal one this time. I meant every word, she could judge me as harshly as she wanted. I understood how much trust was being tested right now, and I could only hope to match the kindness that she showed me the other day. Her eyes shifted, the laser beam changed into something far softer, and she looked back out the window.

"Thank you." She mumbled.

"Anytime."

"I see the hour grows long. I should leave you to it." She stands, but the whiskey seemed to have made a dent in her ability to do so.

"Ma'am, I drove."

She paused, looked at me then back out the window.

"You would be correct."

"Take my bed for the night. I probably shouldn't be on the road myself."

"I cannot impose on you any more than I have."

"Your options are walk, have me drive intoxicated, or that. In fact, I am the one imposing as I don't think you should be alone tonight." I watch her think, apparently it takes two full glasses of 80 proof whiskey to get her to slow down that brain of hers.

"Well…" She looks back at me. "I shall leave myself in your hands tonight then."

"No worries. I'll change the sheets for you." I stood, but she put out an awkward hand to stop me.

"No need. You have done beyond what I expected already."

"It's no problem."

"Good night, Jake." She makes her way back to the bedroom, her gait far more awkward than I had ever seen before.

"Night, ma'am." I linger for a moment, processing, before crossing to the kitchen and getting her a glass of water. Once at the bedroom, I had planned to set it outside the closed door, but it appeared she walked in and fell right onto the bed and almost immediately fell asleep. Silently, I set the glass down and folded my comforter back over itself, so she had something covering her before returning to the living room.

I tossed another log on the fire and sat down on the couch once more with my drink.

~So, you do know how to be a gentleman.~

"Jesus, Lil." I jumped a little.

~Oh, calm down. You did good there.~

Thanks, mom.

~Oh, shut up. Honestly? She is probably going to have the best sleep of her life right now.~

She's going to be hungover.

~Not the point.~

Don't you start with the damned riddles too.

~Hmmm, that could be quite fun.~

Keep it up and I'll drink enough that I won't be able to hear you anymore.

~Not enough liquor in the house for that.~

First of all, fuck you you're right.

~Hehe, and second?~

Just fuck off.

NOVEMBER 8TH, 2023

I barely slept, but what else is new? The sun was just creeping up, and I had prepared breakfast but hadn't started cooking yet. I was certainly curious how this morning was going to go. It had been...many moons since I had a lady stay the night.

I would not need to wait long, as I heard the bed creak. I stood and started cooking, enjoying my second cup of coffee as I went.

~Such a gentlemen!~

Shut up, you.

"Morning, ma'am." I spoke proudly as I heard her footsteps nearing the corner. She grunted as the footsteps approached closer. "Coffee?" I pointed with my spatula.

I chanced a glance, and I can honestly say I had never seen someone look so disheveled and relieved at the same time.

"What time is it?" She asked sleepily.

"0700." I scooped some eggs onto our plates, slid a pair of sausage patties on each and brought them to the table. I had cleared off a portion of the table before she awoke.

"What...Why are you doing this?"

"My dad taught me well. He said 'son, if you have a lady over for the night, you best make her breakfast when she awakes." I grinned at her as I stabbed a sausage. She froze mid step, her expressions going through a series of changes.

"Did..."

"Did...?" I couldn't help myself. She looked around the room as if the answer was in here with us.

"I...Did we conduct ourselves improperly, Mr. Sixx?"

"Mr. Sixx now? Jeez Sarah, after everything I thought we were on first name basis. No need to revert." My comment hit her directly and the color drained from her face.

"I..."

"Sit, I'm fucking with you. We drank and talked, you laid down, I stayed out here." I grin as I come clean and slide her plate closer. "Please, eggs get cold fast."

"You need not toy with me so early in the morning." She said roughly without any real heat in it. She took her seat and started eating. "I appreciate this."

"No problem."

"No...All of this. Last night. Food."

"Seriously, no problem."

We continued our breakfast quietly, I suspected her head was a bit of a mess right now.

We got ourselves ready and headed back to work, the ride mostly quiet except for her confessing that she had a very good night's sleep, but the alcohol and emotions made her out of sorts.

NOVEMBER 11TH, 2023

"Hey boss..." Forsyth met me in front of the door to Fae and mines office. He looked...shifty.

"Everything alright?"

"Just..." He takes a deep breath. "Look, she was trying to be nice."

"Bill." I state curtly.

"I mean, it's Fae. Girl doesn't have a mean bone in her body."

"Bill." I drew out the name a little more.

"Go easy on the girl, okay? She is really proud of herself." He hesitated and moved aside to let me open the door. As it opens, Fae is standing with a giant smile.

"I cleaned your cup for you!" She nearly squeaked. "You don't have a lot in the way of stuff, and it looked dirty." My eyes shot to the cup, and her words hit me like a truck as I saw the insides, gleaming white once more. "I wanted to do something nice for you! But...I didn't know what else to do."

"Thanks Fae." I fight every muscle trying to tighten in my neck as she hands me my once again gleaming cup. "You did good work, that was a lot of buildup." I was trying so hard to not kill her.

~What's the deal? It's just a cup.~

Shut. Up.

"Anyway, happy to help!" She squeaked again, collected some papers and bounded off. I stood there staring at it for a moment as Forsyth slipped in.

"Seven years." I say softly, Forsyth let's out a soft whistle.

"Sorry boss. It was done before I saw it."

"Seven...Fuckin'...Years." I repeat.

~Wait...You didn't clean it in seven years?! That is DISGUSTING!!~

You wouldn't understand.

"Well, no time like the present to abuse it again, eh?" Forsyth clapped me on the shoulder and I glared at him. He smirked. "Pots on in the team room. Come start it off."

Lil, it's a thing in some old circles of the military. You just don't wash it, cause it's being used so often it doesn't have a chance for shit to build up. Same concept as the perfect, pretty uniform is the new guy. Untested.

~Oh...That is still gross. But it makes sense.~

Yeah.

I take a deep breath. Well, Forsyth is right. Time to start anew.

NOVEMBER 16TH, 2023

All of the team leads had gathered again. The air in the room was of frustration, none of us were really looking forward to the next mission. Luckily, everyone accepted it and we grumbled on our own time. Sarah and Fae did their best to coordinate schedules so that some of us only had to focus on Limbo things. However, bills need paid and appearances must be kept.

"Thank you all for your patience." Sarah led the briefing this time. "Due to the manning requirements and limitations, this event will be all teams focus." She turned to look at the screen.

"What's the issue? No one likes pop anymore?" Campbell quipped with a grin, Castanza glared at her.

"That one song is gonna be the death of me." He grumbled.

"Oh, you mean-" Greene started to hum, Castanza immediately threw his notepad at her. A few chuckles from the table and it quieted down.

"Luckily, no Limbo is expected. Honestly, this should be a real easy day for us." Sarah started talking again once the room died down again.

"Comparatively." I grunt. "Keep your eyes open. We may not be fighting demons here, but we could certainly face combat with humans."

"That can't be plausible." Greene retorted, arms crossed.

"Why do you think they called in the entire team?" I asked her, her head tilted to the side.

"Damn, who they piss off?" Castanza asks with a soft whistle.

"Exactly. They have received credible threats on the bands life, so keep your eyes on a swivel." I replied before taking a sip of my coffee. Castanza smirks and shakes his head.

"Fun." Greene speaks softly.

"Okay, take it away boss." I sent the conversation back to Sarah who immediately flows into it.

"Campbell, you get the pleasure of watching the pit." Sarah pointed to the screen which held a map of the venue. "Castanza, Greene, you have this wing, and Sixx is QRF."

"QRF?" Greene asked.

"Quick Response Force. Shit goes sideways and I'll be on your ass before you even know you're in trouble." I added shortly.

"Sounds easy." Campbell spoke up, eyebrow raised with a tone of 'must be nice'.

"QRF requires an intimate layout of the whole facility and constant alert status. Most of my work will be done before deployment and then again if called." I rattled it off quickly, as this was essentially my old bread and butter. Constantly ready at a moment's notice to jump into the fire.

"Huh." Campbell nods, satisfied. "Noted."

"Back on topic, this is the general layout that we expect. Mr. Sixx, load outs?" Sarah turns to me for my part of the briefing.

"QRF will be Limbo ready. Pit team, lightweight. Pistols, armor, lights. Everyone else, light patrol. Rifles authorized. Let's keep the kits normal, no weird shit like bows and swords."

"You guys gonna have a Dreadnought?" Castanza looked at me with an eyebrow raised.

"I said Limbo ready, didn't I?"

"Fair enough, man. Tomorrow night yeah?"

"Yes, showtime will be here at 1200." Sarah started wrapping up her equipment. "Everyone is cleared off until then, except the alert team."

"Damn." Greene grumbled, snapping her fingers in a mock frustration.

"Try to get some rest, gonna be a late night." I finish off the briefing as everyone gets ready to head out.

NOVEMBER 17TH, 2023

Everything was in place for the show. My team even got to meet the singer, some really pretty young lady that I should probably have remembered her name. Yeah yeah, grumbly old man noises. Funny enough, she had taken a real interest in Lancer, much to Ulid's chagrin. His tongue was lolling halfway out of his head, but that singer started asking Lancer every question imaginable, and I could see the shock and embarrassment on Lancer's face. I grinned at Sarah as it happened and she returned it. Sometimes this job had some fun moments.

The show had been running for a while now, everything was quiet. Sarah, Fae, and my team had stationed ourselves in the security room, giving us a solid bird's eye view and central deployment point.

"I was thinking..." Ulid mused. "How are those new coupes?" He showed us his phone, a brand new advert on the screen for a small little import. Forsyth and I immediately exchanged looks. Ulid was allowed to join us as logistical support only. He was still dealing with some fractured ribs, but he could assist with comms and cameras.

"Don't." I grunt.

"Anything modern ain't shit anymore." Forsyth added.

"Okay well...what would you suggest?"

"Classic. Get your hands dirty." I said with a grin.

"I don't know anything about cars..."

"But you wanted a performance car?" Forsyth asked.

"Heh. That little import. Performance." I cackle a little to myself.

"Best way to do it is to learn on your own." Forsyth continued.

"Seconded. Way cheaper, plus you understand the machine." I leaned back in my seat, hooking my hands around the top of my gear. It was one of the most comfortable positions I knew, which probably said something about my life.

"You two talk like a car is some sort of...mythical being." Fae contributed in a confused tone.

"Why not?" I posed the question to the room. "Million different pieces working in sync to provide you a means of transportation." I turned to scan the monitors again, checking on everyone. "Your engine is a precision made contraption that flings large chunks of metal around due to tiny explosions at high rates of speed."

"That makes it sound really cool." Lancer mumbled.

"Dad and I worked on a GSX when I was young." Sarah interjected out of the blue. "71...Maybe 70."

"You did not!" I barked at Sarah, a grin on my face. "Get the hell outta here, big block?"

"Yes, 455 I believe it was."

"Damn, would have loved to have seen that thing. Been thinking about building one just like that."

"Sadly, it is somewhere else now." Sarah spoke matter-of-factly, I genuinely could not tell if she missed it or not, but I suspected she did. "He and I converted it to a 5 speed."

"That would be a slick ride." I grin.

"Yeah, no kidding. I heard about those, they were mean." Forsyth added.

"5 speed?" Lancer asked Sarah with a confused expression.

"Manual transmission. It requires one to use an additional pedal to change gears."

"Gears?" Lancer asked her again.

"When driving, have you noticed how your engine gets louder then softer upon acceleration?"

"Yeah, always thought that was weird."

"Those are gears. It's how your car can go as fast as it does without killing the engine."

As Sarah explained generally how transmissions worked with Lancer, I couldn't help but feel that odd pang of strange thoughts about her...Sarah had started speaking my language, after all.

"Okay! You got me convinced. What would you suggest I look for?" Ulid relented.

"Honestly? A common one. Mustang, Camaro. Lots of parts and info." My comment was cut short as a cleaning lady walked in. Figured they would have waited til after the show, but whatever.

"Easy enough." Ulid opens his phone, I presume to look at cars for sale.

"Let us know if we are in your way." Sarah addressed the cleaning lady, who simply nodded. My eyes narrowed. She wasn't making eye contact, not speaking, and I have yet to see her face. My hand drifted slowly to my pistol. Maybe I was overreacting, but I did not dismiss it when the lizard brain was alerted. The conversation continued, but my attention was on the interloper. Eventually, she emptied the trash and left the room. I stood and followed quietly, making it look as if I needed to use the bathroom, and watched. She still refused to look at me. She stopped in her tracks for a moment and reached in her pocket. My hand tightened on my pistol as my ears exploded with a sudden Limbo opening. Caught off guard, my free hand went to my face, and I grimaced at the sudden shock of pain.

"Clever." I heard that voice again as something slammed against my chest, sending me onto my back and sliding down the hallway. I could feel the armor plate in my vest crack from the impact, and the breath was knocked out of me.

~Oh shit! I need you to buy me some time!~

I tried scrambling to my feet, but Cleopatra leapt and landed on my chest, furthering my lack of breath. Her arms shot out to either side, and gold rings wrapped around my wrists and held them straight out from me.

"Oh, my sweet Liliana…You did choose well this time." She cooed. I coughed as I tried to recover my breath.

"Fuck off!" I squeeze out. She was toying with me, and that smile was a give away. She leaned down closer to my face.

"Hmm, no. Don't think I will." She reached down and touched my face with a finger, and I jerked away as best I could. She just cackled. "You're cute. It's a shame I'll have to kill you one day."

"What's stopping you?" I choked out again, I knew she had me dead to rights.

"I like to savor my food." She grabbed my jaw roughly with one hand and traced my brow line with the other. I growled, as she pulled that same finger up and licked it. "Mmmm. Salty."

~Jake…Having a really hard time here…~

Why?!

~Something is making it impossible for me to connect with the armor!~

Cleo suddenly looked up, sending another bolt of gold into the distance outside of my field of view.

"My my, how rude of your friends to try and interrupt. I only need a few more moments. Don't worry."

"For what?! Why are you doing this?" My voice was still strangled in my chest from the weight of a full grown human crouched on it.

"Why else would anyone go to such great lengths?" She spoke sickly calm, but her face changed as I heard the door explode off its hinges. It sounded like Forsyth used a breaching shotgun to break it free. She looked up quickly, and shots rang out from behind me. A shriek rang out that was unworldly, with a flash of blue, coming from just over Cleo's shoulder.

"Got it!" I heard Ulid scream. Cleopatra deployed a golden barrier with a snarl and retreated.

~That did it!~

I felt the power surge forward into my veins, and I was able to break out of the golden rings with a heave.

"Check fire!" I bark as I start to get up. They lift their fire and I jump to my feet as the armor fully takes hold and the blades swoop from my hands. However, by the time I stood, Cleo was gone and Limbo was threatening its closure.

~Shit, she's gone. Pulling it off before Limbo closes.~

Yeah...

The armor vanished, Limbo closed with a screech, and we were left alone backstage.

"What happened?" Sarah rapidly walked up to me, the others looking around and essentially making a perimeter.

"That cleaning lady was her."

"You must be joking." She said with the hope of a lie. I returned her gaze, making it clear it wasn't. "Well."

"Yeah."

<"Control! Project! I need you down here now!">

"Lancer, with me!" The two of us break into a run, followed closely by Sarah, navigating all the small passageways until we reached the area Team 4 was guarding. Greene was out of sorts, but she was fine compared to an older man on her team who was a blubbering mess. I scan the area, throw open a storage closet, and drag him inside. I try to calm him down but nothing seems to reach him, so I just let him work it out and remain with him. After a minute or so, Sarah joins us.

"Unseelie." She states softly.

"Yeah, no shit. Look at him." I threw back at her.

"What do you suggest we do?"

I pause, considering my options. "Well...If we move him like this, it'll be a bad look on us. If we leave him here, he could get worse."

"I don't like those choices."

"Well Sarah, we got lucky he ain't caused a panic yet." My eyes never left the man. I knew all too well the pain he was experiencing. "Hey, bud, you're safe now. And I know it's hard to believe, I've been there too." I touched his arm, and he finally seemed to be aware of me.

"She...She..."

"Hey, it's over."

"That...That's the problem." He sniffed.

"I'm sorry. But can I ask you a big favor?"

"Yeah...Yeah?"

"Can you keep it together long enough to get you back to the control room? I'll be right there with you the whole time, okay?" I never left his gaze. He stared back at me and finally nodded.

"I can do that." He said meekly. I offered him a hand to help him up.

"Sarah, what if we use the door and ourselves to cover their movement?" Lancer asked Sarah.

"Good call, you get the door, I'll provide a distraction." Sarah replies quickly.

"Come on, warrior." I helped him up and nodded to the girls who assisted with minimizing the crowds visibility of us with the door. We slipped out into the backstage area before anyone was the wiser. As I guided him quickly, I heard Sarah on the radio putting out the warning Limbo was not totally off the table. We got back to the security room, noting that all of our people were looking worried.

"Someone grab water." I escorted him to a chair in the corner, quietly relieved him of his weapons as Ulid brought a bottle of water. I crack it open and hand it to him.

"He looks like he's seen a ghost." Lancer muttered.

"Damn near. Unseelie." I grunt.

"Shit, serious?" Forsyth spoke softly. "How?"

"Remember, Cleo can control Limbo." Lancer spoke up again, almost solemnly.

"Sarah..." I speak with an ominous tone as she enters the room. The implications were very real now.

"I know." Sarah replied heavily. "She is well aware of our operations now. We need to be smart about this."

"Fuck. This is heavy." Ulid spoke absently, his hand on his head.

"You just rest right here, okay? We will get you out of here as soon as we can." I spoke to the man from Team 4.

"Yeah...Yeah. I'm okay." His voice was hollow.

"That's fine, we don't need you to push, okay?"

"That's George." Sarah nearly whispered behind me.

"We all need to take a knee some days, George." I said softly again. He nodded slowly. I was happy to see some life return to his eyes, but he was very much haunted. Satisfied that it was resolved, I rounded on Ulid.

"You're on the bench." I grumbled, a lot more bark than bite.

"Y-yeah well...I had the shot." I could almost hear his knees knocking.

"That one's on me boss." Forsyth grumbled. "I lent him my pistol."

"You're both idiots." I grunt out, throwing a hand in the air.

~Hypocrite.~

"But...Thanks. What the hell did you hit?"

"Some weird little pixie thing." Ulid shrugged, his confidence coming back after realizing he wasn't in serious trouble.

~Yup, Pixie. There are some that can disrupt other entities connection to Limbo, or in my case, the void.~

"Great. Guess we gotta watch for those too." I growled.

"Would that be why you did not receive Liliana's gifts immediately?" Sarah finally took a seat, I could tell she was wired with adrenaline.

"Yeah." I grunted, leaning against the wall and letting my head lightly bump against it. "Only easy day..." I say softly to myself.

Luckily, the rest of the show went smoothly with some minor issues from a few very drunk fans. Once we were wrapped up, Greene ensured George got home safely and we all went back to normal ops.

NOVEMBER 19TH, 2023

"Folks are worried." I sat in the briefing room with Greene, Sarah, and Fae. "And I can't say I blame them. Cleo knows our mission, and she can track us apparently."

"What do you want to do?" Greene interjected. "George is fucked, and I'm not all that great myself."

"Good question." I say heavily. "We can't all just live here. Hell, I wouldn't be surprised if it's already compromised."

"Wait, really?" Fae spoke with a scared tone.

"Why not? Unseelie can access our heads to bring out fears, and they caught us mid mission. Can't be luck."

~You're probably right. I would not trust this place to be a stronghold.~

"What about a relic or something?" I shoot into the dark, already knowing the answer.

"We cannot count on them, as we discussed the other day." Sarah reminded me anyway.

"Shit."

"Radios?" Greene offered.

"Not enough range to cover everyone's home. However, we need a command that's an immediate all hands. Let's call it Broken Rose. You hear that on the radio, text, call, whatever. You come running, fully armed." I leaned back in my chair.

"Basically for Cleo attacking you?" Greene again.

"Yup."

"It's something." She shrugged.

"Otherwise, keep a close eye on your buddies. Probably check in every few hours, be ready for them to try and isolate and pick us all off one by one." The room felt heavier after I finished talking.

"Fair enough." Sarah broke the heavy silence growing around us. "Push it out to the teams. Broken Rose means everyone converges, regardless of where you are."

"Copy." Greene nodded curtly.

"Already writing it up." Fae was tapping away on her tablet.

NOVEMBER 24TH, 2023

"What a surprise, ma'am." I had been sitting on the porch when that MKZ pulled up. "What do I owe the pleasure?" Sarah walks up the stairs with a small bag.

"You left your sunglasses at the office, suspected you'd want them."

I stared at her and accepted the outstretched bag, but my analysis was running overtime. This was not normal, and why would she come all this way for something so silly? "Okay?"

"May I?"

"Well, you came all this way." I motioned to the second seat and she took it. It felt like Liliana was chuckling in my skull for some reason.

Care to explain?

~Nope.~

Ass.

"You truly have chosen a wonderful location to live." Sarah spoke softly.

"Best place to get away. Nature has a way of recharging us, if you let it."

"You speak the truth. I enjoyed camping as a child, I wish I had time to do so again."

"I'm sure I know the answer, but can't you make it happen?" I grinned at her.

"It would be foolish to go alone. Should you wish to discuss leave, one would only need to look in a mirror." She cast a side eye glance.

"Sorry I do so much work for you, I'll stop."

"Could you?" Another side eye with a hint of a smirk.

"Hey, you shut your mouth." I grumble and she cracks a soft smile. It's here I detect a faint whine. "Huh. Fae's slipping."

"You needn't worry about her."

"Pardon?" I turn to look at Sarah as Limbo opens and the colors drain. As the figure of Liliana appears the pieces slide into place. "Ahhh."

"Sarah! So good to finally speak with you again!" Liliana floats to Sarah and extends her hand, a genuine smile on her face.

"You as well. I hope we can speak on…more even terms this time."

"Of course! Besides, do you know how obnoxious it is to use that numbskull as a translator?" She cast me a dirty look.

"Listen. I'm doing my best." I grunted.

"That's what I'm afraid of." She said with a smile.

"Oh, fuck this, I'm getting a drink." I stood and walked inside, the other two followed me chatting idly. "Sarah?"

"Yes please."

I fixed our drinks and we reconvened in the living room.

"Liliana, how long have you been fighting Limbo?" Sarah transitioned into investigative mode quickly as she took her drink.

"Longer than you would believe."

"What insight do you have for us then? What is Cleopatra's motive?"

"I'm afraid I know only a little. The Cleopatra that I knew was actually a kind person. I cannot figure out what happened to her, but my working theory is that something very corrupted leaked out of Limbo at the moment she died."

"So, sort of a combo situation." I offer.

"Essentially. I detect some of the original, but there is something else too. I cannot fathom what the other thing is though." Liliana seemed to truly enjoy being able to communicate openly.

"If we could get the why, we could predict things better." I sigh, swirling my drink before taking a sip.

"You know that won't happen." Liliana returned.

"Limbo's greatest strength seems to be the unpredictability of it all." Sarah added.

"Yup." I grunted and drank again.

"Then how does your relationship work?" Sarah looked between Liliana and me.

"Alright first off, no. Ew." Liliana sarcastically spoke with a fake grimace.

"Really?" I stared at her.

"I know too much, and could you think about something other than cars and guns for ONCE?" Liliana's grin was wicked.

"Oh, fuck off."

"Anyway, I cannot exist in your world. Not normally. So, when Limbo is closed, I remain inside his head like a passenger. During Limbo, I typically stay just in case it closes unexpectedly. If I'm not possessing him, he will probably die immediately. I can support from there, and I can even leave him during Limbo should the need arise."

Sarah was listening intently, but something shifted in her face suddenly. Violently.

"Does that imply what I believe it to mean?" She asked dangerously softly, looking between us both.

"Yeah." I state heavily. "Yeah, it does."

"Unacceptable." She blurts out.

"Only option."

"No. We will find another way."

"No other way, unless you got a time machine to go back to before that scorpio-dragon thing."

"Regardless, Limbo has its own rules that we shall find a way to fix this on our terms." She damn near seemed emotional at this point, in a way I had never seen her before.

"Ma'am, I'm already on borrowed time. I've made my peace."

"This isn't just about you." Liliana interjected softly.

"We will not sacrifice you to end Limbo." Sarah spoke with that tone of finality that meant she would not accept anything else.

"Be that as it may, we might not ever get the chance." I shrug.

"You cannot be so cavalier."

"So others may live." I returned her piercing gaze. "You want to see the tattoo?" I point at my chest.

"No. Unacceptable. There will be another way." Sarah repeated herself. I sigh softly and take another drink.

"He is right though, we may never get a chance to close it for good." Liliana spoke up, I knew she was trying to disarm the tension. I accepted it and looked outside the window as they continued their discussion. There was a soft tap on the window and my eyes focused on the little smokey fox. Its paw was on the glass, looking at me. Softly, it dropped its paw, looked at the ladies and came back to me. It slowly nodded before vanishing again. Huh.

"Hey, lug head!" Liliana's voice cut through my daze.

"What now?"

"Almost time. You ready?"

"Nope." I grunt at her.

"Yeah, well me either. Thanks for the chat, Sarah. It was refreshing." She shook Sarah's hand once more.

"I concur. I wish you didn't have to remain trapped in such a confined area."

"Literally right here, within earshot." I grumble. Liliana floats over to me and puts a hand on my shoulder.

"Finally. Thought you were deaf."

"Oh, shut up." I grunt as Liliana fades and shifts into me again. I could just pick out the faint whine as Sarah stands.

"I mean it. We will find another way." She spoke with a directness that almost made me believe it.

"I won't pull my punches in hopes there may be a solution. If I can end it, I will." I returned her tone.

"I don't think I can expect anything less from you." She sighed. "It's why I keep you around."

"Then we are on the same page?"

"That we are. I shall take my leave and let you enjoy the remainder of your day."

Ch. 8
Jabberwocky

NOVEMBER 26TH, 2023

Back in the control room for the night. Fae had some shindig she requested off for, and I had nothing better to do. While Limbo was expected, there was nothing abnormal, so we let her go. Greene took her team out tonight to patrol a possible entity area downtown. One of her people made the mistake of saying it should be an easy day, and we all know what happens when Murphy hears that line. They had already had a flat tire and needed to come back as their scanner was on the fritz. Lena about blew a gasket, but that was kind of normal.

I was perched in my chair, feet kicked up on the one across from me, listening to the radio. The door creaked open, and Ulid poked his head in.

"Hey, doc just cleared me for duty again."

"Good to hear it kid." I grin at him.

"Yeah, still a little tender but it'll be alright."

"You mentally ready?"

"Yeah, good to go." He smiled as he walked closer. "How's it going in here?"

"Same ol'. Some bozo said it'll be an easy day, they had two malfunctions already." I groan.

"Do they know about Murphy?"

"Shit if I know."

The radio crackles with static.

"Is that normal?" Ulid asked, looking concerned.

"Nope." I stared at the speaker and put my feet on the floor. I hear him come closer and take a seat next to me. "Project, Control. Say again?"

Silence.

"Project, control. Over."

Silence.

"Fuck."

"Why aren't they replying?" Ulid's voice was strained, he matched my anxiety.

"Go get Castanza ready. I'll draw up a package."

"Right!" Ulid jumped up as I collected a piece of paper and started jotting down notes.

"Project, Control, how copy??"

<"Control, Project! We-"> Heavy breathing broke the rest of the call.

"Project, focus! Say again!" I barked into the mic as I finished my notes and the door opened with Castanza and Ulid, Castanza half dressed in gear. I handed him the note as we listen.

<"Unseelie!"> I heard that word clearly.

"Project, do you need back up??"

<"Negative."> The line went dead for a moment. <"Okay, Control, we have 1 wounded.">

"Do you need a recovery team?" I query into the mic.

<"No, we got this, Control. Unseelie really messed us up. Be back soon.">

"Control copies all, I'll have the doc standing by."

"Fuckin' got them again huh?" Castanza grunted, sitting heavily in the seat across from me. "How do we kill this thing, boss?"

"Beats me man. Sick of this bastard." I set the mic back on the counter.

"We'll get it." Ulid nods, his motivation surprisingly stout. "I'll go talk to Jerry."

"Good call, kid. I'll be here."

He nods and runs off, Castanza looks at me.

"You a miracle worker."

"Oh, fuck off, Vic." We exchange smirks.

***

The door flew open, Greene leading the charge. She looked enraged, but it was the kid being helped along by George that caught my eye. Jerry immediately went to work, as George walked right up to me and threw his gear at my feet.

"I'm done. I can't do this anymore."

"George?"

"I quit! I'm done!" He barked in my face and turned on his heel.

"Hey wait!"

"NO!" He screamed in the lobby, catching everyone off guard. "I can't keep doing this! I wasn't built for this!!" His eyes were alight with anger as he stormed out of the lobby.

"Give him some time. He's a hardhead." Greene spoke quickly and quietly to me, I nodded in return. I noticed Ulid quietly retrieving George's gear and disappearing.

"How's your injury?"

"It's mild. She tried to run away but the Unseelie had her under a trance, pretty sure it's a twisted ankle." Greene spoke.

"Sure is." Jerry added out of nowhere. We both nod as he helped her into the medical room.

"Check on George, keep me posted."

"Got it, boss." Greene nodded, following Jerry.

NOVEMBER 28TH, 2023

"Hey boss." Greene had found me in my office. "Got a sec?"

"Yeah, what's up?" I set my coffee down and offered her a seat, which she took.

"George is done. He won't even answer my calls anymore."

"Shit. You think it's done done?"

"Yeah. He's had a bit of a rough year, and I think this just set him over the edge." She spoke heavily.

"He's older too, can't be easy on the old bones." I say softly. "Copy, I'll handle Sarah and the paperwork."

"Got it. Hey…I haven't had anyone quit before." She spoke with a sheepish look.

"Don't sweat it. This job is a huge demand on the easiest of days. This…Isn't an easy time. Do the best you can to keep your people happy and capable, alright?"

"Yeah… Plus Camden is down for a week or so at least." She looks up at me for a moment. "Means I'm solo."

"I'll keep you off the schedule until you're back up, okay? You guys have gotten the brunt of the Unseelie fucker anyway." I leaned forward, towards her. "How are you?"

"To be honest, I'm stressed. This thing has us all on edge and we don't really feel safe anywhere except here."

"Fair. We can never get too comfortable, not until Limbo is settled."

"For real." She chuckled, but it was more of a stress reaction than humor. "Well, that's all I had. I'm gonna…" She sighed. "I don't know. I'll see about helping out somewhere."

"Roger that. Hey, keep your head up, okay?"

"I'll do my best." She offered a forced smile as she left.

DECEMBER 1ST, 2023

There was an odd feeling in the briefing room today. I couldn't place it, almost as if some form of specter was lingering in the shadows, watching. With this life? Who's to say it wasn't. I leaned against the wall as everyone chatted amongst themselves. I caught a glance from Sarah every now and then, but I didn't take the bait.

~You feel it too.~

Liliana's comment was not a question.

Yup. Something...fucky.

~Eloquent.~

Never claimed to be.

I swear I could feel her eyes roll as I took another sip of coffee. The cup never made it to my lips though, as I heard the beginning of that shrill whine of Tinnitus kicking in again. It was far off, probably actual Tinnitus. It was really unfortunate that those noises were indistinguishable. I set my coffee down and stretched my jaw, not like it ever helped, but why not try?

For no apparent reason, the hair on the back of my neck raised and my hand unconsciously rested on my pistol. Then, as if my ears got shredded apart, the shrill whine exploded and took the color of the world with it. I tried to yell, warn everyone to close their eyes, but the words got stuck in my throat as I saw that thing once more.

"You really thought this was for your benefit, didn't you? What, graced by some centuries old entity to save the world?" Liliana stood in front of me, a wicked grin on her face. "You foolish little boy."

"What are you on about?" I looked around into the colorless room, and my team was missing. "What's going on?"

"You forgot Limbo already?" Her voice was sultry, she was toying with me. But this was never how she acted, not that I had ever seen. She began to pace around me slowly as she talked. "Maybe I am draining you too quickly. Really should have gotten a hero in their prime instead of this washed up old rag."

"What the hell are you doing?" My shock was turning to anger, and it was here I noticed my body seemed to weigh a ton.

"Lamenting my choices." She said sadly. Then, as she reappeared in front of me, the frown whipped to a grin. "And you thought you'd save the world."

"This ain't about saving the world, it's about-"

"Doing what's right, yes, I know. I know your type. I've been in your head. Remember?" She sighs. "The white knight routine is so very...Old."

There was a flash in her face, something I couldn't pinpoint. This...Was this the Jabberwocky again? It had to be.

"I'm going to use you until nothing's left, then take my place by Cleopatra's side." She stopped in front of me, her face close to mine. I had never seen her so clearly, but something told me this wasn't her...That flash again. Anger? Sorrow? Her grin came back again, it was wicked. Vile even. "I'll be a hero." She whispers, barely a foot away from my face. "Does that make you jealous?"

"Nope." I tried to shift but my muscles wouldn't respond. "You're not Cleopatra's agent. I saw your realness."

She laughed. Loudly, right in my face.

"Realness isn't even a word."

"Damn, your breath really betrays your age." I hissed at her. That shut her up and brought a hand slapping my face.

"KNOW YOUR PLACE!"

"I do."

Her face cracked again, it was worry. Fear.

"FOOL!" Her face was angry. "You arrogant fool! You have no IDEA what you're playing with!"

It was here I could fully make out the real Liliana trying to reach me. There was a conflict in her eyes. Was she being controlled as much as me? My reality fractured, as if two channels on a TV were vying for which was more dominant. Two versions of Lilana fighting for their time in this reality.

"Stay strong Jake..." A whisper, broken and fragmented but enough to make out. I had to hold the line.

"She won't save you. You can't save yourself." The evil Liliana returned. She seemed to have won, but I know the stakes now. I tried to fight, to use my strength to raise my arms.

"Cute. My little pet is trying to resist." She starts to circle me again, and I focus as hard as I can on breaking free of this control. "Enjoy this fight, it may be your very last one." She whispers into my ear as I force myself through with everything I have, and grab at her neck. To my surprise, I managed to find her tiny, almost frail neck.

"I won't listen to this shit anymore." I squeeze down, focusing on crushing this thing's windpipe. The smirk never leaves, as the form suddenly warps into Lancers face, terrified. I could see the fear of death in her eyes.

"Jake-" She tries desperately to talk even though I had a stranglehold on her. I had to press, this was a trap! Her arms flailed against mine, trying to release the grip I had, but her eyes betrayed the ending fast approaching. "Why...?" She choked out, before a knife appeared in her hand and slashed into my side. I yelp in shock as the very real pain explodes, but I keep my grip.

It was subtle, but reality flickered for a moment before the telltale tinnitus of Limbo departing became evident. The color snapped back into the world, but Lancers face and the searing pain in my side never left. I immediately released my grip, and caught Lancer as she collapsed, she had to be only seconds from unconsciousness.

"Lancer!" I yelp, ignoring the pain in my side, as I help guide her to the floor. She clutches her neck, coughing and sputtering. "Slow breaths!" I speak softly, but very directly. "Fucking hell." I add, mostly to myself.

"Fuck! Medic!" I hear somewhere to my side. Once I was sure Lancer wouldn't die, I looked around the small room. Forsyth was staring at my side, white as a ghost. He still had a bloody knife in his hand. Fae was also white, but shaking uncontrollably in the corner, pressed against the wall as hard as she could be. Sarah, her eyes full of rage, held a Dreadnought in her hand, dripping with some eerie fluid. She looked like she was about to murder someone, and judging by her weapon, she just did.

The doors burst open as Castanza and another from his team enter, half dressed in combat gear.

"What the fuck...?" He mutters, taking in the scene and becoming absorbed by shock.

"Lancer and I need to get to medical." I grunt, looking up at him. The pain was becoming very evident now, and I felt a hand under my arm helping me up. As I move, the pain sharpens and I grunt again. I try to shake the hand off and go for Lancer, but it's a very tight grip.

"Let us help." Sarah's voice, barely audible, hit my ear and I relented my struggle. Castanza and his buddy help Lancer up and we make our way to the doc, Sarah doing what she can to keep me upright.

"Oh, yeah, that...that smarts." I grunt towards Sarah as the adrenaline fades. We enter the medical bay seconds after Lancer was drug in. Jerry takes a single look at me and changes his priority.

"You really are an overachiever." He says softly.

"No, handle Lancer."

"She will be fine and you are far worse. Pipe down, kid." He didn't skip a beat, before directing his patients and caregivers around the room. I wound up on the table, shirtless, as he started on my side.

"What's the word?"

"You're lucky. This is mostly superficial. Shot." His warning wasn't worth much, as he jabbed me with something basically as he said the word.

"God damn it." I grunt.

"Couple stitches and some cleaning, you'll be fine."

"Good. Lancer?"

"She'll be fine, bruised her neck up good, but some painkillers and rest and she'll be back up in no time." He glanced over at her before looking up at me. I was having a hard time looking at her myself. "You both have an Unseelie attack?"

"Correct." Sarah spoke from the doorway. "It won't be a future problem." Her voice carried the weight of the moment, I half expected some form of vindication but that was absent.

"You got it?" Jerry asked with a grin. She simply nodded. "Well done."

I take a glance at Lancer finally. Her eyes were empty and she was softly rubbing her throat.

"You good, kid? You can just nod." I say softly. Admittedly, a bit ashamedly too. She nods, her eyes landing on me for a second before flicking away. "For what it's worth, I'm sorry."

"It's okay." She chokes out, her voice raw and the sound hits me like a brick. "Not your fault."

"Don't make it right, but I'll take it."

"Hey same here boss." Forsyth grumbled.

"The Unseelie takes responsibility here." Sarah states with a renewed force. "None of us were in our right mind."

"Agreed." Lancer chokes out. I looked at her again, and I could feel my heart lighten just a little. She had gotten so much tougher over the past few weeks.

"Guys! Holy shit, I'm sorry I'm late but what happened??" Ulid appeared in the door, breathless.

"You lucked out." Forsyth grunted.

We caught Ulid up to speed as Jerry finished my stitches. Lancer and I swapped places and I sat heavily.

"Ma'am, I'm really tired of being disadvantaged."

"Same here." She said with a huff.

"I got an idea! I'll catch up later." Ulid disappeared once more.

"Huh. This should be good." I grinned at Forsyth, he returned it.

Jerry finally let us go. Luckily everything was pretty mild. I suspected my gear would be mighty uncomfortable from my newest injury, but I refused to sit on the bench. Things were too wild right now. I tried sending Lancer home to rest, but she refused and opted to nap in the break room. Fae had alerted the rest of the teams, but we didn't call anyone back in just yet. So, back in the briefing room with Sarah, Fae, my team except Lancer, and Castanza.

"Joey had a great idea, and it's already started to formulate." Fae spoke at the head of the table. We weren't using any screens or anything at this time, just talking.

"Yeah! So, since it happened right here and we have all our equipment, I asked Fae if we could identify her little Limbo controller thingy." Ulid was speaking excitedly.

"Luck would have it, I got a decent bit of data since she attacked our actual base here."

"Yeah!" He blurted out before motioning for Fae to continue.

"I will spare you the specifics, but I can track where the relics are made. This is all still very early, but I believe there is a source in the Nantahala River."

"Good work, Fae." Sarah contributes.

"I still need to do some digging to isolate it. But I have a decent idea. I propose your probing patrol idea, Mr. Sixx."

"Done. When's the next window?" I ask.

"Two days from now, I'd say it's a decent one."

"I'll take it. My team will be full up." I turned to Sarah.

"I'm inclined for a second team." She looked between me and Castanza.

"Done, big boss." He jumps into the fray, ready as always.

"Okay, Greene on standby. I'll publish the changes." I was already bringing out my phone. "Everyone...I know this is a big order...But try to get some rest."

Ch. 9 The Griffon

DECEMBER 3RD, 2023

One thing was for sure, this area was gorgeous. We were deep into the mountains and forests of NC and the air was fresh. It smelled like rain was on its way, and the sky matched it. We had arrived a bit early, the spot Fae wanted us to check out was way out of the way, but my team made very good time. Castanza was a little behind but was nearly here. I was not worried about getting the teams separated, we were all experienced and we had plenty of time before Limbo opened. Ulid and I sat on a downed tree, Lancer had taken a spot of grass with her head leaned back against the tree. I hated seeing the bruises on her neck, which had gotten quite dark, but she was still hanging on. Forsyth was pacing a little ways off, a cigarette on his lips.

"You're used to this kinda stuff, aren't you?" Ulid asked.

"Yeah. Couldn't tell you how many days I spent out in the field, away from everyone."

"Cool." He said letting it linger for a moment. "Kinda feels...Dunno...Lonely?"

"Sort of, but we always had a team around us. Despite that, having to be dead quiet for hours at a time…" I shrug. "Yeah, I could see lonely."

"How'd you cope?"

"Sheer force of will. Some guys had nicotine, all of us had caffeine. You learn to respect a warm shower too…Always loved that first shower after a long time out." He was getting a little nostalgia out of me, surprisingly enough.

"That's it?" He looked at me, kind of surprised. "Nicotine and a shower?"

"Yeah. You'd be surprised what you miss when you're out of the country for a few months."

"What was your favorite uh…Homecoming?"

"Don't laugh." I grin sheepishly. "But the guys all banded together cause one of our new kids had no one to come to and we came home like a week before thanksgiving. We made this whole big stink about having to go right back into prep for a new deployment and drug him off the plane to a German banquet hall just off base. Huge thanksgiving bash that night."

"That's sweet." Lancer spoke softly, I hadn't realized she was listening, but she was watching intently.

"Work hard, play hard." I shrug again. "God, the liquor we went through that night."

"Why didn't he have anyone?" Ulid looked at me, slightly confused.

"Parents died when he was younger and he was fresh off a divorce. Poor bastard was 22 at the time."

"Damn." Ulid said softly.

"That's terrible." Lancer added in a similar tone.

"Military life is hard." I shrug softly.

<"Prophet, Pathway."> The radio came to life in my ear.

"Go." I replied shortly.

<"In position. All good on our end.">

"Prophet copies, got about 20 minutes."

<Click click.>

"Hey, why'd you let them take the most likely spot?" Ulid asked after a short pause.

"Can't burn out the A Team." I deliver dryly.

"You okay with not being able to protect the big boss?" Forsyth smirks as he takes another drag on his cigarette.

"You know she is more than capable of handling herself." It was a deflection, I knew what he was shooting for.

"Yeah yeah, sure thing boss." He grins and shakes his head. Ulid looked at me confused, but Lancer had a small grin herself.

The next while passes pleasantly with idle chatter. Limbo came about as planned, and we set to work. We scanned for the next hour until finally, Liliana picked up something nearby.

~Ohhh shit....~

What?

~It's a guardian. Corrupted by Limbo. Not gonna be an easy fight.~

Should I get Castanza over here?

~Oh yeah.~

We coordinated our advance over radio and utilized our scanners. Everything backed up Liliana, the source we were looking for was co-located. Standard shit, just a new day.

"All units, execute." I called over the radio, and we made our coordinated attack. Castanza's team was to approach on a hillside as we went up a dried up river bed. Not the greatest choices, but this little alcove had shit for easy pathways. Everyone was silent as a mouse, scanning and watching. I was the third one to enter the natural alcove, following Ulid. We started a perimeter, using stones and trees to hide ourselves for now. The area would have been a great little camping spot, heavily wooden with a small clearing. The only problem was the spectral being that appeared to be cultivating a writhing, color changing mass in the middle of it. The specter was hauntingly pretty. It was partially see through and every bit of nine feet tall. Peaceful, yet menacing at the same time. It's gleaming long sword to its side, stabbed into the ground. Unlike the being, it was very solid. The mass it cultivated just felt wrong. Colors shifting and morphing, vanishing and reappearing. It made the air around it ripple, as if it was bending the very fabric of space time.

Do we jump it? Make contact?

~There…Is nothing to save here. Guardians are prolific fighters, but once they are corrupted, they cannot come back. This poor soul…~

We need the blades?

I clicked off my safety, but I had already begun to feel the power from Liliana take hold.

~On it.~

The armor formed, my weapons turning to the blades.

"Pathway. Cause a distraction. Going in the old fashioned way."

<Click click.>

I only needed to wait a few seconds before his team opened up and I leapt from my cover. As I suspected, their bullets went right through the guardian, but it caused it to break its focus. I lunged forward, rushing for the kill. Their fire lifted and I raised my blades, but the guardian was fast. As I slashed down towards it, that gleaming blade appeared in front of me and my own blades slammed against it hard enough that I could feel the denied attack vibrate through my arms. Before I could recover, it's unarmed fist came forward and struck me in the side of the head with the force of a runaway train.

~Get up!~

FUCK. FIGHT ON.

I pushed off the ground, having been thrown into a heap in the grass. Stars blurred my vision as the air filled with the sound of rifles. I scamper to my feet in time to hear a roar as I turn to see Castanza charging, Dreadnought out and deployed. In one swift motion, the guardian swung its blade and Castanza's roar turned to a scream as his arm erupted in blood and separated at the bicep. In the same momentum, the guardian grabbed him by the head and threw him into the tree line where my team was hiding.

"Fuck!" I heard Forsyth yell, as I charged the being again. I was smarter this time, striking with one blade and leaving a second to parry his counter. It deftly blocked the first blade and easily swept around my second blade before driving another fist into my skull. I slammed hard into the grass again as I heard an unbelievable shriek. I scampered back up, unsteadily this time, as I saw the thing reach out to its distorted mass that it was growing. The shriek grew in volume to a painful level before they both blipped out of existence, leaving us in an eerie silence. I fell to a knee, my head swimming from two massive impacts.

"Thanks for the helmet, Lil." I grumble.

~No problem, but I think you have bigger problems.~

Shit. Yeah.

I shakily examine the area, as I hear some loud voices.

"Shit! This is bad!" A younger dark skin male was motioning me over to where Castanza landed. I made my way over to the commotion, and the sight I saw was gruesome. Castanza had his arm sheared clean off halfway through his bicep and blood was everywhere Apparently, he landed on Forsyth in a way that knocked him unconscious. Liliana had retracted her armor by this point, and my head was still swimming. I took a knee next to the twisted pile that Forsyth and Castanza made, the latter was doing everything he could to save face despite the immense pain he was now dealing with.

~Look…I can salvage this…But those hits you took were bad.~

Do what you can.

~You'll be defenseless until I recover.~

Understood.

There was a hesitation before Liliana's form appeared from my back. Everyone froze or fell back a little at her form.

"It's fine. She's a friend." I say heavily. Sarah put her hand on my shoulder, I had no idea where she came from.

"Seconded." She said with just enough force to shut down their fears. "Let her work." She said softly to me.

"Yeah." I grunt.

A few moments go by, before Liliana speaks up.

"I…I can restore some of his arm and stop the internal bleeding. I can also stop Forsyth's hemorrhage. But…"

I look over them both as she works. "Vics gonna lose a hand and Forsyth is gonna be in a coma."

"Probably a long one." Liliana confirms quietly. I nod softly, Sarah's hand tightening on my shoulder. "Got some more bad news."

"What other kind is there?" I say dryly.

"Limbo…Gonna last a long time today."

"Great." Ulid grumbled from my side.

"Anything we can do to help…Uh…Ghost lady?" Lancer asked Liliana.

"No, you're fine. I'm Liliana by the way."

She nodded, but no one was particularly worried about pleasantries.

"Lil, can we move them?" I ask her quietly.

"Not for a little while." She spoke without looking at me. "You're gonna need that shot. By the way."

"Fuck, really?"

"Yeah. May as well knock it out now since we aren't going anywhere." She floated back over towards me, her job essentially done for now.

"Shit." I pulled off my pack and dropped to a knee as Ulid and Lancer looked at me. "I...Need a shot of B12 every week."

"For what?" Lancer asked.

"Pernicious Anemia." I dropped my pack and fished out the case with the autoinjector.

"You have...Promiscuous Armenians??" Ulid stumbled through the words.

"Pernicious Anemia. Would you like me to help?" Sarah corrected him and held out her hand. I stared at her hand for a moment, confused. "I may not be as skilled as you in the practice of medicine, but I am capable of this."

I looked at her for a second before handing her the case. Truth be told, I had felt a little short in the oxygen department today, but I was so used to it I didn't notice. While she readied the injector, I rolled up my sleeve as far as I could.

"Meat of the shoulder." I direct her before I turn away, not wanting to watch. "Lil, status?"

"All good. I've done what I can." Her voice was shockingly worn. She floated back over to me and sat on the grass next to me.

"Thanks."

Sarah took my arm and set the injector against my shoulder. I grunted as the needle slammed through my skin.

"Fuck." I mutter as she wraps up.

"Did I make a mistake?" She said hurriedly.

"No. You're good." I grumble and roll my sleeve back down. "Those things are great, but they hurt like a bitch. Lil, how you doing?"

"Tired." She says shortly.

"Everyone, I want a perimeter formed around this alcove. Find a defensible position and keep your eyes peeled. Reload, drink some water." Sarah righted herself and started directing the teams.

I looked over at her, thankful she was taking control. My head was pounding by now as I looked back at the two heroes lying in front of me. Castanza had finally fallen asleep, and Forsyth was still out cold, but Lil had made them comfortable. I let Sarah work as Lil and I rested. Finally, Sarah returned.

"Thanks." I said softly.

"Of course. I talked to Fae, she expects this could last for hours."

"Yeah...That guardian was messing with something it shouldn't. Dangerous game. It was essentially tearing Limbo apart and slamming it back again to form a crystal." Liliana spoke slowly, sleepily.

"So that's how she does it?" Sarah asked, taking a knee next to us.

"Yeah." Lil sighed. "It'll find a new place."

"Course it will." I grumble. "So long as everyone else has an advantage, I guess."

"Hey, you got me." Lil said with a grin. I playfully punched her shoulder.

"Yeah. Yeah, we do."

"That is the nicest thing you've ever said to me." She said with a very sarcastic tone.

"Well, you're kind of an ass." I quipped.

"Sorry for telling you what you need to know." She retorted once more with the air of 'well duh'.

"Had I not known better, I'd say you were siblings." Sarah added. We both grinned, until our eyes hit the two heroes once more. That faded the grin quickly for us both. Two serious injuries and a mission failure. Fuck me.

"How long til we can get to the trucks?" I looked at Lil.

"Give them another ten. Do we have a stretcher or something?"

"In the trucks." I grunt.

"I'll handle it." Sarah rose and disappeared. The silence dragged out, before she returned. Over the next half hour, Lil and I ended up resting in the grass and the people Sarah sent out came back with a litter. We only had one, but Forsyth was my biggest concern. We carefully loaded him up, I secured his neck and spine and got one of Castanza's guys to piggy back him. Good thing he had a linebacker on his team. Literally, the boy played for a college team for two years and was built like a brick house. It was slow going through the forest, back to the trucks. Lil returned to my head, saving her the walk which I cussed at her for. I noticed that Lancer had started sticking to my side at this point. I felt like she was trying to be some sort of guardian angel, and frankly? I appreciated it.

***

"We are gonna have to discuss my contract." Jerry was shining a light in my eye, doing his checkup.

"Are you not paid adequately?" Sarah threw at him with a raised eyebrow.

"I have had to work overtime ever since you hired this yahoo," He delivered deadpan while motioning to me.

"Limbo seems to be approaching a crescendo." She replied. It was not normal for her to stay in the room during a checkup, but I could not care less.

"Might be right on that one. Shame I can't stitch Vic's arm together." He moved onto reflexes and got out that goofy little hammer.

"What about Bill?" I asked, worried about the answer.

"Well, I'd say he will be fine, but it won't be soon. So, this passenger of his…?" He turned to face Sarah.

"Liliana. She has some healing powers." I help out, and he turns back to me.

"Gonna put me out of a job."

"She can only do so much."

"She performed a miracle." Jerry started his tests again. "Bill would have been dead from a brain hemorrhage in about 30 minutes from that impact."

"Fuck." I grumble.

"Yup. Castanza will probably be on his feet within a day or two thanks to her."

"I'll let her know." I said simply.

"And you…Maybe a minor concussion at worst. You're fine." he shrugged, looking both shocked and a little disappointed.

"Doesn't feel it." I grumble again.

"Well, yeah. Makes sense. But I don't need to hold you at all."

"Fair enough. Thanks for everything, Jerry."

"Not a problem. I'll work on the other two, you guys just focus on your mission."

"Easier said than done." I mutter and follow Sarah out of the office.

"This is getting bad, Jake." She says softly as we walk through the hall.

"Yeah. Trust me, I know."

She stopped abruptly and faced me, her green eyes burning a hole right to my soul.

"I do not blame you." Her words were direct, sharp.

"Don't have to."

"Stop it."

"Stop what, ma'am?"

She sighs, looks down the hallway and back to me.

"Tomorrow night. Wear something nice, I will collect you at 1800."

"Uh...Ma'am?"

"Consider it a tasker."

"Understood."

She turned on her heel and disappeared into her office. I turn around and immediately run into Lancer and Ulid.

"How is he?" Ulid blurts out.

"How are they?" Lancer punches his shoulder, correcting him.

"Yeah, they?"

"Forsyth should be fine in time, but we don't know how long. Castanza...Well, you saw."

"Shit. What about your ghost friend?" Ulid did actually look concerned as I shook my head.

"She has her limits. She can only handle fresh injuries, and she can only do so much before she needs to recharge." I look between them both. "Go clean up. You look like shit, both of you."

"You too, sir." Ulid spoke with concern, making a stark contrast to his younger self.

"I'll be fine, job needs doing. Go home. Rest up." I turn to leave and stop. "Would...Either of you know what it means to 'dress nice'?" I ask sheepishly. Lancer grins as Ulid smiles.

"Oh man I got you." Ulid blurted out before Lancer smacked his arm again.

"No. Not you."

"What?!"

"You seem to think zippers are a factor." Lancer said with a berating tone.

"Yeah, and?"

"Where should we meet, Lancer?" I broke up their banter.

"I'll send you a pin tonight." She said promptly, Ulid looking between us.

"Alright. Go home." I spoke again, finally turning and left them in the hallway to find Campbell in their team room.

I knocked and entered, she was sitting in a chair nursing a smoothie.

"Shit, Sixx. What happened?" Her eyes widened as soon as she saw me and hopped to her feet.

"I sent my team home. Bad night."

"How bad?" She couldn't keep the dread from leaking out with her words.

"Castanza and Forsyth are going to be benched for a while." I said heavily.

"Fuck."

"Yeah. You guys ready?"

"Damn straight, we will hold the fort. Can we do anything for those two?" She crossed her arms in front of her chest, her expression one of resilience.

"Not really, Jerry has it." I pause, a silence settles. "Be careful. You and your team."

She nods sharply. "Always. Go home, boss."

"Yeah." I nod, turn and leave. I make my way to the ready room, stripping off my gear and storing it. Since most of the combat I was using Liliana's gift, my gear was surprisingly clean. After that, I went to Sarah's office and knocked on the open door.

"Yes?"

"Hey. Campbell's up, I've sent my people home." I leaned heavily on the door frame, noting that Sarah seemed surprisingly put together.

"Good. Your turn." Those green eyes hit me once more, and I felt like they were reading my soul.

"Next stop, ma'am. Are you okay?"

"I am. Don't forget, 1800 tomorrow."

"Good to go. Leaving from here or my place?"

She considered it for a moment before using a tone that told me she disapproved but wouldn't fight it. "Might as well be here, as I suspect that's where you will be."

"Fair enough. Phones on if you need me."

"I'm sure we will be fine." She cracked a soft smile this time, a hesitant one. "Rest well."

I raised my hand in a farewell salute and departed.

***

It was late. The moon partially lit up my front yard, and I had the lights off so I could see the stars. I don't know why I thought a simple beer, even my heavy weight Oil Fire clocking in at a whopping 14% would be enough tonight. I leaned against the railing, the empty bottle clinking as I bounced it off the top rail.

"FUCK." I barked, and in one fell swoop motion, I pitched the bottle at a nearby tree, the glass cracking into a few pieces.

~You blaming yourself again?~

"Fuck off." I turn back inside, fixing a much stronger drink.

~This is how you handle it, like always.~

"Like I told Sarah. You won't like my answer for how I get through this."

~This is a dangerous game you play.~

"And?" I sigh, sipping my fresh drink.

~Just hold on, hero. Tomorrow will be a new day.~

"Do not call me that." My voice was flat, and a new anger boiled.

~Noted. So, the plan is to drink until you have to sleep?~

"You're catching on."

~Is that what they would want?~

"First, they aren't dead." I return to my seat on the porch. "Second, they ALL need me to be effective."

~Getting wasted is going to accomplish...?~

"Something akin to sleep. The ability to press on."

~What about you?~

"Oh yes." I take another drink. "What about the dead man walking, who already has a signed death certificate? What about the man who seems to be stalked by death and injury?"

~You are not the cause of this!~

"Bullshit. Look through my memories and all the people I failed."

~THOSE AREN'T YOUR FAULT! You fucking idiot!~

"Maybe. But it was my job to save them." I sit heavily on my chair on the porch once more, savoring my new drink.

~Fine, you're not going to listen to me. But you still deserve peace of mind. Maybe even some form of happiness.~

"Fuck off."

~You haven't truly smiled in a while now. You're not dead yet.~

"I have a mission to complete, and the rest is secondary."

~You are hopeless.~

"Yeah, yeah pretty much." A heavy admission, spoken lightly.

~Look...It's not over yet. Maybe Sarah finds another way.~

"Cool."

~Jake...~

"They call me Atlas for a reason."

~Yeah, because you make everyone worry. Share the damned load, you don't need to shoulder this burden yourself.~

"I can handle it. I take this, and everyone can keep fighting and put an end to this."

~Hypocrite.~

"Survivor."

~I really wish I could turn off our connection at times.~

"Sorry." I felt it, it wasn't just empty words. But I didn't know how to articulate anything more. "For what it's worth, I appreciate the concern."

~I can tell.~ She 'speaks' heavily, and I can tell I pissed her off. I sigh heavily, as I feel the alcohol doing its thing.

"Never was supposed to be like this." I spoke softly. "Supposed to be a damn war hero. Go save the world, come home and win the girl. Steel guitar playing a slow, epic outro as the sunset." I take a deep breath. "Now? I dunno." I pause. "It's not that I don't care. It's not that I want to die. I want to give them a chance to have what I never will."

~How can you so boldly say something so brutal?~

"Look at the field, Lil. Take a good long hard look, then tell me there is any chance I'll have the storybook ending."

Silence.

"Don't cry for me. I've made my peace long ago. I may never come home. This time, I know if I don't, it won't be in vain. I will have found a way to save the world"

~Lug head.~

"Yup."

I found some form of peace that night, sadly it was at the bottom of some premium whiskey.

DECEMBER 4TH, 2023

I spent the day researching and training swordcraft. I had done some work before, but the Guardian laid an absolute beatdown on me and I was intent to never let that happen again. I poured over videos and books, then I went to the training room and went at it until I broke a practice sword clean in two. Sarah had done some sword training with me in the past, and she was shockingly good, however she was unavailable today. Her busy schedule led to more confusion as to what this fancy dressed tasker was for me later in the day. I had to settle for Ulid to beat up on today, who was an impressively willing victim. I had just laid a particularly brutal take down on him a few moments ago, and we both were sitting against the wall cooling off.

"I'll hand it to you, kid. You have some resilience." I grunted.

"Comes with the territory."

"Yeah?" I looked over at him, picking up an odd tone.

"Well yeah..." he paused, chewing his words. "The foster care system will do that."

"Wait, you're an orphan?"

"Yeah." He wiped his brow from sweat.

"Had no idea." I took a drink.

"Yup, story is my mother dumped me shortly after birth and I have bounced between families since I was a baby."

"Makes sense that Sarah was able to recruit you so young then."

"Heh, yeah. The social worker had a field day on that one, but they all worked some legal shit. I may be young, but I've had my own place for...two years now?" He said with a smirk.

"Ya know, explains a lot." I said softly.

"What about it??" Ulid immediately got defensive.

"The ego, the reckless behavior. Makes sense." I said simply. He glared at me for a moment before shrugging.

"Guess I had something to prove."

"How about now?" I asked him, wiping sweat off my brow.

"Eh." He paused. "Been meaning to tell you…Sorry for running away. I…That…I was terrified."

"It's in the past now, kid."

"No, I need to…" he took a breath. "When they started to circle around us…There were so many…"

"Overwhelmed you?"

"Yeah, like…Big time. I panicked. I'm sorry."

"You've proven that by now. You keep holding your ground like you have been, you'll be alright in my book."

"Thanks…" He said softly.

"You ready for the next round?"

"Oh, hell yeah, old man, let's go!"

***

"Hey Jake!" Lancer said sweetly as I walked up to the entrance of some department store, which I had never heard of before.

"Hey kid." I had my usual on, jeans and a T-shirt. I knew it was nothing special, but it worked.

"So, something nice? What's the occasion?"

"Not sure, Sarah told me to be ready. Nice dress was most often service dress, which has explicit regulations on what I needed."

"Oh brother." Lancer sighed with a soft grin. "Come on, I'll get you fixed up."

"Thanks kid."

"No worries." She led us inside. "I helped my brother a lot. He has absolutely no fashion sense."

"I can relate…" I mumble.

"Agreed." She pulled a few things off the rack and put them next to my chest. "Hmmmm."

"Is it that challenging?"

"Sometimes." She spent the next few minutes doing the same thing. Grabbing a shirt, looking at me, and sometimes handing it to me and sometimes putting it back.

"What got you into archery?" I asked after I had three shirts in my hand.

"My mother." She plucked another shirt out but returned it. "She was so close to competing in the Olympics a little ways back, but she could never quite place high enough."

"Damn, that's impressive."

"Yeah, until the wreck." Her tone dropped a little, but she was still very much present.

"Wreck?"

"Parents got hit by a drunk driver one night. T boned them as they pulled into a restaurant for an anniversary, and the best part?" She grinned at me. "I was there, in her belly."

"No wonder you're so tough."

"Evading death as a babe, just like my new boss." She said simply, but I felt the feeling she put behind the words. "Anyway, she got a lot of nerve damage from the wreck, so she hung up the bow, stayed home to raise me, then taught me everything she knew when I was old enough." We had moved onto the pants by now, and she pointed at the black slacks on the rack.

"I can handle size." I said and started looking at the sizes. "She sounds pretty impressive."

"She is. I got lucky with my parents."

"Dad still around?" I pluck off a pair of slacks and straighten up.

"Yessir, he works in IT and they are pretty comfortable."

"Glad to hear it. Try these?" I raise up the haul in my hands and she nods. We head to the dressing room, and I start on the first one. Deep green button down shirt that admittedly did look sharp. So, I stepped outside.

"Well?" I ask, a hair awkwardly.

"Oh yes, first try!" She grins mischievously.

"What's with that look?"

"It'll match Sarah's dress perfectly." She spoke in a knowing tone.

"Do what now?" My eyebrow raised.

"You'll see, boss. That one wins, do that." She grins again, dismissing my question.

"Alright, works for me." I return to the room and put my old clothes back on. She put the other stuff back on the rack and met me at the counter as I was starting to check out.

"Have fun with Sarah." She said brightly.

"Dunno if fun is part of the plan."

"Sure." She grins knowingly at me as we walk outside. "I'm betting she has a plan."

"She always does. But again, doubt fun is part of it." I repeat and Lancer rolls her eyes.

"Sure thing." She grins again.

"Wel thanks again for this. Hope it wasn't too much."

"Not at all, it worked out well. Well, I'm off to play some games with Joey."

"Oh?"

"Not like that." She shakes her head. "He needs an older sister."

"Does he ever." I snort.

"You have helped him a lot though. I can't tell if he reveres you or is terrified of you." She tilts her head, thinking.

"Probably both. But he has come a long way."

"I'll handle the rest. He's finally showering every day."

"Oh lord." I rub my eyes. "You know, he isn't the only one."

"Hmm?" She tilts her head once more.

"You too. You've come a long way in a short time. You're doing well."

"Aww..." She turned away from me, clasping her hands in front of her. "I've got good role models." She admits sheepishly.

"Still, happy to have you on the team, kid."

"My honor to be here. Now go on, you have a…Mission to prepare for." She smirks. "Have a great one!" She waved as she started to leave.

"You too. See you around!" I turn, my mind racing once more. She clearly knew something about this evening that I did not.

***

Sarah was still being tight lipped on this tasker, but here we were in her car on the way. I will never forget seeing her for the first time tonight, her hair was in a perfect braid and she wore a deep green dress that plainly stated her elegance and position with a dangerous slit that went clear up to the side of her hip. It took me aback and I had to recover my thought line.

The ride was mostly quiet, as we pulled up to the Biltmore Estate outside of Asheville. A beautiful estate that became a fancy tourist destination full of fancy buildings and food. I had never really been here before, but I was marveling at the grounds as we arrived at a very fancy restaurant. She pulled the car around the loop, and a pair of tuxedo clad gentlemen met us at each of our doors and let us step out.

"Ms. Steel, shall I park the vehicle for you?" One spoke with the air of upper class.

"That would be wonderful, thank you." She responded kindly, the man on her side nodded and hopped in, driving off. The second one stepped around me to greet her.

"Ms. Steel, your table is ready."

"Good evening, Gerald. The usual?"

"Of course, ma'am."

Sarah stepped closer to me, putting her hand under my arm indicating I was her escort for the evening. A subtle nod, and I scanned the area assuming I was a form of bodyguard for some business deal.

"This way, please." Gerald guided us through the main entrance and down the beautiful halls until we made it to the dining room. I was watching every face as we went and began cataloging exits as she squeezed my arm.

"Rest easy, soldier. I do not anticipate the need for those skills." She nearly whispered to me, which just raised my confusion more.

"Here you are, ma'am." Gerald led us to a two seat table near the fireplace which was pleasantly crackling. I shot her a look as two more tuxedo dressed gentlemen pulled our seats out and we sat at the table.

"Thank you, Gerald." She spoke softly to him, as he produced a bottle of wine from a fancy cooler stand by the table. Without a word, he poured some in both glasses and left. She had picked up the menu, while I looked intently at her for a moment.

"So, what is this tasker?" I ask softly after a moment. "I assumed some form of business dinner."

"In a way." She laid her menu back down. "I felt the need to treat you to a wonderful dinner after everything you had been through recently."

I took pause to that, and my jaw set.

~She's trying to be nice to you, lug head.~

Why?

"What for?" There was a hint of an edge in my tone, which she picked up on.

"Is it wrong for me to treat you well?" She asked softly.

"So, what, is this pity? Or this a last meal before firing me for fuckin' up?" I felt the anger rising but I kept my tone under control. This wasn't a place to make a scene. She seemed to match my energy as she calmly took a sip of her wine before setting it down, and blasting a hole into my soul with the piercing green gaze that I swore had become a super power of hers.

"I have watched you set aside yourself for everyone in the Roses. I have watched as your soul, or what is left of it, gets torn asunder as you place the weight of your team, the Roses, and the world on your shoulder. I have watched as you ask for absolutely nothing in return. I am well aware of the extent you have, and will go to, in order to secure a future for us all." She let the words linger, each of them hitting me dead on in a vulnerable spot. "You do not treat yourself with the honor and respect you have earned. I have decided to assume that role to ensure you are treated accordingly."

I stared blankly at her.

"Staring with your mouth agape is uncouth in such a place as this, Mr. Sixx." She spoke with an edge I couldn't place, but I snapped my jaw shut, nonetheless.

~I told you. Men...~

"This is...far more than I deserve." I say sheepishly.

"Leave that for me to decide. I encourage you to choose what you will without looking at the cost. I will handle it." She picks up her menu again. "In fact, they told me the ribeye is wonderful tonight."

~Stop staring, for fuck sake.~

I shake my head, coming back to earth and look at my own menu. It was undoubtedly the most fancy menu I had ever seen. I had opened my mouth to speak, but Sarah cut me off.

"I will not hear you say you don't deserve this."

"Understood." I shut my mouth and made a decision, the ribeye did sound good. We placed our orders when Gerald had returned, and I looked at her.

"Well, if I can't complain about the reason, tell me this. Have our missions gotten more dangerous?"

"Sadly, yes." She chewed her words for a moment. "Injuries are an expected side effect of combat, as you well know. But up until now, they have not been severe."

"So, what changed?" My eyes narrow a little, trying to understand. "And when?"

"I believe I told you before that Limbo is everywhere but has moving hotspots. My counterparts in England, India, Alaska, Japan, Nigeria, and the Antarctic have all informed me that we are relieving the threats in their areas."

I had to take a moment to process the fact that so many other operations were going on worldwide. I knew we were not it, but the reach was impressive.

"So, we kicked them somewhere it hurts." I add.

"So, it seems. It all seemed to pick up around the time I hired you. I do not intend for this to be blame, it is a fact." She added the second half with a hint of hurry.

"Yeah, I got it." I wasn't insulted and wanted her to continue.

"I have a working theory, however." She continued. "You are aware of the secondary reason I hired you, not simply for your combat ability?"

"I figured that part out, yeah." My eyes widened. "Wait, you made us a threat? With my services, I made a cohesive battle team instead of an organized, reactive police group?"

"That would be my insinuation. It would seem we have become a victim of our own success."

I lean back in my chair. "Well, shit."

"Indeed."

The silence lingered for a moment while I processed everything once more.

"It's nice to have your work recognized." I smirk. Sarah looks at me quizzically. "When your enemy decides to focus solely on you, it means you're doing something right."

"You certainly have an interesting perspective on the situation." Sarah's face broke into a smile as she spoke. I couldn't help but marvel for a moment at how the room, her dress, and her smile made for a moment of bliss.

"But I can't help that, miss Alice. We're all mad here. I'm mad, you're mad." I grin as I speak.

"Good evening to you too, Mister Cheshire." She replied in kind.

The tense moments of early dinner were long dissolved by the time food had come. We had a friendly chat as the evening progressed and I learned a few things about her past and her high end schooling. After she dropped me off, I was certainly impressed by her. Even more so when you take it in contrast with me. A smart ass, plain dress, grumpy old fool who would rather be out chopping wood than wearing anything with a collar. What the hell was she doing being interested in me? Wait, was she even? I shook my head to clear my thoughts. Didn't matter really.

Hey, Lil?

~Yes, dumbass?~

Did I just get ordered into a date?

~I'm not dignifying that with an answer.~

Heh, got it.

DECEMBER 5TH, 2023

I was getting frustrated, stuck at my desk, alone in the office. I had been pouring over profiles of our people trying to find someone to stand in for Castanza, who had finally been cleared for visitors this morning. Depression had hit him like a train, so it was a short visit, but it was long enough to break my heart.

After Vic, Frank was my next best bet, but he was out for God knows how long. Greene and Campbell are next, they already had their team. No one else had leadership experience. I slammed my fist down on the desk, making everything shake.

"Fuck." I grunt and lean back in my chair, crossing my arms behind my head while staring at the ceiling.

"Everything okay?" Sarah appeared in the doorway. I glared at her from across my desk.

"Nah, I need a cloning machine." I grumble. She approaches and sits side saddle on my desk looking at the folders.

"I understand your struggle." She said simply.

"Yeah, no wonder ya'll didn't wait for me to sit around. This is a soup sandwich." I moan, and Sarah smiles.

"Your word choice is colorful." She picks up one of the folders, still smiling.

"No leadership experience, confidence problems, horrible aim. That one isn't even a consideration."

"Noted." She picks up another.

"Some combat ability, but no one ever understands what she says."

"Ah yes. I believe she is from New Orleans." She swaps another folder.

"No one fits the bill. Leadership is garbage on all of them, and I don't know if I trust them to even try to lead. Not right now and not with where they are at." I sigh again, dropping my arms finally.

"What do you propose?" She lays the folder back down as our eyes meet.

"Honestly? Dissolve Castanza's team. I'll take the linebacker, give the two older ones to Greene. I hate the idea, but I just cannot see them surviving any other way."

"Do it." She said simply.

"Fair enough." I say heavily. "Castanza will be pissed. What do you intend for him?"

"That largely depends on him at this stage. He has been resistant to any conversations that entail the future."

"Understandable. He's going to need time to accept that stump of his."

"Jake..." She threw me a glare.

"What?" I blink. "Oh, too brash?"

"Suppose I should expect it from you." A soft smile cracked her face.

"Always aim to please, ma'am!" I grin back at her. "I'll handle the roster and see if I can coax out another team lead."

"Thank you. I have been chasing down another potential member, but alas, they have another plain background."

"Numbers help, but I need someone who can do real work."

"Beggars cannot be choosers." Sarah spoke softly as she left the office.

DECEMBER 7TH, 2023

I shut my truck's door and leave the parking lot once more. I was heavy tonight. We still had three teams, we still had fighters willing to do the job.

Lil? Be straight with me. Odds are against us.

~Well I wouldn't say that...~

I just asked you to be straight with me.

Silence.

Yeah, I figured.

~Sorry...~

Part of the territory.

The drive home was fairly quiet until I recognized the shrill announcement of Limbo once more. I sighed, pulling the truck over to the side and hitting the flashers. I honestly didn't know if that would help or not, but it felt like the right thing to do. So, each time Limbo hit and I was driving, I pulled over. I put it in park and Limbo opened shortly.

A strange gust of wind seemed to blow, taking a few leaves across my hood. Intrigued, I stepped outside, my hand on my pistol.

~I'm picking up...The Guardian?!~

That one??

~Yes! But...Something is different.~

I stepped to the side of my truck and scanned the area. In the tree line, sure enough, the Guardian appeared. It almost floated out of the trees, that amazing sword sheathed on its back. A breath of air curled around us, almost trying to speak. It approached closer, until it stopped a few feet away. My hand was tight on my pistol, as it slowly raised its arm, and dropped something shiny from its hand. The rock clattered to the ground between us, and it lowered its arm.

"*Use...It...Wisely...*" A breathless voice seemed to carry on the new breeze that circled us once more, and the Guardian slowly stepped backwards, disappearing into the tree line once more.

"I'll fix this!" I called after it. I didn't know why. "I'll find a way!"

"*Not....alone....*" The voice carried once more and silence fell.

~It's a crystal!~ Liliana exclaimed in my head.

Is this a Limbo control crystal?

I asked as I stepped closer, collecting it.

~Yes! This is fantastic. Finally!~

One is better than none.

I pocket it and return to my truck. Use it wisely...What did it mean?

~Good question. You know, Limbo may have proven me a liar. Once Guardians were corrupted...They never acted like that before.~

Maybe our fortunes are turning?

~Sarcasm, even in your own head?~

Heh, yeah. Guess so.

Ch. 10 Red Queen

DECEMBER 8TH, 2023

Lena met me at the door today, once again brandishing a screwdriver.

"You gonna ask me to join the fight?" She scowled.

"Can you?" I duck as the screwdriver flies towards my head.

"Which team you want me on?"

"You talk to Sarah?"

"Yes, mom said I can go out to play." She glared once more.

"Campbell or Greene. Take your pick, both are even."

"I'll help Campbell. She needs some toughening up." She turned halfway around. "Hey...You okay?"

"Fit as a fiddle."

"Fuck off with that military bullshit."

"Ain't been okay for years, but I'm still fit to fight."

Lena looked around before facing me. "That's not good."

"Yeah, well. Job needs doing." I shrug.

"I told you, knock it off. Don't lose yourself to this, okay?"

"No problem, Lena. Thanks." I gave her a half smile that she didn't buy.

"Seriously. You're no good to us dead." Her eyes showed a level of gravity and concern I had not seen before.

"I can't die." I grin again.

"Shut the fuck up." She jabbed my chest with a finger again. "We are all counting on you, asshole. Every person I send out with my equipment, every time Limbo hits…" I see her eyes start to get glassy.

"I've got this, Lena."

"No, you don't!" A tear broke free from her face. "I know that look! I've seen it before, you fucker!" She jabs me again and begins punctuating her sentences with jabs. "You may win, but at what cost?! I see your eyes, I noticed the reduced sarcasm and the new intensity of your training. You look haunted!" She pauses, and I stare into her eyes once more as another tear drops. I reached up and took her offending hand in both of mine.

"It's cause I am." I smile softly. "Which is why I know what must be done. Why I am doing this. It has to be me."

"No, it doesn't!" She barked.

"Name one other person who can. It has to be me, everyone else will get it wrong." I held her hand as another tear fell, and I could feel one trying to form on my own face. With her free hand, she punched my chest and leaned into me, her forehead hitting my chin. "I'll end this, Lena. I'll make this go away."

"Not at the cost you're trying to pay."

"Ah, you talked with Sarah."

"Of course, we are trying to find another way." She picked her head up and looked at me, I still held her first hand in mine. "You idiot."

"Do you know the PJ motto?"

"Who?"

"Pararescue." I pause. "My old life." I paused again before letting her hand go and pulling my shirt up to show off the cursive writing tattooed on my chest, right over my heart. She looked down, read it, and immediately turned away. I let my shirt fall. "I know it's not what you want to hear. But this is war."

"This is bullshit." She said heavily. "And you have already given up."

"I have not."

"Bullshit!" She yelled, whipping around to glare at me once more.

"I promise you, if there is a way out, I'll take it. But if it's me, or Limbo, I have made my choice."

She opened her mouth to retort, closed it, and tried again before storming off.

What a fucking great start to the day.

***

In a continuation of fun, I made my way to medical. I pushed open the door and looked around the room. At some point, Jerry had summoned a third bed which luckily remained empty currently. I quietly walked over to Forsyth's bed first, patting his leg as I looked over his chart. I sigh, it looked as if he would be bed ridden for a while now. Jerry made a note of two weeks to a month with a question mark.

"Hang in there, Bill." I patted his leg once more and put the chart back before walking around the curtain to Castanza's side. His eyes flicked up at me before going back to the phone in his hand.

"Boss." He grunted. His voice was eerily weak.

"How you holding up, Vic?"

He glared at me for a second before sighing and putting his phone down.

"That good, eh?"

"Fuck you, man." He grunted. "Can't believe this. All those fights and that thing took my damn hand." He raised the stump, still heavily bandaged.

"If it's worth anything, I'm sorry."

"You didn't do it." He glared at me again.

"I coulda been better."

"Shit, maybe. But weren't you the one that told me not to dwell in what ifs, Hermano?"

"I swear..." I sighed. "You jokers only listen when it can be used against me." I shook my head as Castanza grinned a little.

"You bet your ass." His face fell again. "Don't know what I'm gonna do now. Can't fight like this."

"Sarah come chat with you yet?"

"Once..." He replied, looking away with a sheepish tone. "I...Might have told her to get the hell out."

"Heh, how'd that go?"

"Well, I'm still breathin', man." He shrugged before looking back at me.

"Sure, she will be fine. No decisions need to be made just yet, Vic. Take your time, heal up."

"Rich, comin' from you, Hermano." He smirked.

"Okay, okay, guilty as charged." I put my hands up as if I was surrendering.

"You need some sleep, boss." He grunted.

"Alright, mom."

"Serious man. You look like shit."

"Job needs doing." I shrug. "I can sleep when I'm dead."

~Getting some Deja vu here...~

Oh, fuck off.

"Yeah, well the reaper gonna find you before jobs done if you not careful, boss."

"I'll see what I can do." I pat his leg, not unlike Forsyth. "You need anything, give me a shout, okay?"

"Yeah man, grab me a fuckin' hand while you're out." He shot me a halfhearted smirk.

"Sure, but you get a Walmart special."

"Feelin' the love, Hermano." He shook his head as I walked back out of medical.

DECEMBER 10TH, 2023

Snow had fallen today. Just an inch or so. I remember when it was cause for excitement, the beauty in this region is unmatched when the mountains were capped with white. I used to love the untouched snow, especially as it was still falling. I stayed up late with the porch lights on just watching it fall, the light catching the flakes and dancing down as if I was soaring through some galaxy somewhere.

Today, however, Limbo beckoned.

"This area seems to be a new congregation of injuries and deaths." Fae pointed to the map, showing multiple dots. "It's still really early, but I think there may be something here." She turned to face us, all of my team with the linebacker kid who was named Freddie Lancaster. He was quiet but seemed to get along well enough with my kids.

"Are these confirmed or suspected?" I ask her.

"Combination. I'm kind of taking a little liberty here on this one." She said softly, I could tell she wasn't used to being so bold.

"Fair enough. We can scout that area out." I look a little closer. "My bet's on the north east sector."

"I was thinking the same." Lancer spoke up. "Looks like some really good hiding spots."

"Exactly. How long we got, Fae?"

"About two hours or so. I'll get you guys signed up for this area." Fae turned to her computer and started typing.

"Hey, good work on this one Fae. This is way more precise than before." I stood but watched her reaction.

"Thank you…" She said softly, I grinned a little as she still hadn't gotten used to being thanked.

"Alright, load up, team." I pushed my chair in as the room got loud with the sounds of shuffling chairs.

"Hey, Jake?" Fae called out as I was about to leave. I stopped, turned and let the door close after Lancaster walked out.

"What's up?"

"Just..." She looked around the room. "Be careful out there."

"You too?" I smirked. "It'll be fine." We locked eyes for a moment before she finally nodded.

"You mean a lot to everyone. Come back safe, okay?"

"No problem. I'm unkillable, after all." I grin and she shakes her head. "Anything else?"

"Nope, that's it." I saw a hint of a grin on her face.

"Alright, see you in a bit."

***

"It. Is. COLD." Ulid grumbled.

"Chicken." I grunt, as we make our way past another park, down a well-known backpacking trail. We were all bundled up, the snow sticking to our shoulders and helmets.

"How are you not cold?" He threw back at me.

"I'm fueled by caffeine and hate." I grin back at him. Lancer was up front, barely making a noise, followed by Lancaster, then me, and Ulid taking up rear guard. I had finally started to trust him again, and that position was vital for making sure we didn't get flanked.

"Bullshit." he grumbled.

We were making good time, despite the deteriorating conditions. Lancaster was not the most sure footed on this trail, but he was lugging around a M249 with about 500 rounds of ammo so I couldn't be surprised. How Castanza secured him a belt fed machine gun, I will never know. Limbo began to slip into place once more, and the snowflakes froze in midair.

"Eyes open." I speak softly, and the team got much quieter with each step. Each of our feet still made a soft crunch on the snow, which slowly got louder as the flakes accumulated. The path had taken us up the side of a valley, there was a deep ravine to our left that rose again to a matching mountain, and a sheer cliff face to the right. There was nowhere safe to go here, and I hated being so exposed. Our only saving grace right now was the lack of ice buildup. Lancer understood, and coached Lancaster on how to cover each other the way our team did best.

The path emptied out to a valley, so I had Ulid hold the rear while the three of us spread out and searched. I pulled out my scanner, but it was largely fruitless. Nothing came up, no lair to be found here.

"Control, Prophet. Not getting anything over here. ETA on Limbo close?"

<"Copy…About 20 minutes. Recommend RTB."> Fae called back a little disappointment in her voice.

"Prophet copies, RTB." I had noticed Lancer already starting to make her way back towards the truck, Lancaster close by. It was here that I heard a terrifying cackle echoing around the woods.

"What was that?" Lancaster muttered. I waved at him to get him to shut up, then motioned for everyone to get down. I know what that was. I keyed the mic softly.

"Broken Rose." I whispered into my radio as I felt Liliana charging my veins again. I could tell the radio failed, and no part of me was surprised.

~She's close. But she's not the threat.~

The air overhead sizzled briefly, and then again.

"Holy shit!" I heard Ulid bark out.

"Contact!" I yell out as Liliana deploys the armor. I charge forward into the tree line, on the hunt. Lancaster opened up on the M249 spewing his rifle's promissory note of death by volume. Another woosh, and a sizzle. I spotted the Graal, it was close.

"AMY!" I heard the guttural scream from a distance. Ulid's voice. I pause and look back, my heart stopping for a moment knowing what that meant. Anger bubbled and I returned to the hunt. It was maybe 50 feet away, the Graal had returned with a new lacing of gold. It moved like a lightning bolt, Cleo must have increased its speed.

~Cleo is helping it!~

"IT WON'T SAVE YOU!" I roar and bolt forward, swords poised. It saw me, dodged and got behind me, sending another pair of spikes screaming my way. It moved unreasonably fast and one of those spikes sparked off my thigh armor.

I screamed in anger once more, changing direction. I had to draw it back and get fire support. I also needed to be faster. Luckily it chased me, and shortly I heard Lancaster's rifle going wild again. I rounded a boulder and landed heavily to catch my breath and reorient myself to the area. As I did so, the weird relic watch seemed to float up in front of me, and it began to flicker and phase. It reminded me of the rift the Guardian was tending but not as severe. Then, it pulsed and flashed brightly, and the entire area seemed to freeze even more so than Limbo normally did. I looked over at Lancaster, his bullets were frozen in the middle of the air, a stream of pain paused in mid-flight. I could see his face, snarling in combat anger, frozen in time.

I turned and saw the Graal once more. I didn't wait, I took the advantage and sprinted dead into the trees, right at the golden Graal. Whatever this relic did, it had made it slow down so much that it was just drifting instead of nearly teleporting as it had before. I closed the gap quickly and plunged both blades into its torso, retracted them and slashed down again. I effectively chopped the thing into three, before taking a horizontal slash and making it six pieces as the area around me began to pulse once more. Time was up, my relic had done its job I suppose. Right before it hit a crescendo, I dove out of the way as Lancaster's bullets came back to life and slammed into the trees around me and the Graal, which immediately erupted in viscera.

"Hold fire!" I holler back, and his shooting stopped.

Deep breath.

Get back up.

~Well done. The relic is done now, you won't be able to find it.~

That's fine, it did what I needed it to.

I moved quickly back to our little area and reunited with Lancaster.

"Shit, that's cool." He said stiffly. I nod and make my way to Ulid and Lancer. I knew before I arrived. I could hear Ulid sobbing. I rounded the tree and my heart nearly fell out of my chest.

~Oh my god...~

"Lil! Go!"

~It's...It's too late.~

Lancer had been skewered against the cliff wall, a nearly perfect shot directly to her heart. Her feet dangled limply where Ulid sobbed uncontrollably. She almost looked peaceful, had it not been the blood that had poured from the wound, and her head hanging limply with hollow, vacant eyes. The little pool of blood in the snow at her feet tore me up inside.

"No, it's not!" I yelled, my grip tightening on my blades.

~Why would I lie?!~

"FUCK!" I yell into the woods.

~It's too much, and she's been gone too long. Jake...I am so sorry.~

"Lancaster. Eyes up." I speak heavily, fighting the tears trying to form. I knew there was no point in getting Ulid up. Lancaster nodded and started scanning the area again. We were still in Limbo, I can't let up. Not now.

But my heart felt empty.

"Sixx..." Ulid clawed at me, barely discernible. "It's my fault..."

"No, it's not." I step over to him, taking his hand.

"She saved me...She pushed me...She..." His words dissolved into blubbering insanity once more.

"Then you honor her memory." I grip his hand, and he looks at me. "Make it mean something." I didn't have the pretty words this time. I only had the point.

"Yeah..." He nodded. His eyes were vacant too, behind the tears.

Finally, Limbo closed. The spike vanished and Lancer's body crumpled to the ground which brought another wave of Ulid sobbing uncontrollably. I stepped forward, repositioning her and closing her eyes with my hand. "Ad Astra, Amelia." I whisper softly. I leaned forward and pressed my forehead to hers. "I...I am so sorry." I felt a tear break free. I lean back and try my radio.

"Control. Prophet."

<"Prophet, control. You guys good? Been quiet a while.">

"Negative. Graal eliminated. One KIA. RTB."

Silence on the radio. Today, I didn't care. I collected Amelia's body in my arms.

"Lancaster, help him back to the truck." I motion towards Ulid with my head.

"Sure thing." He immediately went over to him and tried to get him to his feet. I could tell it was mostly Lancaster doing the lifting.

I lied to her.

~You did not.~

I did. Told her I'd bring her home.

~And you are.~

Stand amongst the craters where your friends died and tell me the semantics fucking matter anymore.

It was silent except for the sounds of nature, unfazed and unmoved by our trauma. I hated everything, myself most of all.

***

<"Prophet, Rose."> I barely heard the radio, as I was putting Amelia into the truck.

<"Prophet?">

"Go for Prophet."

<"Confirm, KIA?">

"Confirmed. RTB now."

<"Who is it?">

"Lancer."

Pause.

<"Copy."> Sarah's voice was as heavy as I felt and the line went silent. We got in the truck and headed back, everyone silent as a church mouse.

***

I put the truck in park and stared out the windshield for a moment. By the time I got out, Ulid had already opened Lancers door, and despite tears flowing freely, he managed to pick her up as I was carrying her before. He turns, and we lock eyes for a second before nodding at each other and I lead the way into the office. I opened the door and was met with a gaggle. Sarah and Fae stepped around me, helping Ulid into the door and making sure everything was out of the way. Castanza and Jerry opened the next door and guided us too medical. No one spoke. They saw the looks on Ulid and my face and no one uttered a word. Ulid laid her down on a gurney, Sarah rested a hand on my shoulder before I leaned forward and arranged Amelia in a respectful way. Ulid collapsed to his knees and began to cry again. I touched Lancers shoulder one more time and walked out of the room. Out of the office. I was still fully equipped in gear as I stepped outside into the late day sun. My heart had finally broken. A girl died today and I couldn't stop it.

Again.

I punched the dumpster hard enough that it sent a shockwave down my arm and the echo lasted for seconds.

"Jake?" Sarah's voice.

"Not now."

"This isn't your-"

"Don't finish that fucking sentence!" I rounded on her.

"It's not. You once told me that you have to expect more to die."

"Fuck you!" I bark. My fist ached. "Stop using my words against me, I know what you're doing."

"Then listen to yourself."

"The same asshole that seems to be stalked by death but only he can evade the reaper's scythe?! When does it end, Sarah?!"

"It ends when we put Cleo in the dirt."

"Yeah, so we're fucked."

I glared at her, and she simply looked back at me.

"I had not taken you for the type to give up." Her words slammed into me.

"I don't quit."

"Sure, that's what Atlas would say. But you sound like you just gave up."

"Fuck off!" I roared again. "Walk a mile in my shoes then fucking talk! I'm at a dozen failures now! A fucking dozen! How many more can my soul take?!"

"Then I guess you better end Cleo before we have to find out." I hated how calm she was. I hated how collected she was. And most of all, I hated how right she was. With a roar, I slam my fist into the dumpster again, making another wave of pain. The lid broke free and slammed shut with a loud clang. I knew it didn't do anything, but I wanted to feel something, and I knew it wouldn't break. I let everything settle, looking to the ground.

"Fine." I mutter after a moment. "Find the bitch. I'll take her to hell myself."

"May want to get that hand looked at." She spoke softly. I looked down and I had dislocated a finger, to which I promptly popped back into place. "Or not."

"I'm fine."

"You're not. But I get it." She took a small step forward. "None of us are." We locked eyes, her green eyes once again blasting a laser directly to my soul. "I am not capable of doing your job. I do not believe anyone else can either." She didn't back down despite my glare. If anything, her eyes burned even hotter into my soul as I realized what she was doing.

"I'm gonna be honest with you, Sarah. Don't know how much I have left in this old soul."

"Then I will help keep it flying until the end."

"Can't ask you to do that."

"You're not."

Silence once more as the stare down continues. Finally, I exhaled heavily and looked away.

"Yeah." I hung my head for a second and Sarah steps closer again, this time putting her hand on my shoulder.

"Please. Lean on me."

"You're hurting too."

"Not as bad as you are." She spoke softly, her other hand placed upon my other shoulder, and she slowly applied pressure to get me to face her. "You are not alone, warrior."

I looked back into her eyes, the laser replaced with a soft warmth. I leaned forward until our foreheads met lightly, and I closed my eyes. I have no idea how long we stood like this, but once we straightened up, there was a layer of snow on both of our heads.

"You keep acting so nice to me, I might get some wild ideas." I murmur softly.

She grinned and chuckled softly, not saying a word.

"Okay. I…" I take a deep breath. "Job needs doing."

"It does. Together." She nods.

"Yeah, yeah. Together."

"Better."

"But I want that bitch in a grave."

"We all do. Fae may actually have an angle." She said softly, lowering her arms.

"Guess we have a briefing to attend. After I pull Ulid off the floor."

"Let's." She said simply and turned, leading me back towards medical.

***

It took a lot of work to get Ulid back on his feet. Apparently, they had become very close and treated each other as siblings, which I had seen developing over the past few weeks. He seemed to be taking after me and took the blame of her death solely on his own shoulders. The details were still unclear, but apparently, she pushed him out of the way of one of those spikes, taking it herself.

We made our way to the briefing room once more, Fae standing at the front of the room shaking like a leaf. Summoning all the courage I had left, I walked right up to her and gave her a hug and felt her fighting against the tears she barely held back. After a few moments I broke away, she wiped her face and we all got started.

"I've been trying to isolate and track Cleo's movements." She spoke shakily. "I have narrowed it down to a hot spot here. The old Warnkin movie theater. It's been deserted until a year ago when they brought it back up so it's a relatively popular place right now." She moved some maps around on the screen. "It's...Not a promise. But there has been a collection of odd issues all around this area and this seems to be the center."

"So, their HQ?" I ask.

"That would be my guess. However, it seems to be exceptionally active. Every Limbo lately seems to have multiple signatures, but I cannot get any verification. I haven't said much until now, but I think they are somehow jamming our scans."

"Course they are. Ten bucks says we got a jammer relic of some kind." I grunt.

"That would be quite possible." Sarah adds.

"So...Go in, cap the bitch, get out?" I ask hesitantly. "Seems too easy."

"Well, we have no idea what you'd be stepping into and there will be innocents all around. They have been doing marathon runs of Christmas movies all month up until the 24th."

"Weird promo, but okay." I grumble. "Sounds like recon time."

"Campbell and Greene are already briefed and preparing for the next two Limbos to gather intelligence." Sarah offers, I glare at her wondering why she was trying to sideline me. "You will go on the third night. That way, if anything goes wrong you are fully aware of the stakes and can execute immediately." I nod, somewhat satisfied at her reasoning.

"Copy." I cross my arms. "Don't like the delay, but I get it."

"We need to play the right card at the right time, Jake." She spoke softly, and I looked over at Ulid who was barely here, then at Fae who was still shaking. We were running out of fighters, fast. She was right. Smart trumps violence today.

"Limbo schedule?"

"Tomorrow morning, the 12th has one around midnight, and then again on the 13th." Fae checked her notes confirming what she knew, looked up and nodded.

"I'll be ready. We will be ready." I kick Ulid's chair, bringing him back to life.

"Sir. Recon and assault on the 13th." His voice was still hollow.

***

Ulid and I returned to the team room for a bit, neither of us interested in talking. He played on his phone, I sat in a borderline meditative state nursing one of his Gatorades. I knew he was zoning in and out as the screen kept lighting up his face and turning off after a while. Eventually, the door creaks open.

"Hey boys." Castanza enters, his feet heavy. I looked over and he had a hospital gown on still, and his eyes were glazed as if he was under some good pain killers.

"Vic." I grunt. Ulid doesn't respond.

"I won't bother asking." He grunts back, I nod simply. "I'm here though. Doped up on the good shit or otherwise." He grinned sloppily as he took a seat next to me.

"You flying high?"

"Yessir." He flowed through the word, the r lingering an alternating between a regular and the rr of his native tongue.

"Jerry gave you the good stuff." I smirked at him.

"Huh? Oh. Yeah!" The dopey grin came back. "Man…You hanging in there?"

"Best I can Vic. Getting real tired."

"Go to bed then."

"Not like that."

"Oh?" He looked at me for a moment, I returned a side eye glance. "Oh…" I nod in reply.

The moment settled.

"Well, boss, once we cap this bitch you need a vacation. More than earned." He grinned again, clapping me on the shoulder with his good hand. "I got a guy, take real good care of you."

"Thanks man, but let's finish this fight first. Can't get too excited." I return his grin, knowing how empty of a sentiment it would be. The only vacation coming up was a permanent one for me.

"You got it, Hermano. Hey, whatever I can do from here, I got you." He leaned back in his chair. "Ain't much, but I got you."

"You and Sarah talk?"

"Nah, but she won't kick me out. Even if I gotta be Fae's bitch." He grinned again, I was beginning to think he had two expressions right now.

"She's a slave driver."

"Fuck, I had worse." Silence settled for a moment. "Real sorry about Amelia." He added softly.

"Thanks." I grumble in return. "Think the kid may be taking it even worse." I flicked my head towards Ulid, the light turned off and he had closed his eyes at some point. Good, he fell asleep.

"Yeah?"

"Yup. Ain't easy losing a sister. Blood, combat, choice, don't matter."

"Yeah. Fuck." He took a deep breath. "My boy taking care of you?"

"Lancaster? Dude, that 249 helped big time in killing that Graal."

"Heh, he likes that thing a lot."

"I see why." I stretch my neck. "Suits him."

DECEMBER 11TH, 2023

I barely slept again.

~You need to stop doing this to yourself.~

I need the world to fuck off and give me some room to breathe.

~You and I both know that won't happen. You've gotta make the best of it.~

Trying.

~You know what? I finally believe you.~

I sigh, as I put the truck in park and walk into the office.

~You have actually tried to confide in someone, I'm happy to see it.~

Drop in the bucket.

~Progress is progress.~

Yeah. Well.

~Stop. Don't say it.~

I won't say that it still won't bring them back.

~Seriously, Atlas.~

Didn't say it.

~Whatever. You should be taking the day off.~

Negative. Handling Amelia's affairs.

~Fair enough. Take it slow, okay?~

I did actually take my time today, moving slowly and working through the paperwork. Sarah and Fae took care of next of kin, I collected her belongings to send off with them before they left. Afterwards, I worked on the paperwork, took care of chores and maintenance and mostly stayed quiet. I met the recon team in the briefing room and they confirmed our suspicions. A large amount of entities are drifting around but they were not able to get close or get a good read. I left them to work with Fae on trying to figure out what forces they had as I wandered to the team room.

"Ulid." I spoke shortly as I saw him curled up in a chair. He looked up at me.

"What's up?"

"Come on. Errand time." I turn to leave.

"We aren't on duty."

"Trust me, kid." I grumble, and he stirs getting off his perch.

"Where to?"

"A ride." We walked in silence to my truck and I started driving off.

"This where you tell me it's gonna be okay?" He broke the silence finally.

"Nope."

"Then what are we doing?"

"Our fuckin' best. There is nothing I can do or say to relieve your pain."

I saw him shoot me a look and turn to face the window.

"It's not fair." He mutters after a little while.

"Nothing in life is."

"Fuck that." he grunts. He was almost starting to sound like me and Forsyth with that tone.

"Sorry. But we can do the next best thing." I pulled into the parking lot and put it in park. "Honoring those we lost."

"A trophy store...?"

"Yup." I open the door, reach into the back seat and pull out Amelia's bow. As soon as Ulid saw it, his face fell.

"Why do you have that?" His tone was aggressive, not the type of aggression I was used to hearing out of him.

"Making sure she won't be forgotten."

"How??"

"Come on, kid." I led him into the store, I could feel his glare as I approached the counter.

"Good afternoon! How can I help you?" The clerk spoke happily but caught our expressions and his mood seemed to change.

"I'm here to commission a few things."

"Would this be an honor plaque, by chance?" He spoke smoothly, with reverence now.

"Yes." I placed the bow on the counter. "One for this, and another for a sword."

"Certainly." The clerk got out a pair of white gloves, taking the bow with great attention.

"Hey, be careful with that!" Ulid snapped, I set a hand on his shoulder.

"I will treat this with the utmost respect, sir. I'm familiar with these types of works."

"He's the best in town." I added.

"Ah, Mr. Sixx. Thought I recognized you." He nods at me before placing the bow in a very nice, wooden desk towards the back. It was velvet lined and everything was nearly pristine. We put everything on order, and made sure the details were right on Sire and Lancers plaques before returning to the truck.

"Kid? Make sure you collect these when they are done. Hang them in the team room."

"Me??" Ulid gasps.

"Yeah. Who better?" I give him a solemn grin as I back the truck out of the spot and start driving back.

"Why not you?" He finally asks softly.

"Cause I got that funny feeling the 13th might be my last mission." I speak normally, despite the implications.

"What? Why?"

"Just a feeling."

"No. You're not allowed. You can't. Aren't you unkillable?" I could sense the bargaining stage starting already.

"Yeah maybe." I grin at him again.

"Besides you got that…Liliana girl, right? No way, you're gonna be fine." He looked out at the road. "You have to be. No way, no chance you're gonna die."

"Well, I sure won't make it easy on Cleo either way."

"Well yeah. You're gonna kick her ass. Bam, slash, bash, boom." He punched the air with each word. "Avenge Amy. That's what we are gonna do." He went silent for a moment. "That's just the way it's gonna be." He added softly.

DECEMBER 13TH, 2023

Today was the day. Fae compiled what she could, and we all met up in the briefing room. It honestly wasn't a lot. There seemed to be another shadow swarm guarding the perimeter preventing access. They noted some flying entities that appeared to be dragon human things that no one saw before. Greene saw something resembling a Minotaur enter as well. Yeehaw, it sounds like a party.

The briefing room was packed and my roster wasn't great. I had Lancaster and Ulid. Greene was deploying as well as a reactionary force and Campbell was to stay here in case something else kicked off. Lena was in the corner, absently working on a pistol someone brought her. She looked nervous but determined. We were about to wrap up and leave when Castanza slaps the table with his good hand.

"I'ma join you, boss."

"And do what, Vic? I need you here to assist with coordination."

"Fuck no, I'm going."

"Vic, look at your hands." I glared at him, I knew what he was trying to do.

"I still got one, Hermano!"

"Vic." Sarah broke in. "I require your assistance here. If Cleo flees, or does something we are not prepared for, I need someone strong to back us up." It was refreshing to see that laser beam eye of hers on someone else for a change.

"Alright. Fine. But shit goes south, I'm coming." Castanza relents, barely. I nod softly at Sarah as the teams filter out to get ready. The air was expectedly heavy today, and there was nearly no chatter as the room emptied. It was Sarah and I left in the room after a moment.

"Come home, Jake." She spoke directly, no pretense at all in her voice.

"You know I can't promise that." I looked away towards the screen. It had turned off and was just black.

"Yes. Joey told me what you discussed. Look for a way out." She stepped closer to me, breaking the normal social distance line.

"That why you're not going out tonight?"

"Fae and I are going to coordinate from here and see if there is something else we can crack. Lena had an idea. Don't give up on this, Jake."

"Sarah…"

"I mean it." She placed a hand on my face and turned me to face her. Her eyes betrayed a vulnerability I had never seen before. "You need to come home."

"I'll do my best." I put my hand on top of hers, fighting the brewing cauldron of emotions in my stomach.

"That's all I can ask. Come home and we can figure it out from there. It's not over."

"I wish I could share your optimism." I gave her a solemn grin, which seems to be my default lately.

"Then I will exercise it for us both." She leaned forward slightly. She paused for a moment before leaning the rest of the way and pressing her lips to mine. My nerves radiated a shockwave as I breathed in deeply, a faint hint of the tropics filled my nostrils as I leaned into her, returning her affection. My every fiber wanted to stay here at this moment, but it was a fleeting moment on the grand stage today.

After a few seconds I lean back.

"Now you have no choice but to return to me." She said with a soft smile.

"I am certainly motivated." I mutter softly.

"I won't keep you any longer. I will be here." She nodded and opened the door for me as her usual mask slipped back into place. I hesitate before stepping out into the hall.

Duty calls once more.

***

We found a nice spot, away from prying eyes. It was an excellent overlook of the theater, which was at the end of a strip mall and surrounded by trees. We were on the north side, looking down into the flattened area below, facing the entrance. It was nothing abnormal, buildings and a big parking lot in the front which wrapped around the side. We were essentially looking down into a little valley with everything nestled comfortably inside. A major highway was to the East, only way in and out of this place except a dirt road heading north east. Greene took the south approach which was likely a harder path, but she had more bodies. Everyone had been extra quiet, we all knew the stakes. We were hot on the heels of a lot of bad luck, and no one wanted to press it farther. Without much ado, Limbo opened and we started the mission.

The shadow swarm had a solid perimeter around the building. The scanner was useless and was completely spoofed as soon as I tried using it so it went back in the case as we looked for the leader. I couldn't tell you if it was the swarms or some kind of relic, but it was expected. Time to work things the old fashioned way.

~There! See that dark spot moving from left to right?~

Got it. Dreadnought time.

~You don't want my help?~

Not yet. I can move quieter this way.

"Eyes on lead. By the van at the edge of the parking lot, moving left to right. Cover. Approaching." I spoke softly on the radio as I crept forward from my hiding spot, securing my rifle against my back and readying the Dreadnought. I heard a pair of clicks on my headset confirming Greene heard. I snuck silently, weaving around bushes on the side of the road and plotted my course to appear near the leader. It occurred to me that we only used this thing on a single shadow creature and Campbell said it worked for them, but I always had Liliana in reserve if need be. Fingers crossed, this works.

This? This was what my life was about for years. Slip in quietly, take care of business, and disappear into the night.

I had made short work of the distance and almost made my move as I heard one of those dragon things swoop overhead. I looked quickly, and it didn't appear to see me. It looked more like some goblin bat thing than a dragon to me, but it was ugly with a big ass mouth either way. It flew off towards Greene's team. I resumed my approach, only a few feet away as I heard an unworldly screech and gunfire from Greene's side of the theater. No time to hesitate, I lunged forward and the Dreadnought found its mark. I drove the sleek device deep into the center mass of the most dense shadow of the group. It began to spasm and convulse before it collapsed inward on itself, and the shadow perimeter faded into thin air.

"Greene, SITREP?" I called as I reset my rifle, holstered the Dreadnought and hunkered down behind a large truck, motioning for Ulid and Lancaster to join me.

<"Busy!"> More gunshots and unworldly screeching.

"Hey, two more coming in!" Lancaster spoke and pointed to the east, spotting two more of those things swooping out of the sky.

"Greene, two more heading your way." I called over the radio but no response, just the staccato of gunfire. "Control, Project is engaged.

Passport eliminated shadow swarm. Proceeding to support Project." I stand and motion for the boys to follow as I move closer to the building, eyes flitting between cars and frozen humans. Despite what we knew, constant vigilance was a requirement. We needed to close the distance to support them in case they needed back up.

<"Control copies.">

<"Hey, Prophet! Press! We're fine!"> Greene came over the radio finally, sounding stressed.

"Prophet copies. Call if you need me." I swear under my breath and redirect our team towards the theater itself. I seriously doubted they were handling it well enough to not need us, but I had grown to trust Greene. I hope I don't regret that decision one day.

The closer we got to the theater, the more humans were clustered around the area. Must be nearing a showtime. We bobbed and weaved all the way up to the doors and entered quietly. I could still hear the gunfire outside, but I also heard what sure sounded like a death scream, so I chalked that up as a win for them as it was not a human noise.

"Spread out, eyes open." I hissed at them both. We kept to the walls and hunted. The center had your usual concessions desk with all the normal theater going goods, a few reception tables around the walls and frozen humans were everywhere. The lobby had a raised ceiling, and it split off into two wings in the rear that appeared to empty into the theaters themselves.

An eerie laugh seemed to originate in one of the theaters and seep out into the lobby. I motioned to stop, Lancaster behind me and Ulid on the opposite side of the hall. A deep growl seemed to follow suit, and then heavy footfalls. This thing sounded big and angry. Out of the right wing, closest to Ulid, I saw it. A massive hulking minotaur that took up the entire hallway. It stepped into the lobby and stood up farther, it had to be a full twenty feet tall. Each step it took I could feel through the floor. I clicked the mic.

"Watch your shots. Try to lead him away from people. Ulid, on you." I saw him nod and line up his sights, Lancaster behind me shifted his 249 and set up the bipod on a reception table. It noticed Lancaster first and roared, throwing its head back and stretching its arms wide. This thing was truly massive.

~Want my help?~

Not yet. Be ready.

~These things have a big ass blind spot to the rear, weaknesses are pretty easy to tell. Go for the optics.~

Rog.

Gunfire, Ulid opened up, followed immediately by Lancaster and the beast was caught in two streams of fire as I maneuvered away from the group to get a third line of fire. It roared again, angrier this time, and charged towards Lancaster. I dropped to a knee, firing a few rounds into its eye, as it started to move. Unfortunately, it wasn't enough. Each step it took got closer to the lobby people, and it was too big to miss any. It was pissed and partially blind, so it flailed a good bit. I could see each frozen human body that it slammed into with its massive legs and sent them flying. Or at least, beginning to fly, as they froze again in grotesque angles as soon as they weren't connected to the minotaur's legs.

"Get it back in the hallway! Minimize casualties!" I bark through the radio and Ulid starts moving around its rear to draw it back.

The minotaur recovered from being blinded in one eye and grabbed a person at its feet roughly. It hurled the old man at Lancaster who dodged, narrowly avoiding getting slammed.

~Fucking convenient the bodies used as missiles don't freeze ain't it?!~

So long as everyone else has an upper hand. Focus!

Once again, the body was frozen in a grotesque lump as Lancaster tried to reposition, but the Minotaur threw another and slammed him into the wall. Lancaster and the innocent crumpled into a heap. Ulid and I opened up on the Minotaur's back, but I could see Lancaster was down for the count, he wasn't moving and the 249 lay on the ground a few feet away.

"Not working!" Ulid barked.

"I see that! Lil!"

~Already started.~

No sooner than she finished talking, the armor started flowing as I kept back tracking deeper into the theaters, away from the innocents. Once the blades were ready, I reversed and charged forward, slashing against its leg and bringing it down to a knee. A massive fist came firing from my side, but it was a hair too slow and I backstep just in time before slashing with another blade. It sunk deep, and the second blade came slashing down after it and finished the job. The minotaur was down an arm, thick black blood falling from the new wound as it screamed in anger and pain. I pressed the advantage, driving both blades deep into its chest.

Explosion.

Outside.

"Greene, you got eyes??" I yanked the blades free as the beast collapsed and bled out rapidly.

<"Stand by!"> A few seconds pass. <"Truck exploded outside. It's still burning? How?!">

"Fall back! Point Bravo! Go!" This was an ambush, I could feel it. This much combat and no Cleo? Ulid looked rattled, but I punched him in the arm, and we both made for the lobby as the cackling came around again.

"Where's Lancaster?" Ulid barked, I was already leading him towards where he fell. Luckily, he was already stirring. I dropped and skidded on my knee, sliding to a stop next to him.

"On your feet, Lancaster!" I saw Ulid grab the 249 as Lancaster struggled to stand, unsteady on his feet. Once he processed the twisted body that had slammed into him, he violently puked onto the floor. "Come on boy! Get it out and let's go!" I stood with him and had my hand on his shoulder to steady him. He wipes his mouth, nods, and accepts his 249 from Ulid and we start going towards the door.

<"Prophet, Rose. Calvary en route.">

"Rose, Prophet, I never called for you."

<"Project has taken injuries and we have something that may help."> Shit, did that mean we lost radio for a bit?

"Prophet, copy." I slammed through the door, leading the way once more. "Heading to point Bravo."

<"Control, copy. See you soon.">

"Get to the trees, now!!" I set off at a dead sprint once I ensured everyone was outside. Before anyone could make any distance, however, a nearby truck began to levitate, all of us beginning to slow our pace and watching with concern. "What the..." As the words slipped my lips, a golden rope encircled the truck.

~IT'S HER!~

"Control! Passport Actual! Broken Rose, I say again, Broken Rose! Parking lot, outside theater entrance!"

The radio response was delayed by a few seconds as the rope began to crush the truck. <"I copy, final team already en route!">

"Help is on the way, watch your back!" I echo to my team.

A unified 'copy' came from both Ulid and Lancaster. The sound of wrenching metal, shattering glass and pieces of vehicle filled the air now, as if a large crash just happened in front of us. The truck was toast, turned into a pile of scrap metal.

I felt the subtle weight of the sleek black armor around me. It gave me comfort that we at least had a fair shot at this fight. The wreckage of the truck finally fell to the ground in a heap, almost unrecognizable as Cleopatra's form floated and landed on top of it, smiling from ear to ear.

"Cute clothes, child." She murmured.

"Light her up!" I directed Ulid and Lancaster who started firing madly into Cleo as I sprinted forward out of the line of fire. She produced another shield that absorbed their shots like they were nothing. It bought me time to close the gap though, and I lunged forward, launching off the hood of a nearby car and bringing my blades crashing down on her as my team lifted their fire a moment before. She saw it coming, another golden shield appeared and I slammed into it, hard. I hit the remains of the truck and then the cement.

<"We got a problem! More of those goblin things are here!"> Greene over the comms.

<"Hold on Hermano, I'm coming!"> Castanza?!

<"ETA?"> I hear Greene call back as I scramble to my feet. I see Lancaster out of the corner of my eye providing cover and distraction as best he can. She floated down to the ground, her shield taking everything the boys could throw at her.

<"Four more minutes, we runnin' every light!">

I rallied and charged forward again, kicking off on the debris of the vehicle, hoping to catch her off guard. I was still close, and I was off to her side enough that I was hoping she wouldn't see, maybe even thought she had taken me down.

Success, she was distracted by Lancaster's latest volley of fire, and I was able to catch her with my shoulder. I didn't have time to bring the blades around, I needed her off kilter. I made a solid impact, and we both went careening across asphalt and landed apart. I was up on my feet first, but only just, and her smile had been replaced with anger. She produced a slender golden khopesh this time, and it was her turn to lunge. She struck fast, each attempted hit I managed to block was barely in time, and it was pure luck I hadn't been slain yet.

~Keep it up! You got this!~

After several furious strikes, Ulid poked around the wrecked car and distracted her long enough with a few rounds from his rifle, enough for me to take the offense finally. My blade barely missed, and she grabbed my wrist with her free hand, smashing her head into mine. My vision exploded in stars, despite my helmet.

<"Greene's hit! Oh shit, this is bad."> Couldn't tell which voice that was. The simultaneous impact from Cleo and the words hit me like a train. I stumbled as Cleo swung her blade and made contact with my side slamming me through the remains of the truck.

Get up.

I was dazed, everything was swimming.

GET UP.

~Nothing I cannot manage, keep up the pressure! She's losing her edge!~

I found the ground and struggled to my knee, the armor had taken the hit, but it was clear it couldn't take much more. I could feel Liliana's fatigue through her words and tone.

~Stop worrying about me!~

"You two! Go take care of Greene!" I turned and barked at the boys behind me, and they looked at me like I was crazy. "Go!!"

"I'm not leaving you!" Ulid barked.

"That's an order, boy!" I growled and turned to face Cleo who was watching, savoring the exchange.

"Fine! I'm coming back though!" Ulid barked, and I heard their footsteps as they disappeared from the field.

"Lil?"

~I'm with you but that took a lot.~

"Rog."

"You don't get it do you?" Cleo spoke smoothly. "This world will be mine, whether you suffer or not."

"Why are you even doing this?"

~Keep her monologuing. Buy them time.~

That's all we have left, Lil.

"Because this world is just silly. Wrong. All of you pathetic humans scampering around like you know what's right and wrong...Have you not seen the chaos? The destruction? This world doesn't even look like it used to." She stepped forward, motioning around her. "All this...Concrete. Metal. It makes me sick." She lunged, her blade flashing through the air, and I blocked it with a loud clang. "You take, and you take!" Her anger boils, another slash. I can tell she's only toying with me right now. A sick thought crosses my mind, she knows she has won. She's playing with her food right now. "As if this world is yours! But guess what...Once I kill you and finish off the conversion?" She smiled wickedly, another swing of her blade which clanged off my defense. "Everything will be chaos and your true forms will all be revealed. Wrong, twisted, corrupted...But REAL!" Another slash, this one faster. "Not that it hasn't already!" Her eyes were showing her insanity at this point. "Look at your media, the way you treat each other! All I see is humans consuming products and treating each other like shit. You are all nothing more than the embodiment of greed. You want to see greed?? I WILL SHOW YOU!" Clang, clang, clang. Another flurry of strikes, each getting closer and closer to making contact.

The sound of skidding tires erupted behind me as a vehicle came sliding to a stop.

"Get down!" Sarah's voice barks, and I fall quickly to the side as her door fully opens and she leaps out. Her rifle barks, a flurry of rounds with deadly accuracy at Cleopatra. Quick as a flash, the golden shield was up once more. She cackled.

"Silly girl, why announce yourself?"

"I required your attention." Sarah spoke with resolution. It was here that I noticed the shield beginning to disintegrate where each round impacted. Sarah raised her rifle again as Cleopatra gasped in shock. Sarah got off one single shot before Cleo took aim with her blade, morphing it to a spear, and letting it fly in the span of a second.

"NO!" I yell, launching myself at Cleo but it was too late, the spear had already been thrown. I continued my assault, ramming Cleo with my shoulder once more and sending her to the ground as I heard impact and shearing metal. I look back seeing Sarah's thigh pierced by a giant golden spear, sticking her to the front of her Lincoln.

I must have frozen for too long and Cleo had come back with a strike of her own. A golden blast from my side had sent my flying into the side of a work van, crumpling the door and sending shattered glass all around me.

"Lil. Take care of Sarah."

~What about you?~

"I didn't stutter." There was silence for a moment before the armor reverted back to my normal gear and I saw Liliana's form fly off to take care of Sarah. As the power left, I could take stock of the damage, and it wasn't good. I tasted blood, my head was swimming with a probable concussion, the entire right side of my torso felt like ground beef. I spat the blood out of my mouth onto the ground.

"You foolish, greedy little pests." Cleopatra's voice as she walked towards the wreckage cooly.

"Fuck off." I growl, stretching out my shoulders. "Pests or not, we made a mess of your shit today."

"I could have used someone with your tenacity. Such a shame to waste you."

"Funny, we thought the same thing about your dog. Your Graal had a new paint job, but it still fell to us. Ants. And your best buddy, the Unseelie?" I found my footing and stood up. I felt like hell, but I wasn't done yet. "Staked through the head, by one of our inventions."

"And you have the gall to call me a corruption." She growled and charged me once more. I emptied the magazine of my rifle into her and used it to block her blade coming at me from my left side. The impact jarred my arms, and I could feel the shrapnel of the rifle shattering as she sliced through it. It was enough to avoid a critical hit and deflect the blade to the side, but not enough to stop her from causing a deep gash in my left arm. She cackled and kicked my chest, hard, sending me flying back into the concrete. I felt the rear plate in my vest fracture and the bladder of water burst.

"Give it up, child! You have no chance, not with your precious master gone!"

I knew she was right.

"Everyone, fall back to base. Someone get Sarah out of here." I called in the radio, my voice rough at this point. I struggled to get back up on my feet, my body screaming in rebellion.

<"Say again?">

"Everyone. Back to base. Now."

<"I...I copy. All teams, recall back at base."> She didn't understand and I wasn't going to say anything else. I ignored the calls for clarifica-

tion on the radio and pulled my pistol. I aimed and fired at Cleopatra's form, each shot doing nothing at all.

"Jake, fall back. I can't help you anymore, not after everything." Liliana had reappeared, floating over some of the wreckage behind me.

"It's fine Lil."

"Jake!"

"Grab Sarah and fucking go!"

Cleopatra raised her khopesh, the glint of red from my arm still visible. "Oh, the taste of sacrificial blood..." She licked the blade, ensuring she tasted my blood while doing so. "It has been far too long.

"LILIANA! GET HER OUT OF HERE!" I bellowed at her, Cleopatra just stood there, relishing the exchange. Liliana finally moves away, I didn't need to look at her to feel her regret and defeat. It echoed my own, but my job was not over yet. I had to buy them time to retreat and regroup.

Cleopatra started cackling as they disappeared into the distance. "Let's make this interesting, shall we?" She pulled out another item. I couldn't make out what it was, and she crushed it. Limbo immediately snapped out of existence, and the world's color started to return.

Fuck, not good. Lil isn't here to keep me alive. I immediately plunge my free hand into the pocket with my own crystal, slam it on the ground and fire another shot, shattering it. It was the last round in the magazine and the slide locked back. Limbo seemed to halt sharply and attempt to reverse itself as Cleo cackled once more.

"You won't learn. It's fine though, you won't need to anymore." She pulled another one out and crushed it. "You really thought I was so stupid? I knew that the Guardian helped you. He was a fool too." Limbo was shearing itself asunder, being forced to open and close in such rapid succession but eventually the color began to return, and the whine screeched into existence.

We stood in a battleground of a movie theater parking lot, and it didn't take long before the screams of unaware innocents filled the air. I could only imagine the carnage inside the lobby. A truck that had snapped back into motion slammed on their brakes as they careened towards Cleopatra, who stuck out her hand and sent a burst of gold at its hood, slamming it into a stop. Judging by the horn now blaring, the driver was knocked out cold, or worse. Somehow, I was still alive, but I wasn't complaining.

"Neat trick." I choked out.

I took a deep breath. Something was calling to me from somewhere. My pistol was empty, rifle destroyed. I lost Liliana's help. I was alone. My mind flicked to the stories of my heroes, had they felt the same? Did they feel the same terror, defiance?

So be it. My destiny awaits.

> *There was a green mixing with Mr. Sixx's veins. The color was ugly. Poisonous. It kept mixing, spreading up his legs from the ground.*

My veins felt hot, like I had fire boiling under my skin. It fueled me somehow, it cleared my head. I assumed it was the clarity that came with embracing your final moments in an insane move, hoping against everything that it was going to count.

"Attention on the net." I keyed the mic, dropping my pistol's empty mag and grabbing a new one. "It's been an honor." I shoved the fresh mag in and dropped the slide. "Prophet actual, out." I threw my headset to the ground as my entire world shifted.

The mixture of green and blood had fully mixed and began to glow. Not entirely in a traditional glow, it seemed to radiate light in a unique way. His armor, once a gleaming, empty black was long gone. The ground cracked, and the earth snaked up his legs. It moved quickly, wrapping his body in an intricate, beautiful design. It wove around him to his hand, a darkened hilt of black appeared from the mass. Make no mistake, this was not charcoal. There was an unspoken, subversive strength here. The earth continued to snake into his hand and grow the hilt, morphing itself into a new sword. It gleamed in the sun, as if multiple elements of the world were fighting for control over its form. It was ethereal. It's as if Mother Earth herself had cast her vote in this battle, and she was angry.

Cleopatra's face was contorted in anger, and a blob of gold erupted around her left arm, morphing into a kite shield. Her right, a viciously curved khopesh, barbed and very sharp.

"That's...Not possible." She spat.

"Let's dance, bitch." I did not know who to thank for this, but I wasn't going to stop and ask questions. I holstered my pistol and readied my sword.

She screamed and lunged, my blade catching hers in a fast parry. It seemed she expected it as her shield smashed into my side, sending me off balance. She was so fast, like a strike of lightning she was bringing her blade again. I glanced the blow with my blade, planting my feet to absorb the force before bringing my knee into her wide open gut, knocking the wind out of her. I try to bring my sword around, but she blocks me with her shield. My footing was still secure, so I lurched forward, sending her careening off balance, her shield smacking the ground with a metallic, ringing tone. I seize the advantage, closing the gap and bring my sword to bear, a high slash to end this shit once and for all.

A glint of gold metal flashes in the corner of my eye.

I recognized that feeling all too well. Cleopatra began to cackle, as I could feel her blade digging into my chest cavity from the side, deep.

"You FOOL!" she screeched, her accomplished laugh filling the air, as blood began to fill my lungs. I could hear the relief in her voice, I had her scared up until now. So that's something, I guess. The shock, the pain, the rapidly disappearing strength forced me to drop my blade with a loud clatter.

I smirked, as something told me I wasn't done. A whisper. A request of faith somewhere in my soul, blowing in on the breeze.

Gunfire. To my rear. The final volley of a UMP sending rounds down range before the bolt catches, leaving an empty chamber. I looked behind me, Sarah was pale as a ghost with a bloody leg. She used the last few rounds that smacked into Cleopatra with a deadly precision. Sarah promptly went even whiter as her eyes rolled back and she fell hard against the hood of her Lincoln. I turned back to Cleo, whose grin widened before it disappeared sharply. Those rounds Sarah fired began to dissolve Cleo from where they hit. I reach forward and grab the golden bitch roughly by the neck, the same power as before whispering to me.

"For Frank" I choke out. Cleopatra's face shifts, morphs into confusion and terror. "For Amelia." I slam my helmet against her forehead and pulled my pistol. I pressed the barrel against her temple as the warm metallic taste of blood filled my mouth. Cleo's eyes showed her disbelief as I pull the trigger, her assured victory snatched in the last second.

POP.

A deep red geyser of viscera erupted from the side of Cleopatra's head. Her eyes were frozen in that same disbelief as life immediately left her body. "So...Others..." Blood flicked from my lips as I forced out the words. I put the pistol against the front of her skull this time, I had to be sure she was gone.

POP.

Another splash of ethereal blood, and I released her neck, her lifeless corpse flopping to the ground. "May...Live...." I cough out a big wad of my own blood as my strength fails and I collapse to my knees. My head hits my chest. My job was done. Others were going to live.

Speaking of others, I could hear the crowd murmuring, taking their photos. They must have come to see the commotion.

Sirens in the distance.

I chanced a look up, wondering if maybe she was wrong...

Maybe...

Maybe there was a place left for me here. But I could see the colors, the edges, all starting to disintegrate. Guess that's it for me. No sunset, I didn't get the girl.

I fall forward onto all fours, coughing up blood weakly. My reward for a job well done was this blood stained concrete. I looked towards where Sarah fell, where she saved us all. I tried to crawl towards her. She was too far for me to see...

Guess I don't even get the slow electric guitar outro...

I'd make a terrible action hero.

I smirk weakly at my shitty joke, and I would sigh, if I could, as my own vision begins to swim and everything turns into a fever dream.....

***

"Hey man, everyone knows the hero gets the girl in the end!" Reggie slapped me on the shoulder.

"Shit, Reg, you know that's Hollywood bullshit." I smirk as I hop out of the truck and shut the door. "Besides, you think some bimbo is gonna find you out here in the sandbox?"

"Man, you don't dream, Atlas!" Reggie smirks, throwing his arms wide. "You think that some fuckin'…I dunno…Lady Gaga looking girl is gonna find me one day?!"

"With a face like yours, Reg, I'd settle for a butterface." I unclip my helmet as we walk under the netting. "Have you seen a mirror recently?"

"Have you?? Shit man. Not even sure a mother would love that face."

***

"That's really cool!" She spoke with a smile, her fingers gently on my bare chest as the raised letters marked my intent for the rest of my life. "Does it hurt?"

"Not at all." I grinned, smiling at her as her blonde hair caught the setting sun. "John got one too. Is it… Weird we have matching tattoos?"

"Not at all babe." She leaned forward and kissed me. "You're all a little weird."

***

I kept my slow pace because my leg was still mending. I could tell I had a soft limp as we moved.

"Are you okay?" Lancer asked softly.

"Yeah, just got a little roughed up in the last go."

"Is...Is that common?" She asked even more hesitantly than before.

"Combat of any kind could get you injured. But you have me. You'll be fine." I gave her a soft smile over my shoulder. *"I'm unkillable."*

I opened the door to the armory before she could fully process my words. I spoke before Lena could bark. *"Morning, Lena, did you miss me?"*

"You're still alive?!" She tried to sound angry, but I could tell there was a relief in her voice, hidden deep. Very deep.

"Sorry to tell you, but yeah. Still breathing."

"Damn, next time I'll cut the brake lines." She had actually stopped what she was doing to talk.

"You sure you know what those are?" That got a glare, as I walked up to the counter, leaning against it more to keep weight off my bad leg than anything else.

"You drive that F250 yeah?" She almost sounded like a viper.

***

"Boys and girls, I present to you the key to our salvation. BEHOLD!" Sire held up the sleek Dreadnought. *"The Dreadnought! So named for the fear it will strike in your enemies!"*

"What a ham." I whispered to Ms. Steel She had her arms crossed watching, I had my back against the wall, one leg bent against it. She smirked. We have gotten a lot more comfortable in the past few weeks, working closely on improving our people's abilities.

"Are you surprised?" She whispered back.

"Nah. Almost jealous."

"You??" She looked at me, a smile with fake shock on her face.

"Yeah, you right." We grin at each other before returning to watching the scene unfold.

"To deploy this wondrous machine, you hit this button." He did so and the Dreadnought extended, the barbs deploying. Some of the younger members were in awe. "Our own Lena assures me it will vanquish your enemies in the Limbo! Now, step up and take the training stick. Let's get started!"

"At least they take to him. It's goofy but it works." I speak softly to her as people start pairing off to train.

"He does have a way." She nods. "Even if it may be...Out there."

***

Well...Looks like I'll be joining up with you all soon enough. Hope you saved me a spot.

***

"What time is it?" She asked sleepily.

"0700." I scooped some eggs onto our plates, slid a pair of sausage patties on each and brought them to the table. I had cleared off a portion of the table before she awoke.

"What...Why are you doing this?"

"My dad taught me well. He said 'son, if you have a lady over for the night, you best make her breakfast when she awakes." I grinned at her as I stabbed a sausage. She froze mid step, her expressions going through a series of changes.

"Did..."

"Did...?" I couldn't help myself. She looked around the room as if the answer was in here with us.

"I...Did we conduct ourselves improperly, Mr. Sixx?"

"Mr. Sixx now? Jeez Sarah, after everything I thought we were on first name basis. No need to revert." My comment hit her directly and the color drained from her face.

***

"That's all I can ask. Come home and we can figure it out from there. It's not over."

"I wish I could share your optimism." I gave her a solemn grin, which seems to be my default lately.

"Then I will exercise it for us both." She leaned forward slightly. She paused for a moment before leaning the rest of the way and pressing her lips to mine. My nerves radiated a shockwave as I breathed in deeply, a faint hint of the tropics filled my nostrils as I leaned into her, returning her affection. My every fiber wanted to stay here at this moment, but it was a fleeting moment on the grand stage today.

After a few seconds I lean back.

"Now you have no choice but to return to me." She said with a soft smile.

"I am certainly motivated." I mutter softly.

????

I could hear birds chirping. Singing. It was a pleasant song, it reminded me of the scrub jays in Florida. Playing in the short trees, darting back and forth making a ruckus. How did I get here? I opened my eyes, and what greeted me was a lush, verdant forest. Trees, plants, flowers, everything. It seemed like a dream. Over the rustling of leaves, and playful animals chittering about, I heard a noise to my side.

"Liliana?"

She stirred softly. I heard her grunt, as she lay curled up in the grass nearby.

"Liliana?" I ask again, I lean over and touch her shoulder. I noticed her wings were gone, but she was still in the same cloak. Her gray eyes slid open, looking at me.

"How…?" She muttered sleepily.

"Your guess is as good as mine. Are you okay?"

"I think so." She pushes herself up into a sitting position, we check ourselves over quickly. "Yeah, I'm fine. What is going on?"

I shake my head. "Last I remember was fighting Cleopatra." The realization hit suddenly. "If we are both here…"

She looked at me, thinking for a moment. "I mean, maybe?" She stood up. "Is this what's beyond the void?"

"Girl, we are so far out of my realm, I couldn't even point to which map we need." I remained sitting for now. "Can't really complain though. It's gorgeous here."

"Yeah." Her tone was almost sorrowful.

"Lil, ain't enough room for two martyrs. You served for 2000 years, and it seems we ended the blight. Let yourself feel some happiness?" I smirk at her as she glares back.

"You first."

"Gimme another 1900 years." I grunted as she rolled her eyes at me.

"My children. Welcome. I have been watching and waiting." The words were utterly surreal, Liliana and I looked at each other. The voice seemed to emanate from the forest around us, but it didn't even seem like a voice? *"Forgive me my metaphors, but you are in Eden."*

"Mother Gaia?!" Liliana gasped out. No spoken voice greeted her, but the sudden breeze through the trees seemed to say yes.

"Who?" I asked Liliana.

"Mother Gaia...I had only heard rumor..."

"Gaia, like Earth?" I ask her once more, reaching into old memories from school. Liliana nodded as another breeze swept through. It seems like everything just gets weirder as soon as I think I have it figured out.

"Thank you for ending the blight dispelled across my realm."

"Yeah... No problem..." I spoke a little thickly, of all the oddities, talking to the trees had to be the strangest.

"I am the keeper of this world, and I have summoned you here before your return to the void. My connection to the Terran plane you know is weakened as I repair the damage done by Cleopatra. I have little to give, but I wish to thank you myself."

I looked to Liliana, afraid this may be a trap. It seemed the mental connection was severed, and I admit...It felt a little quiet in my head. I...Did not know how I felt about that. Her expression reflected my concerns, but she was not alarmed.

"You two had been unknowingly entrusted with the entirety of this plane's salvation. Cleopatra caused a significant amount of damage, but I was still able to offer assistance. In fact, it was I who kept you alive during the final battle as Liliana had vacated you when Cleopatra closed Limbo."

"Holy shit, I didn't catch that." I muttered.

"You were a little busy." Liliana replied just as softly.

"Wait, did you help Sarah too?" I asked pointedly.

"That was under the brilliant design of Sarah, Lena and Fae. They weaponized aqua regia, one of the only weaknesses Cleopatra possessed."

"I knew I liked those ladies for a reason." Liliana grinned at me.

"God damn, I owe 'em…Well…Everything."

Liliana threw her head back into a deep laugh.

"Lil?"

"After everything, the all-powerful Limbo bitch got taken down by human bullets!" She smiled widely at me, and I couldn't help but match it. We both started laughing like insane fools for a few moments. It was the primal laugh that only those who cheated death could share.

"Speaking of debts owed, in repayment for your services and sacrifice, I can return life to the vessel recently slain. For I have the ability to mend the scars Limbo caused, but the damage is not completely reversible."

"What, so you can bring us back?" I ask, hope rising in my chest.

"The answer would not be so simple, my child. In order to return this life, I would have to erase the curse you refer to as Limbo. It would be as if it ceased to exist."

Liliana's head drooped. "Give it to him."

"Sorry, what??"

She looked at me with heavy, but intense eyes. "She hasn't said anything in plural yet."

"Plur-wait, one of us goes back and the other goes on??" She nodded. "Hold on, let's talk ab-"

"It's your life! Your body!" She became angered, fast. "I don't want it!"

I hesitated before I stepped towards her. You can't share a mind with someone for so long without getting to know them. "Lil…" I touched her shoulder, I could tell she wanted to hit me but couldn't do it. The anger was replaced with a melancholy look. Things clicked into place in my head. "You're mission complete, aren't you?" There was a hesitation before she slowly nodded again, and I embraced her. She didn't move, she didn't speak, but I felt her begin to melt into my chest, and the faint sound of suppressed crying broke through the happy forest noises. "You did well. Enjoy your retirement, Lil."

"Thank you." Her voice was broken, pushing through her tears. "Thank you for bringing me across the finish line."

"Team effort, Lil."

"Fuck you." I could hear the hint of a smirk, as she talked into my shoulder.

"Fuck you too." I paused. "I'm gonna miss you."

"Fuck you will." She pulled back and I could see the smile on her pale face. "I'll save you a spot wherever I end up."

"Oh, make sure it's the lava pool with the spikes."

"You moron, that's not real." We grinned at each other. "But...Atlas...I need you to promise me something."

"What?"

"Don't be so willing to sacrifice this new life." She grinned at me through the tears staining her cheeks. "Round three? Make it a good one."

I was lost for words, as she jabbed a finger into my chest.

"And for fuck sake, if you don't kiss Sarah again, I'll come back from the beyond and do it myself."

"I am pleased you made such a conclusion. Far less will be changed with this modification than with the latter. I must advise you, this will not be so simple as just stepping back into your vessel. I must modify the timeline with the erosion of your Limbo."

"What does that mean?" I turn towards the trees, confusion and a little dread seeping in.

"You will return to the day before you joined the Steel Roses, yet you and no one amongst you will have ever experienced Limbo. Your dreams

never happened, your friends never died. Things will be very similar to what they once were, without the stain of Limbos corruption."

"That doesn't sound bad, why do you make it seem so?"

"Because you alone will have to bear the burden of memory, as this requires an anchor to secure the end of your Limbo."

"What...Does that mean?" Liliana asked. "Like, only he will remember?"

The gentle breeze of acknowledgement came around again.

"So...I will live alone with the knowledge of what was done and sacrificed..." I hung my head. "And this, too, will kill the bonds and connections we formed as a team." The breeze again.

"Jake...That means-"

"I'm aware."

"You going to be okay-"

"You know my answer."

"Jake...Atlas...You'll be alone."

I stare at her, my eyes locking onto hers. "So others may live. Fate has decided to call my bluff for the third time." Her turn to put a hand on my shoulder. "What's that saying? Better to have loved and lost than never loved at all? I guess Atlas is more applicable now than ever before."

Her eyes showed her sorrow. She paused, then nodded. We each respected the other's sacrifice to bring about the restoration of sanity.

"Do it, Mother Gaia."

"Is this what you both wish?"

"Yes." We spoke in unison, eyes locked.

"As you wish, my children. I wish I could do more for you. For what it is worth, I believe you have both fought valiantly and should be honored to have made it this far. I will take it from here, you will no longer be plagued by corrupted souls."

"Wait, so you're back? In control?" I asked the trees. The winds of acknowledgment swept through.

"Good." I sigh, looking at Liliana before hanging my head. "Good…" I pause and look back up at her, a single tear escaping my eye. "Not all warriors get to know their sacrifice was made for a purpose."

"Yeah. Guess we got lucky, hero." She grinned softly at me.

"Maybe…" I return her smile with a somber one of my own. "Maybe I'll accept that this time. Fellow hero."

***

It felt like I had just blinked. I was sitting on the porch once again…A severe amount of Deja Vu as I looked at my drink in my hand and my phone on my thigh. Well…Looked like she didn't lie. I still remember it all, and my head and my heart felt….empty. I took a drink, checked the time. I wish I could remember when that Lincoln came up the driveway, but something told me it wouldn't.

I took a deep breath. It was worth it. Whatever that thing was would have wrecked everything. Society was kinda fucked up, but at least this time it had a chance to make it, not get corrupted to hell and back. Subconsciously I put my hand on my chest, touching the motto I dedicated my life to. All…All three of them. As the sun began to set as I finished my beer. I didn't know what to do now…I honestly felt a little lost and aimless. And empty. Very empty. I picked up my phone, not knowing what I was doing.

I tapped out the letters "GSX" into the marketplace. Maybe I'll paint it red? I already knew the exact shade it needed to be.

Epilogue

AUGUST 11TH, 2026

I sat alone at the bar of the local VFW. My glass was near empty, my eyes red, my soul heavy. The bartender could tell I was working through something and had the decency to let me do so. What better place for a warrior to think? To process? It wasn't long before an old man sat next to me. It was Jed, a very old vet that took to sitting silently with me for a while. I suspected we both had things to deal with but couldn't voice it. He ordered his drink and we sat in silence for…I don't know how long.

"Who were they, kid?" His voice was like gravel but there was a warmth to it. Guess he decided to break our silent pact today.

"Dunno how to answer that."

"That bad?" He paused, taking a drink of his beer.

"Yeah."

The silence dragged on, heavy. I pulled out the worn Roses patch I used to wear every day, the flipside was stuck to the old Cheshire patch I wore before that. They were both worn, almost a physical representation of my own soul. I set them down on the counter in front of me, and I could tell he noticed. I appreciated him not saying a word about it.

"Noble thing you do here every Wednesday." He grumbled.

I grunted at him.

"At what cost?" He pressed.

"I know what I'm doing." My voice was low, almost a growl with the liquor in my system.

"You can't bring 'em back."

"No, sir. But I can help those that are left."

He grunted this time and silence fell again. I had decided to go back to the Roses after everything reset, serving for about two years before I quit. I couldn't handle the ghosts, I couldn't separate the memories of the world that no longer existed and the one that did. I was saddened that Lancer never joined up but I looked for her. She had a good life without Limbo. If I'm honest, it was being a stranger to Sarah that finally broke me.

"Sometimes..." He started softly.

"You wish it was you instead?" I interjected, cutting the silence this time. I saw him nod out of my peripheral vision. "Universe is a bitch." I mutter, he nods again. We sat in silence again, it felt like hours but the clock on the wall begged to differ. How could I put into words how I felt? I feel like an entire world has left me behind. I was a ghost now and the worst part...I let Liliana down. She asked me to make the most of things, and here I am...Unemployed, taking in retirement, moping in a bar. I sighed deeply.

Eventually, the bartender walked up. No one knew why, but she only answered to Fraulein and if anyone tried saying anything else, the patrons immediately corrected them. She was older, maybe 50-60 range with medium length blonde hair, and almost always had a flower in one ear. Kind, but only as kind as you could get with a bunch of salty veterans. Probably once a week we all heard her open up on some sorry sap that didn't know the rules. The lack of accent just made the name confusion worse.

"This one's on one of your kids." She slid a fresh bottle to me. I looked up at her, forcing a soft smile.

"Thanks."

"Things happen for a reason, boys." She leaned on the bar looking at us both.

"Trust me, I know." I felt my smile fade as Jed grunted. She patted my shoulder as she stood up to get back to work. We resumed silence as Jed's granddaughter showed up, told him his ride was here and went to sit at a table with a man.

"She joined up cause of me."

"She seems like a squid."

"Good eye, kid." He grunted.

"She's a good egg though, taking care of you."

"Yeah…Just glad she made it out in one piece. She was such a sweet little thing when she was young." I nod, listening. "Couldn't tell you how many times she made me play dress up with her growing up."

"You in a dress must have been something."

"Yeah. Drafty." Jed grunted, looking up at the TV. "Funny. Never thought I'd live to see two space races in my time." I looked up to see a story about the establishment of a colony on the moon.

"Clock waits for no man." I say softly, he simply grunts in agreement. Fraulein walked back up, phone in hand.

"Lady at the door said she's looking for some guy with a number for a last name." She looked rather annoyed as I looked up at her. "Probably some punk ass kids again. Know how many times I get a call about a Seymour Butts?" She shook her head.

"Sixx?" I offered.

She looked at me with a little shock. "Really? Oh lord, yeah that's right. I only hear folks call you Atlas."

"She a red head?"

Fraulein nodded.

"I'll handle it. Old timer's tab is mine." I got up and walked off before he could fight back, I heard him say 'thanks' roughly. I'll be honest, I had no idea why she was coming to this VFW or asking for me. I quit about a month ago. She didn't somehow remember, did she? Shit, I forget to return something? Nah, Lena would have come to collect. I felt a jolt as I touched the handle to open the door. This had to be some kind of coincidence. I opened the door and was greeted by the exact image I expected.

"Ma'am? Looking for me?" Her eyes locked onto mine, some kind of expression I couldn't place. Some things never change.

"Mr. Sixx. I find myself in the precarious position of asking for your audience." Her voice was...Soft? Weak? I've never heard this before, not out of her mouth.

"Well, you found me, ma'am. What can I do for you?"

"Is there somewhere we can talk, alone?"

I stepped aside, letting her through. She stepped forward with a hesitation. "It's pretty dead on Wednesdays. Just an old vet, his kid, me and the bar keep." She nodded, a nervous apprehension I've never seen before. I followed her in and called out to the bartender. "Fraulein, whiskey, neat please." She nodded, and Sarah gave me another look. Another one I couldn't analyze. You'd think I would have gotten better at this by now.

"Thank you. I...Must admit I feel a little out of place." Sarah took a seat across from me.

"Understandable, but you're here as my guest. You're fine."

"What...How do you know I like whiskey?" The fascinating expression continues.

"Lucky guess?" I offered, as Fraulein brought both of us our drinks. I had no disillusion she could see through me, but I was not in the mood to bare my soul.

"Please don't lie." There was that edge in her voice once more. Guess she was calling my bluff.

"Magicians don't reveal their secrets, ma'am."

She glared at me, before taking her drink and tossing back a fair bit of it. "Then allow me another question. Why do I feel like you know more about the world than I do?"

What kind of question was that?

"And just how do you expect me to answer that?"

She paused. I could recognize THAT look. It was her version of 'give me the truth, regardless of how it will hurt.'

"I..." She paused again, taking another drink. Truth be told, I'd love to capitalize on this confusion, but I couldn't bring myself to do so. I...Well....I missed the old days. I missed the old team, torturing her with kindness. This was not the place or time, however. "I feel like something is missing, Jake."

"Missing?" My eyes narrowed as I spoke. Was she remembering? "Missing in what way?"

There was yet another heavy pause. When she spoke, it was quiet.

"Why do I feel like my memories are wrong?"

I stared at her. This shouldn't be possible. I took a drink this time.

"Jake? Your silence..."

I took a deep breath. "And what is it you think you should remember?" And what should I tell you? How much pain should I summon by telling you the truth?

"I feel...I feel like my memories are wrong. Sanitized?"

"Like you experienced something that the world is hiding from you?"

She nodded, her green eyes boring into mine. "Why? How do you know?"

I turned away, staring at the TV blankly. I don't even know what it's playing, but I take another drink. How in the HELL do I proceed? What should I do, or say?

"Jake...You know something." She spoke softly, and I finally turned back to her. The pleading and fear in her eyes broke me.

"Please don't..."

"I need to know."

"I assure you. You fucking don't."

"So, what, you alone carry this burden?"

"Fuck off, Sarah."

"No."

I sighed. "For once, would you listen to me?!" I hissed.

"You are haunted by something that only you know!" She hissed back. "And I know damn well I am involved! So, tell me what the hell is going on!"

I gritted my teeth, my hand balled into a fist on the table. "Fuck. Off." She stared at me, ignoring my threats.

"I feel pain when I walk down our corridors! I feel sad when I look at Fae! I don't even know HOW to feel around you!" I could feel her eyes burning holes into my skull. "What is going on?!"

I downed the rest of my glass, staring at the table. "Last chance. Walk away. Please. Let me protect you, one last time."

"Fuck you, Jake." My eyes flicked to hers. "Talk."

I sighed, my fist slammed the table, rattling the glasses and napkin holder. I took a quick breath. "I....was not granted the gift of ignorance everyone else was." I turned my glass in place with my other hand, spinning freely from the condensation. "These memories...They are a beast of a burden. A curse."

"I don't care. I need to know."

I met her stare. Something inside me begged to tell her, something else screamed to keep it locked away forever. "Sarah..." She didn't flinch. She didn't back away. An old memory surfaced and my eyes started to tear up.

"Jake? Are you okay?" She sat up straight ready to go. I shook my head softly, wiping my eyes.

"You son of a bitch, you found a way..." I mumble.

"Pardon?"

I took a deep breath, steeling myself. "I warned you." I paused, Fraulein had amazing timing with bringing me a refill, and I took a big gulp. "Promise me, you won't call me crazy?"

She nodded. "You have my word."

"Well, ma'am...I remember it all. From the first fucked up dream, until the fall of Cleopatra. So...You asked for the full story. Don't forget your promise." I spun my drink around once more and began to tell her the story. All of it.

Memory can be a curse, no? However, it is far better when it can be shared. A vague memory surfaced as I started to talk...One of the Guardian whispering that I was 'Not....Alone....'

Afterword

More is coming on the horizon............

    https://dot.cards/sixxatlas

    https://www.goodreads.com/author/show/67935211.Jason_Nadle

Also by

SV Silverfish: Moon Rise

(Coming soon to Amazon and other bookstores, Fall 2026)

I had it all. A great job, a great ship and the best fighter ever made by humanity. Nothing lasts though, and now here I am, two years later on my 30th birthday sitting in a seedy bar.

This is my last chance to get back on my feet...No idea what the next step is, but I know it won't be pleasant. The vaguely named 'Cap' walks up and offers me a job on an eclectic cargo ship. Without many choices, I embark upon the next adventure on the Silverfish.

It's made clear to me quickly that the crew is unique but work well together. I hope to myself that this could be a new purpose, but these types of ships are known to venture deep into the gray area on morality...Either way, Cap seems to speak as if he's being charged by the word and the ship doctor (Wait, why do we have one of those??) is certifiably insane.

Well, time to launch. Wish me luck?